A PASSING FANCY

Copyright © 2021 by Kaye Dobbie
2nd Edition

ebook 978-0-6489371-4-2
print 978-0-6489371-5-9

All rights reserved.
Except for use in any review, the reproduction or utilization of this work in whole or in part in any form by any electronic, mechanical or other means, now known or hereinafter invented, including xerography, photocopying and recording, or in any information storage or retrieval system, is forbidden without the written permission of the publisher.

This is a work of fiction. Names, characters, places and incidents are either the product of the author's imagination or are used fictitiously, and any resemblance to actual persons, living or dead, business establishments, events or locales is entirely coincidental.

Cover Design and Interior Format

A Passing Fancy

KAYE DOBBIE
PREVIOUSLY PUBLISHED AS DEBORAH MILES

PLEASE NOTE:
This book was previously published under the penname Deborah Miles and has been reissued without editing.

ALSO BY KAYE DOBBIE

THE BOND
THE DARK DREAM
WHEN SHADOWS FALL
WHISPERS FROM THE PAST
FOOTSTEPS IN AN EMPTY ROOM
COLOURS OF GOLD
SWEET WATTLE CREEK
MACKENZIE CROSSING
WILLOW TREE BEND
THE ROAD TO IRONBARK

Also books previously written as
Deborah Miles

A PASSING FANCY
SWEET MARY ANNE
JEALOUS HEARTS

AUTHOR'S NOTE

Mention is made of Bendigo. At the time of the novel, 1858, Bendigo was in fact known by the name of Sandhurst. However, to avoid confusion, I have used the name Bendigo throughout.

CHAPTER ONE

THE BUSH WAS so dense and silent that Cleo felt awed. The afternoon was drawing long shadows over the track before her and the sun, shining for the first time in days, was low and golden through the bush. It really did seem like spring, and the golden wattles, bedraggled by the rain, were beginning to dry out.

Cleo sighed. This morning, it had seemed quite reasonable to set out alone. She had taken one of the new Cobb and Co coaches from Melbourne over a week ago, and since then had been sitting in Bendigo, waiting for the weather to clear and paying exorbitant prices to the innkeeper there. There was a coach service to Nugget Gully, but it did not run every day and it did not run when the weather was wet, and, at the moment, even though the sun was shining, the roads were impassable to any vehicle larger than a wheelbarrow. So Cleo had waited, her funds being eaten up, until she could stand it no more.

And so, being a girl of quick decisions and high courage, she had set out for the gold fields of Nugget Gully on a newly purchased horse with only her carpet-bag and a saddle-bag for company.

It had seemed a sensible thing to do at the time, though the Rawlins family, with whom she had travelled to Bendigo, had claimed she was mad. 'You'll see, the road will be passable in another week,' they had said. But Cleo had been waiting a week now for the last part of her long journey and had felt unable to wait another day, let alone another week! Now, with darkness not many moments ahead, it did seem foolish and... yes, even dangerous.

Cleo took a breath, and brushed tendrils of her chestnut hair back from her eyes, where it kept escaping the firm chignon. She straightened her already ramrod-straight back, and tried to think calmly. She must be nearly at the inn. She had been told that it was halfway along the road between Bendigo and Nugget Gully, and that if she rode at a steady pace she must reach it before nightfall. But it was growing dark now, and she had seen no sign of human life, and certainly not a bustling inn.

Cleo sighed again, and irritably brushed at the moth which blundered against her cheek. If only Papa were here! But Papa had died and been buried at sea, not two weeks out of Plymouth, and all his hopes of a new life in Victoria had ended with him. But his daughter had travelled on, not believing at first that he was gone, and then determined to make his dreams come true.

Papa would be proud of me, she thought now, hoping it was so. More likely he would be angry with her for riding out alone into the bush, where there were wild beasts and bushrangers. He had often called her impetuous, and sometimes even pigheaded. Cleo denied them both angrily. *She* knew she was neither.

Cleo's mother had been dead for twenty years, since she was five. As she grew up, she had gradually taken over the job of running the house—cleaning and cooking—as well as dealing with her father's business accounts. He had been a milliner, and quite successful among the fashion-conscious in the city of Plymouth. Cleo had helped there, too, sometimes sewing late into the evening to finish some lacy concoction for Mrs. So and So's head or some feather bonnet for Mrs. Such and Such's daughter.

'You have a flair for it,' her father had told her with pleasure. 'I always thought to have a son to leave the business to, Cleo, but I know it could be in no safer hands than yours!'

But Papa had become ill, and Plymouth had been too cold and too damp. He had needed a drier climate, and Victoria it must be. The decision had been a difficult one, and Cleo knew he would have preferred to end his days in the place where he had been born. But his health had been bad and, after many enquiries and discussions, he had even become enthusiastic about the move.

Victoria, he had told her, was a forward-moving colony. Gold had been discovered there in 1851, and since then a great number of settlers had arrived to make their fortunes. Although now, in this year of 1858, many had returned home—rich and poor alike—many others had remained to build towns and cities. There was a need for men such as her father. So, the business had been sold, and with it their tidy house, where Cleo had spent her entire life. They had had to uproot themselves from all they had known and travel thousands of miles into the unknown.

There had only been one moment of doubt, after they had boarded the ship. 'Am I doing the right thing by you, my dear?' her father murmured to Cleo. 'Should my health be the cause of your unhappiness?'

'Papa, I am not unhappy!' she cried, surprised by this last-minute wavering in such a positive man. 'We will have another shop, and be rich in no time, you will see.'

He smiled, but still looked at her pensively. 'You are twenty-five, Cleo; old enough to be wed with children and a home of your own. Your mother wed me at eighteen! There was no one in Plymouth you will be sad to leave...?'

She laughed. 'Papa, you know there is not! I am too old to marry now—I'm on the shelf, and glad of it too. What do I want with a husband and children? I am content to be my own mistress.'

'I was afraid of it,' he retorted, but gently. 'I brought you up too much like the son I never had. I fear you frighten your admirers off.'

Cleo shuddered elaborately. 'Indeed, I hope so, Papa!'

And, within a week, Papa had gone—taken off by a simple chill—and their savings belonged to Cleo, who must make her own way in the new land. She thought, then, through her sadness, that it was just as well he had brought her up as a son. How would a weak and clinging woman manage, alone in a strange land, with not a single friend to shelter her?

When the ship docked in Melbourne, she had found accommodation there at an exorbitant price. All the prices seemed high, and she disliked seeing her money being spent where it did little good. She had met the Rawlins family in Melbourne; a young couple with one child, travelling to relations in Bendigo.

'When gold was first discovered,' Mrs. Rawlins told her, 'there were few women on the fields. Life was very hard, and the miners were always moving from strike to strike, looking for gold. But now the camps are more settled—those that remain. They are building in stone and timber instead of living in canvas tents. Bendigo is quite a city now, you know. Much of the gold you could find in the creeks and pick up off the ground has gone. They are digging deeper under the ground now, following the reefs.'

They all booked on the American coach run by Cobb and Co to Bendigo, and Cleo enjoyed riding in the well-sprung vehicle, watching the scenery flash by. Bendigo was a large, sprawling place, with mining constructions dominating the town whichever way she looked. The buildings seemed wonderfully grand for such a young city, opulent brick and stone, rubbing shoulders with timber verandas. Bendigo seemed to be trying to throw off her rugged frontier image for one of sober respectability.

The Rawlins were concerned for her safety. That she should be travelling on her own at all seemed to them very shocking. But Cleo merely smiled, and as always did exactly as she pleased. But even she could not fight the weather, and the rain prevented the daily coach from its journey to Nugget Gully. The road quickly became boggy and impassable. A week went by, and Cleo become more and more impatient. Her savings were disappearing fast and she had yet to even reach Nugget Gully!

'But why Nugget Gully, dear?' Mrs. Rawlins asked her, watching Cleo pace up and down before the windows and the grey drizzle beyond. 'Bendigo is so much more civilized. You could make your home here. I'm sure you will make many friends, and perhaps in time some nice man will offer for you and... why, then, you will not have to worry about your future at all!' Mrs. Rawlins smiled at her from the comfort of her own married state.

Cleo grimaced. 'As to that... if I sat waiting for some "nice man" to make me an offer, I would probably starve to death.'

'But Nugget Gully is isolated and rough ...it's still a shanty town, Miss Montague! Not like Bendigo at all.'

Cleo waved her hand a little impatiently. 'My father spoke to a man in Plymouth, who had mined there. He said there were many Devon and Cornish folk there. He had his heart set on it. I know he would want me to try there first.'

'But a young woman like yourself, alone... who knows what dangers you might encounter?'

'As to that, I should say I am older than you, Mrs. Rawlins. And I am used to taking care of myself—I have done it since I was five years old.'

'But England, Miss Montague, is quite, quite different from Victoria! I believe people have died only by wandering into the bush and losing their direction...'

But Cleo had stopped listening. She did not consider herself in need of such advice. She certainly did not mean to let Mrs. Rawlins tell her what she could or could not do, at this late stage. She saw herself as well past marriageable age, and was determined to make her own way in the world, despite the handicap of being a woman.

'Cleo...Cleopatra,' she had said once to her father. 'Why such a fanciful name, Papa? I should have been a Jane or...or a Martha!'

He had smiled. 'Your mother was a romantic, my dear. After we were wed, I took her to see a play. She had her heart set on it. I don't remember the name now, but Cleopatra came from that play.'

Cleopatra for such as she! A tall girl—'Junoesque', someone had once called her—with chestnut curls, thick and riotous, and dark eyes surrounded by thick lashes. She was beautiful, but she disliked her looks—the fashion was for petite blondes—and sought to disguise them with plain clothes and severe hairstyles, making of herself the sort of woman she felt she ought to be. A sensible, middle-aged housekeeper, she considered herself, and so assumed the style. She had never thought of herself as attractive, or wanted to be. She was too big, too brusque and too capable. Beautiful women were like her mother, tiny and delicate, fragile creatures who needed looking after and never seemed to live very long. And if sometimes she would catch herself dreaming or feeling lonely and longing for someone to admire her, Cleo would speak to herself sternly and tell herself such things were not for her.

So it was not surprising that she had laughed at Mrs. Rawlins's worries, and bought herself a horse and set out, alone, into the Australian bush. The sun was almost down.

Cleo found herself thinking that at home now, in September, the weather would be cooler, the
leaves falling yellow and brown. And here it was spring, with the trees blossoming and the days getting longer and warmer. Somehow it was not right.

The horse, until now walking slowly but quietly, suddenly jibbed, startling Cleo out of her reverie. She tightened the reins and made soothing sounds, but the horse jibbed again, jolting her and almost unseating her.

'Blast you,' she whispered. 'What is wrong with you?'

But the horse sensed danger and sidled away from the path ahead, try as Cleo might to force it on. A bird, chattering angrily, flew up into the branches, and the sun glinted off bright wings.

The man seemed to appear from nowhere, a shadow among shadows. He was filthy, and the parts of his face not covered with grime were covered with beard. The horse reared, threatening to toss Cleo off, and she fought to control it, jerking on the reins and making things worse from inexperience. The man was closer now, and she realised he held some sort of makeshift cudgel. She could smell the stale, dirty scent of him, and tried to kick at the horse's side, and turn it back the way she had come. But the man had hold of her bridle and pulled the animal back around.

It seemed to recognise the hand of authority, and suddenly stopped struggling, standing quiet with head down. Cleo felt her heart begin to hammer in her breast. The man was even filthier at close quarters, and the warm, rotting odour of him almost made her retch. He was looking up at her, slapping the cudgel against his leg, and when he grinned his white teeth shone strangely through his beard.

'Well, isn't it my lucky day?' he said, and his voice grated like a knife on stone. 'Get down off the horse. Now!'

Cleo forced herself not to cower. She sat straighter than ever, her fingers gripping the horse's mane, her face a white blur in the twilight. 'I should warn you, I have friends travelling close behind me,' she said in a loud voice which did not waver. 'They have guns.'

He looked at her a moment, and then cleared his throat and spat. 'Friends? Well, even if that's true, I'll be well gone before they arrive. Now get down or I'll knock you down.' He lifted the cudgel at the words, and Cleo felt the violence like a cloak about him. She slid down on to the soft, debris-strewn roadway. It was still soggy from the rain, and smelled of damp and rotting vegetation.

'What do you intend to do?' Her voice was husky despite her resolutions, and her fingers were digging into her palms. 'If you mean to rob me, I will give you what little money I have if you will not harm me.'

Fool! she thought, for saying such a craven thing. But the man's eyes were level with hers, and something in the way he was looking at her made her blood run cold.

The sun was almost gone now, and the air had turned chill. Another bird flapped up, startling them. Cleo stepped back, away from him, but it was too late. The man lunged at her. Cleo, her reflexes heightened by fear, fell to one side and, nearly losing balance, grabbed at the cudgel. But he swung it, and it caught her upper arm. The pain, for a moment, nearly made her faint, and then they were on the ground, rolling over and over in a desperate, silent struggle.

Silent? Her heart was thudding in her breast, and her breath whimpered through her lungs and throat. Cleo scratched at his face, feeling his own hands tearing at her hair, her clothes. The horse snorted, somewhere to her left. A piece of branch scratched at her cheek. She tried to pry the cudgel from his hand, but he wrenched it away, tearing at her desperate fingers. She felt her life, like a tunnel, receding from her, and Papa's face flashed into her mind. What an ignominious end! To have come so far, and for what? To be murdered by a bushranger in the lonely bush.

The foul clothes and body of the man who was trying to kill her were pressed on top of her now, suffocating her. Cleo cried out for breath as much as through terror. He was pulling at her bodice, and she heard the ripping of the cloth, exposing her white chemise. His blackened nails clawed at the soft lace, and it seemed suddenly so obscene for such as he to touch her that Cleo felt dizzy and thought she would faint. Now he was forcing his forearm against her arched throat, and her breath was going. She was a strong woman, but the man had a strength born of living like a wild animal, and Cleo knew that nothing now could save her from the horrors of rape and murder in this lonely place.

Strangely, it was not of Papa she thought then, or her home in Plymouth, but a dream which often came to her in unguarded moments, and which she dismissed as ridiculous. The dream that there was a man beside her, a lifelong companion, someone to love Cleo and only Cleo. She would never now have the chance to find such a love, Cleo thought, as the clouds formed in her mind. Or even to dream of it.

A shout. Suddenly Cleo realised that the thundering she had heard growing louder was not her heart, but a horse's hoofs, coming closer. Her own horse began to stamp its hoofs dangerously close, and snort in reply. The attacker didn't seem to hear. He had torn apart her chemise now, and she felt his hands on her breasts. The horse reared, whinnying, and at last the man on top of her lifted his head, listening. But it was too late. The rider came out of nowhere, dark, like a nightmare.

Something struck Cleo's attacker so hard that he was lifted off her body and thrown several yards away. He hit the ground with a dull, muffled sound, and lay quite still.

For a moment, Cleo couldn't believe she was free of the stinking weight of him, and lay on the ground as if she too were unconscious. Her breath was coming in loud sobs, her head was spinning, and wave upon wave of nausea threatened to overwhelm her. She had never felt so helpless, so lacking in control.

The rider, who had arrived so providentially, pulled his horse to an abrupt halt and dismounted. Running feet approached where she lay, too shocked to move, wondering if this was yet another attack upon her unprotected person, or maybe part of her dream.

In the gathering gloom, another man looked down at her, and Cleo knew then that it must be part of her dream. For here was the man she had always seen at her side, when her mind wandered into those forbidden thoughts of a future which was not possible for her.

His face was creased with concern beneath a broad-brimmed hat, and the eyes which met hers were as dark as his hair. She stared back at him, fixed to the spot, and, gradually, as the concern in the dark eyes turned to speculative amusement, she became aware of her skirt rucked up over her lace-trimmed pantaloons and button-up boots, of her hair falling riotously about her, of her torn bodice and sleeve, and dirt-smeared face.

'Are you all right?' His voice was deep with concern, and Cleo felt the blood rush to her face. This seemed almost worse, this helpless, embarrassing position, than the bushranger's attack.

'Perfectly, thank you,' she said, her voice harsh, and started to push herself upright. The pain in her arm was excruciating, and she caught her breath, biting her lip to stop herself crying out in earnest.

Through her dizzy pain, Cleo felt his arm about her, helping her to sit up. He smelt of horseflesh and sandalwood, so clean and wholesome after the other. Cleo shuddered, remembering, and felt his grip about her tighten. She forced herself to meet his dark eyes, and was shocked at his closeness. He looked weary and unshaven, as though he had travelled a long way in a short time, and his black hair curled at his temple...in short, he was the most handsome man she had ever laid eyes on.

'Did he hurt you?' he asked, and she shook herself, rebuking her foolish, ridiculous thoughts. She must be delirious!

'I... yes, my arm. He hit me.'

He hesitated, and then caught her sleeve and, taking what appeared to be a knife from his boot, slit it all the way up to her shoulder.

'Please,' Cleo said, at her most acid, 'don't concern yourself about ruining my gown!'

The dark eyes slid back to her, and there was a curious, searching look in them. 'From what I can see, the gown is ruined already,' he said, and his voice was full of mockery.

Cleo bit her lip, feeling foolish.

The stranger was inspecting her arm. There was an angry red mark above her elbow. 'Does this hurt? Wriggle your fingers.' And, when she complied, he said, 'It's not broken, only badly bruised, I think.'

'Thank you,' Cleo whispered, ashamed of her earlier sarcasm. She noticed he still held her arm, and his eyes had slid towards the torn bodice. Cleo clutched at the cloth nervously, and looked across to where the prone body of her attacker lay, still and untidy as a bunch of old rags. 'Is he dead?'

'Does it matter?' He flung the body a look of contempt. Then, turning back to Cleo, he demanded, 'Are you alone? Are you travelling alone?' And, when she didn't immediately answer his question, the amazement grew on his face, followed swiftly by anger. His eyes narrowed to black slits.

Cleo lifted her chin as bravely as she was able. 'I . . . I could not wait for the coach to run. It was delayed a week already, with the rain and. . . I had business on the gold fields and—'

'Of all the idiotic things to do,' he cut in rudely, and rose to his feet. He reached down and, grabbing her uninjured arm, hauled her roughly up beside him. She swayed a moment, dizzy with pain and fright, and he held her steady, with barely concealed impatience, until her head cleared.'

'It's none of your business,' Cleo said breathlessly. She pulled away from him, walking towards her horse, trying not to drag her feet. She felt bruised and battered all over, and there was still a curl of nausea in her stomach. As she checked that her belongings were still in place, she tried desperately not to let him see how much her hands were shaking.

'Oh? Not my business?' he retorted. 'The fact is that you would be murdered by now, if not for me. And if not murdered, then certainly raped. Don't women like you consider that to be a fate worse than death?'

Cleo glared at him. 'Thank you, sir, for your help. But, as you can see, I am quite all right. If you will just help me to mount I will continue on to the inn...'

He shook his head at her in amazed anger. 'If you think I'm going to let you ride off alone, you're mad,' he said sharply. Two hands came together at her waist, and, amazingly, he lifted her like a feather up on to the seat of the saddle. Cleo sat, staring down at him, as he brought his horse over. It had been standing obediently waiting throughout the entire incident. He stooped over the prone man, and fetching some rope from his own saddle-bag proceeded to truss him up like a Christmas turkey. When that was done, he mounted his horse and brought it up beside hers.

The final rays of the dying sun shone, just for a moment, capturing them in light—it had only been minutes since the man had first attacked her and yet it seemed like hours. Cleo looked at her rescuer and saw him properly, for the first time. Dark, thick hair and dark eyes in a brown, handsome face. Broad brow, straight nose and curling mouth. He looked broad and strong enough to be a blacksmith, and his clothes fit him like a glove. Cleo flushed, suddenly aware that he had noted her perusal and it amused him. No doubt he was used to being looked at by women! The thought made Cleo even more angry, and that she could have, even for a second, confused him with her secret dream caused her cheeks to whiten with rage.

'If you're ready,' he said with a drawl, 'we'll find this inn.'

'There is really no need...'

But he evidently didn't think such a foolish protest worth answering, and they passed the body of her attacker in silence. The bush was becoming alive with the hum of crickets and cicadas. Cleo thought she saw a bat flutter past, and hoped she was mistaken. She followed the stranger as best she could, wondering how he knew his way so well.

'What the hell are you doing out here alone?'

His angry voice startled her, coming as it did out of a long silence. Her arm was aching from the jolting of the horse and she felt dizzy and faint. For Cleo, her own mistress for so many years, it was a confusing and frightening moment. She had never felt less in control of her destiny than she did now, and he had to pester her with his questions!

'I'm going to Nugget Gully,' she said at last in repressive tones.

'Oh. And you have friends there? Relatives?'

'I...' She was tempted to lie, but lying was not

natural to Cleo. 'No,' she admitted, reluctantly.

She felt him look at her in the darkness, and wished herself a thousand miles away. But all he said, after another moment of silence, was, 'Where are you from? I mean, originally?'

'Plymouth.'

'How long have you been in Victoria?'

'Almost two weeks.'

'Two weeks.' And now the mockery was as heavy as the growing darkness. 'A whole two weeks, and you set out for Nugget Gulley, alone? Good God, that anyone could be so naïve, or stupid, or both!'

The blood rose to Cleo's cheeks, but she didn't answer. The usual words, 'I can take care of myself' were bitten back from her lips, because it was plain to this arrogant man that she could not!

Suddenly, ahead, there was the faint glow of light through the trees. Cleo caught her breath, thinking for a moment it was another bushranger, this time with a lantern. But the mocking, drawling voice beside her said, 'Your inn, ma'am,' and Cleo realised that the light was much brighter than that thrown by a single lantern. She had never been so relieved in her life!

Voices drifted out, as they drew into a clearing and the inn appeared before her. At least, she supposed it was an inn. It was a rough, wooden dwelling, with stables to one side, and an open doorway with a little porch over it. Voices came through the doorway, and the smell of beer was quite strong even at this distance. It did not look the sort of place to which a woman, alone, would be welcomed. Cleo bit her lip.

'Exactly.'

Her big brown eyes swiveled around to meet those darker ones, gleaming in the light from the inn. There was mockery in them, and they slid over her disheveled appearance like a spoken insult.

'Not exactly a Plymouth inn, is it?' he went on. 'Or, come to that, a Melbourne one either!'

'I never expected—'

'The host is respectable enough,' he went on, ignoring her excuses, 'but even a respectable man may demur when it comes to welcoming a single woman travelling alone at night.'

Cleo clutched at her torn bodice, covering her bosom. She knew that her gown was dirty and ripped beyond repair, and her body ached, even, her bones ached. Anger and stubborn pride turned suddenly to despair. She looked down at her fingers, clenched on the reins, and wondered what her father would have said to her. She had a fairly good idea, and shivered suddenly, imagining his anger.

The softness of cloth about her shoulders startled her. Cleo looked up into dark, mocking eyes in a handsome, grim face. He pulled his jacket closer around her, bending so close for a moment she thought he meant to kiss her. The thought was so sudden and so ridiculous that she blinked back at him like a frightened rabbit.

A smile quirked up the corner of his mouth. And then he had turned away and slid down from his mount. 'Wait here,' he ordered, and strode towards the inn, vanishing inside.

Cleo held her breath. She felt inclined to take the reins and whip her horse into a gallop, anything to escape the embarrassing mess she had got herself tangled up in. But the darkness beyond the bright, welcoming light of the inn was frightening and alien, and she had lost all of her confidence. Besides, she didn't put it past her so-called rescuer to come after her and drag her unceremoniously back.

But there was to be no escape. He had already returned, striding back towards her. A plumper, shorter figure hovered in the doorway behind him. 'Come on,' he said, and held out his hands. Cleo hesitated, but plainly there was no choice, and she slid down to the ground. He was taller than she, and bigger, and for a moment she felt overwhelmed and almost—dared she think it?—tiny. He planted his hands firmly on her back and propelled her towards the innkeeper.

'Aaron, this is the lady. An accident a couple of miles south. Send your sons out to fetch that vermin I was telling you about; he is parceled up nicely, so they shouldn't have any trouble. Is there a back way to the room? No? Well, then, ma'am, we must brave the taproom.'

They were both looking at her, the stranger with mockery and the innkeeper, Aaron, with some curiosity. Cleo pulled away from his grasp, and tightened the jacket about her bosom, then without looking back she strode boldly on through the door and into the light.

For a moment, Cleo stood swaying, blinking in the gleam of the lamps, stunned by so many faces turned in her direction. There was a silence in which she could hear her own breathing, and then a murmur started, followed by a few laughs, and she felt ready to sink.

An arm came suddenly about her waist, and in a moment Cleo was steered on through the stables, and out through another door at the back. They stood in a narrow passageway on to which opened yet more doors. Aaron, who had followed, opened one, and, avoiding her eyes, said, 'Comfortable bed, miss. I'll get someone to bring you water to wash and... tidy up.'

The door closed behind him. Cleo, who had been holding her breath all the while, let it go with a rush. She closed her eyes. It was a nightmare. In a moment, she would wake up at home, with all the chores still to be done, and a house to run, and a life to get on with. A tear of self-pity rolled down her cheek, and impatiently she brushed it away. If only there was someone... someone to hold her, to comfort her, to scold her and yet love her for the foolish thing she had done.

Her thoughts came to an abrupt halt, and she wiped her face again. How foolish! What need had she of anyone but herself? She might be impetuous, but she did not lack courage. She needed no man to stand guard over her, like a mongrel over a bone!

A sudden pounding on the door made Cleo start. She tightened her grip on the jacket again, her eyes huge in her white face. 'Come in,' she said rather cautiously.

He did, and dumped her bags on the floor at her feet, with her saddle. 'Best not to leave it to the temptations of the stable-boy,' he said, gesturing to the latter. Then, glancing about, he added, 'Is the room all right?' Cleo looked about her too, realising that she had not even bothered to view it yet. The lamplight showed it to be small and cramped, but at least warm and dry and, presumably, safe.

'Yes,' she said, at last. 'Yes, thank you.'

A boy appeared in the doorway behind him, and, with a smirk at Cleo, placed a jug of steaming water on the wash-stand, the top covered with a rather worn-looking towel. He paused then, flickering another look up at Cleo. Flushing, she was about to give him a piece of her mind when the stranger fished into his pocket and handed the lad a coin. The boy scampered out, well pleased, and shut the door.

'Thank you,' Cleo said again, stiffly, 'but that was not necessary. I'm sure he is being well paid for his work here.'

The man laughed abruptly. 'By Aaron?' Then, before she could argue, he told her, 'Your horse has been rubbed down and settled. You have water to wash in, and a bed to sleep in. Is there any other service I can perform for you, ma'am?'

Cleo was sure she must have misheard him, or perhaps was imagining more to his words then he had intended. And yet... the look in his eyes, the lazy smile on his mouth, both gave credence to her incredible belief that he meant... that he could be suggesting...

'You can go away and leave me alone,' she said in a breathless voice.

'I don't even know your name,' he replied, as if she hadn't spoken. 'Surely, having rescued you from a fate worse than death, you can tell me that?'

She was tempted to rebuff him and send him from the room. No man in all her admittedly rather sheltered life had ever spoken to her or behaved to her as this man had. She had never met such a man, and had no experience in dealing with his kind. She feared... she very much feared that he was what was called in hushed voices a 'rake'. Someone who preyed upon women, seducing them and abandoning them. That he seemed to think Cleo a suitable victim was astonishing enough. After all, she thought, she was no beauty, especially in her present disheveled state. Or was it that which appealed to him?

She drew herself up stiffly, and eyed him as coldly and sternly as she could. 'My name is Miss Montague. And now I wish to be alone.'

'Miss Montague,' he repeated and bowed slightly. 'How do you do?'

He was mocking her. He was trying to make her foolish and she had already been made to feel quite foolish enough for one day.

'Will you please leave?' she hissed, and moved to open the door.

'I will leave when you return my jacket, Miss Montague,' he retorted and watched her flush. She all but flung it at him, folding her arms across her bosom. 'Thank you. In the morning, Aaron will see to it that you travel with someone head-ing in your direction, someone respectable. I have instructed him precisely. If I hear that you have set off alone again, I will put you over my knee. Do you understand me, Miss Montague?'

The mockery had gone, and his eyes were dark and quite serious.

Cleo opened and shut her mouth, speechless with rage.

'I have to leave tonight,' he went on, evidently feeling she had nothing to say. 'I have things needing my urgent attention. Otherwise, let me assure you, Miss Montague, I would remain and ride with you myself to Nugget Gully.'

'Then,' she breathed, 'I am very glad you have to leave tonight. I could think of nothing more unpleasant than continuing in your company for another minute! Goodbye, Mr...?'

But he only smiled, and said, 'Until we meet again, Miss Montague.' The door closed, and Cleo stood staring at it, alternating between fury and fear and confusion. She didn't even know his name. He was arrogant and infuriating, and, despite the fact that he had probably saved her life, she could not like him. But it was his final words which came back to haunt her, while she tried to sleep. 'Until we meet again.' A strange thing to say, when Cleo had already decided quite definitely that she never wanted to meet him ever again!

CHAPTER TWO

CLEO LOOKED DOWN upon Nugget Gully and wondered whether to laugh or cry. It looked as though there had been some natural disaster. The earth had all been dug up and turned over, and there were little hills of it everywhere. Once, there had been many tents too. A canvas town of miners, all seeking their fortunes with pick and shovel. But most of them had gone now, with the alluvial gold. They now sought it deep underground, as the towering poppet heads bore witness.

Beyond the few tents and outlying shanties lay the town. It seemed to consist of one main street, on to which faced the more important buildings, and other narrower tracks leading off it. The main street was a wide, dusty thoroughfare, busy with horses and drays and, today, a flock of sheep. The noise engulfed Cleo, floating up into the blue sky.

Nugget Gully had been a gold town for six years now, and had a hotel, a music hall and several stores to show for it, as well as the more usual smithy, butcher, and coach depot. The hotel was the grandest—a two-story building with a veranda around the front. As Cleo paused to view it, a man, evidently the worse for drink, was ejected out on to the street in front of her, and lay a moment on the road before getting to his feet and weaving off in the other direction. The music hall was next to the hotel, plastered with large advertisements of the latest 'star' to visit the town. Further down, there was a stolid, stone-built bank, various other official-looking buildings in blue stone, and an emporium which seemed to sell everything from nails to face lotions. There were barrels and sacks at the front, and someone loading a dray with enough supplies, Cleo decided, to last a year at least. A woman, her long dress dragging in the dust, ran after a shrieking child, threatening dire consequences if it failed to stop.

Cleo sighed, and climbed down off her horse. A store-owner, pausing in his doorway to light his pipe, glanced at her curiously, and after a moment she made her way purposefully towards him.

'Please, sir, could you tell me if there are rooms to rent in this town?'

The dark eyes narrowed, and he finished puffing on the pipe before replying. 'The hotel,' he offered. 'There'll be rooms there if you've the cash. You've not come to work there, have you?'

The idea plainly appealed to him, and Cleo felt herself flushing. 'No, I have not. And I'd rather not stay at the hotel. Isn't there somewhere more... more respectable?'

The man smiled. 'Well, there's Mrs. Smith just down the road a bit. House with the white fence and garden, on the way out of Nugget Gully. She rents rooms to those she considers respectable. Other than that, there's Finnigan's Hostel, but mostly miners and labourers stay there.'

'Thank you. Mrs. Smith sounds just what I'm looking for.'

The man met her smile with a nod, and watched her climb on to the mounting block by his horse rail and remount her horse. She felt his eyes on her back, and held herself as stiffly and proudly as she knew how.

So this was Nugget Gully. The place her papa had dreamed of all those thousands of miles away, in Plymouth. The place she had risked everything, yes, even death, to find. It seemed small and hodgepodge, and yet... there was wealth in the buildings, and in the quiet assuredness of the place. Perhaps it would be all right.

The journey, since the inn, had been pleasant enough. Cleo had travelled with two men whose wives were back in Melbourne, awaiting the letter to join them when they had made good. They were friendly and kind enough. She had been safe with them from bushrangers and had learnt, if she hadn't already known, how reprehensible had been her actions in leaving Bendigo alone. Their excitement and enthusiasm had infected her, and erased some of the misery from the night before. Her arm still ached, but it was merely bruised, as her rescuer had told her, and would be better soon. She had tried to repair the gown, but it was beyond repair, and in the end she had bundled it up in her bag. She had worn her grey gown, which, she thought, was exactly what she was—plain and uninteresting.

A dog barked, startling Cleo out of her reverie, and she looked up to see a neat building, with a white picket fence and a garden which might have come straight from England. A little dog barked through the gateway, and a large woman in an apron, who had been stooping to pull some weeds, straightened and eyed her curiously.

Cleo slid down from the horse's back, smoothing her skirts and trying to slap some of the dust out of them. She felt gritty and sweaty from the road, and longed for nothing more than a hot bath and a long sleep.

Mrs. Smith was eyeing her with the professional interest of a landlady, and must have liked what she saw, for she smiled warmly at Cleo's approach, and hushed the dog as it continued its shrill yapping. Yes, she had rooms to let, and yes, indeed, there was one spare at the moment. She must come in, instantly, and have some tea. Had she come far? From where? And... alone?

Cleo followed her into the cool of the house, blinking in the dim light after the bright sun. Mrs. Smith was saying, 'Women do things here that they would never dream of doing in England. All sorts of work. They even take up the shovel themselves—mining, I mean. I've known many a miner's wife or widow to do so! But women—respectable women, that is—do not usually travel alone about the country when they are fresh from England, Miss Montague.'

The disapproval was faint, but there. Cleo

flushed angrily, but her voice was cool enough. 'Needs must, Mrs. Smith. I trust you will not think I am less than respectable because I have acted... acted in a forthright manner.'

Mrs. Smith laughed. 'Goodness me, no! From the first moment I laid eyes on you, Miss Montague, I could see you were nothing if not respectable. I've seen enough of the other sort in my time to know.'

Cleo's room was small, but clean and fresh, and the windows looked out over the back garden.

There was a narrow bed and a wash-stand, and some shelves and, behind the curtain, a rod to hang one's gowns on. Cleo thought of her own room, in Plymouth—no doubt full of strangers now. She would have wept, if she had been made of lesser stuff. But, being Cleo, she cleared her throat and said, 'Thank you, it is just what I wanted. How much did you say it would cost per month?'

Mrs. Smith named her price. 'And that was a week, not a month, Miss Montague. But it is worth every penny. You have all your meals provided and I do your washing for you. You'd not get such service within fifty miles, no, not even at that grand hotel!'

The price took her breath away, but Cleo swallowed and agreed. She had no choice. But she determined that she would find her own place as soon as possible, and begin making money rather than squandering it.

Mrs. Smith was chattering again. She was a hearty

sort of woman, as broad as she was tall; and her eyes were pale and blue and shining with curiosity. Cleo made a mental note to always lock her door, in case Mrs. Smith was the sort who went through her boarders' belongings.

Downstairs again, in the parlour, Mrs. Smith poured some tea in flowered cups, and offered Cleo some biscuits. There was a thin, harassed-looking servant girl, Milly. Mrs. Smith, after sweeping a glance at Cleo, instructed her to boil up some water so that Miss Montague could take a bath. Cleo sipped her tea to hide her smile.

The parlour was dainty and cool, with lace curtains and ornaments crowded on to the many little knick-knack tables, as was the fashion. It reminded her of home. After Mrs. Smith had shown her some photographs of her late husband and her son, who was away in Melbourne, and asked Cleo numerous questions about the voyage, they turned to Nugget Gully. Mrs. Smith seemed to know everyone and everything concerning the place. Cleo half listened to her, thinking instead of the bath which awaited her, and hoping Milly would hurry with the water.

'You've seen the hotel?' The abrupt question brought Cleo up with a start.

'As I came into the town, yes. It looked quite...grand.'

Mrs. Smith laughed. 'And so it is. They have had quite a few of the famous from Europe staying there, when they were performing at the music hall. Lola Montez—shocking, she was! But they showered her with gold nuggets and ten-pound notes. She must have left here far richer than she came!'

Cleo sipped her tea, and wondered if she could take up singing, like Lola Montez. Still, it was hardly a respectable occupation, even if one didn't do some of the more shocking things which Lola was renowned for.

'And he owns most of the town,' Mrs. Smith was saying. 'The store, the hotel and the music hall. And, of course, the land. Used to have all this land, to run his sheep on. He still runs them to the north. Most of the food he sells to us he grows himself. Rich as Midas, they say.'

'I beg your pardon? Whom did you say this was?' Cleo asked suddenly.

'Jacob Raines, Miss Montague. He owns most of the land in Nugget Gully. If you stay here you are sure to meet him. He thinks he owns the people as well, though he doesn't own me! He's not even very respectable...if you know what I mean. Comes from a good family, I believe, but a black sheep. He may be rich, but none of the really respectable families would ask him into their homes, let me tell you!'

'He sounds a thoroughly unlikeable person,' Cleo replied. Then, purposefully, she went on, 'Tell me, Mrs. Smith, is there a shop here which sells bonnets and the like? Good ones, I mean?'

Mrs. Smith chewed her fingertip. 'The emporium sells some, and the draper's, but they aren't what I would call "good". Those that have the money get their clothing sent up from Melbourne, the rest of us make do.'

Cleo smiled. 'Well, Mrs. Smith, I make hats. Indeed, I make very good hats, and I intend to start making hats in Nugget Gully for you and all your townspeople. As soon as I can find somewhere to start my business, you will have as many good hats as you like.'

That night, Cleo took her money out of its hiding-place in her petticoat and counted it on the bed. There was enough to buy a small place, and arrange for the proper furnishings and the bits and pieces she would need to make her wares. Cleo sighed. Her hair curled about her shoulders, and she tossed it impatiently back; the chestnut lights glowed in the lamplight, turning to fire. After a moment she put the money back into the hidden pocket and then under her pillow.

But as she closed her eyes to sleep, for some reason the face of her rescuer came to her. She had meant to ask the innkeeper his name, and now it was too late. She was glad she would never see him again. He did not strike her as being particularly respectable. Something Mrs. Smith had said played teasingly at her mind, but she was tired, and fell asleep before it could become quite clear.

The next day, Cleo was up bright and early, and out into the beehive-like activity of Nugget Gully. She wandered through the town, even to the shanties on the outskirts, watching the miners at work with their picks and shovels, and the cradles— wooden boxes which were filled with water and then rocked to extract the heavier gold from the other debris. Women and children worked alongside the men. Cleo felt sorry for the families living in such close, unsanitary conditions. Mrs. Smith had already informed her that there was sure to be typhoid this summer, carrying off large numbers of the weak and the young.

There were people from all over the world on the Victorian gold fields—Britain, the Americas, China... Cleo had never seen a more colourful bunch. A lot of them were employed in the quartz mines, now that the more easily extracted alluvial gold was running out. The quartz mines went deep underground and followed the reefs of quartz, and, hopefully, its partner, gold. Poppet heads dotted the landscape, and great mullock heaps grew where the earth from underground had been brought up. A gold battery thundered noisily, crushing rock from the mines, while men swarmed like bees.

A few of the more enterprising miners called out to her, but Cleo ignored them. Besides, she was so bound up in her own thoughts that she had no time for chit-chat. For the first time she could remember, Cleo felt free. It was a good feeling, though a little frightening to one whose life had always been so structured. A woman had to do a man's job in this country, if she was to survive without one. You could be respectable and still do the work of a miner. It sounded ideal to Cleo, who was, despite her impulsive streak, very respectable.

In time, she wandered back towards the boarding-house, thinking that it must be getting on for lunchtime. Mrs. Smith was prompt with her meals, and Cleo didn't want to miss out. There were others boarding there, too, whom she had met at breakfast. A couple of men in suits whom she thought might be speculators, and a young woman who appeared to be rather 'delicate'. Blonde, pale and interesting, the fashionable ideal.

The main street was busy, rushing with vehicles and people. Cleo hastened her step as she reached the hotel and, seeing the men gathered about its veranda, along with a somewhat gaudy woman, went hastily to cross the road. The men called out something, and the woman went off into peals of laughter. It was, doubtful whether their joke was aimed at Cleo, but, being sensitive, she felt it was, and hurried all the faster. She failed to see the wagon bearing down on her until the driver shouted, dragging on his reins. The horses reared, and Cleo, turning and seeing her danger, cried out in terror.

She smelt the dust, and the horses' hot breath, and the brilliant blue of the sky blinded her eyes as she fell. Someone screamed—was it herself? There was an agonising pain as she landed on her bruised arm, and then darkness.

Darkness, darker even than her rescuer's eyes. For a short time she thought she was back in the bush, fighting off the bushranger. She did not know of the group who gathered about her, and carried her into the cool depths of the Nugget Gully Hotel. She did not know of the plush, red-carpeted steps they climbed, and the richly ornamented and dimly lit private parlour where they finally laid her down. She only knew that the jolting had ceased and the cushions beneath her head were soft as down, and it was cool and peaceful and smelt of polish and perfume.

A hand rested on her brow, and then brushed back her escaping curls. Whispering, and then a door closed. Light peeped through her lashes, and then she felt someone removing her button-up boots, leaving her only in her stockinged feet. That this was a shocking thing to do crept slowly into her mind, and she could only think that she was back in her own room, and Mrs. Smith was making her more comfortable. It therefore came as a great shock to Cleo that, when she opened her eyes at last, it was not the bulky form of Mrs. Smith bent over her, but the broad-shouldered form of a man.

Startled, Cleo cried out, clutching her hand to her throat, and tried to sit up. The man straightened then, his eyes narrowing as they met hers. She knew him instantly, and made a strangled sound, still struggling to sit up.

'Have you a death wish, Miss Montague?' Black eyes raked her down, and then he made an impatient sound, and pressed her back down upon what, she saw now, was a couch covered in scarlet brocade and emerald velvet cushions. It made her head ache. 'Lie down!' he snapped at last. 'You may be concussed. You were certainly out of your senses.'

'I...' she gulped, and clutched her head. 'I was almost run down.'

'Yes. You stepped into the road, they tell me, in front of a wagon. Luckily for you he managed to stop in time. They brought you in here. No one seemed to know who you were. Unfortunately, I did. Will you lie still?'

Cleo made a petulant movement. 'I am perfectly all right. I hurt my arm again, that is all… And if you intend to rip this sleeve as well, I shall scream!' This was hastily added as he reached out towards her arm.

A reluctant smile curled his lips. 'I was only going to feel if it was broken, Miss Montague. I don't make a habit of slitting women's gowns.'

She let him feel her arm, wincing. For some reason her heart was hammering in her ears, and she felt hot and cold, in turns. The fall had certainly unnerved her—she felt light-headed, and when her rescuer met her eyes again she had the impression she was going down into their dark wells.

'Miss Montague?' he said, frowning at her. 'Should I call the doctor? I was about to, when you woke.'

'No, I am perfectly all right. I must be getting back. Lunch, you know.'

'Is that what you were thinking of, when you were almost run down? Lunch?' The amazement was back in his eyes.

'No, I. . . I didn't wish to walk past the hotel. I was crossing the road.'

His dark eyebrows lifted at her. 'Indeed!' he said coolly. 'Were you afraid you may become contaminated by the building, or was it the people in it?'

'I would hardly think it a suitable place for a woman of respectable habits to be seen, sir.'

For a moment, he gave her a long, cool look, and then, striding to the window, he pulled back the heavy velvet curtains. 'Come, Miss Montague,' he said, in harsh, ringing tones, 'look from this window and, tell me, where do you think you are?'

Frowning, Cleo turned and looked. She could see the roofs of the town, and the smoke from many chimneys, and the poppet heads of the underground mines on the outskirts of town. In fact the view was lovely, and if her arm and head hadn't been aching so much... Good God, was it? Could it be? 'Where am I?' she gasped, but already knew.

'You are in that den of iniquity, Miss Montague, the hotel. You were carried here, when you were unconscious. Is your reputation in tatters now?'

The cool sarcasm of his words silenced her, and she blinked at him. His arrogant, handsome face, his tall, broad form in what she now saw to be perfectly fitting, richly wrought cloth. 'Who are you?' she whispered; a terrible fear had taken hold of her mind.

He met her eyes, his brows rising again, and then bowed his head briefly, and with a smile said, 'I am Jake Raines, Miss Montague. I own this place.'

Cleo closed her eyes. Her arm was throbbing abominably, and she still felt faint. But after a moment she drew herself up and stood, with the help of the back of the couch. 'I must go. Mrs.

Smith is very strict about her meal hours and, really, I cannot stay.'

He caught her unhurt arm, and pulled her closer to him. For a moment he was so close that his breath fanned her cheeks. Her hair was untidy, escaping its pins, but she didn't move to rescue it. He was taller than she, and far bigger, and there was something overpowering about him which made her stare up at him like a silly mouse mesmerised by a serpent.

'You cannot stay?' he mocked her softly. His finger touched her cheek, and slid, light as a feather, down to her mouth. He traced her top lip, slowly, his dark eyes gleaming with the knowledge that she found herself helpless. 'I think you are a prude, Miss Montague. A prude who cannot even unbend enough to have lunch with a man who saved her life not three days ago.'

'Please, stop,' she whispered. 'If you wish I will lunch here. I only...please, let me go.'

Something changed in his face, softened almost, and then he had let her go, and strode to the door. He opened it and called down the stairs, 'Gert, come up here!' He turned, flickering a glance over Cleo's frozen form, and then smiled. 'You will be quite safe, Miss Montague. I am perhaps not a gentleman, but I have not sunk to those levels.'

Cleo didn't answer. She turned to the window. She was a fool to have thought he might have dishonourable intentions! When he could have, and probably did have, many other women to keep him company. Why should he bother with such as she? He had been teasing her, enjoying watching her quaking before him. He was despicable.

A young woman in a black uniform with white apron and cap appeared at the doorway. Her eyes went from Cleo to Jake Raines. 'Ah, Gertie,' he said, 'we will have luncheon for two. And quickly, please. We're hungry.'

'Yes, Mr. Raines.'

She closed the door, softly.

'Would you like to tidy yourself after your unfortunate accident, Miss Montague? There is a room through there...'

Cleo looked into the mirror, after she had closed the door firmly after her. She had a smudge of dirt on her cheek, her hair was a mess, and her gown was soiled. No wonder he had been amused by her! Hastily, she put herself to rights, pulling her hair back severely into a chignon, and smoothing her gown as best she could. Perhaps there was some way of slipping out without his seeing her? But, even as she thought it, she knew she would not. Because he had saved her life, or because he had mocked her as to his intentions? She did not know, but she was not about to run from a rake such as he.

Was he a rake? Wasn't it obvious? she thought sarcastically, her brown eyes glinting. He was the sort of man who believed every woman he met could hardly wait to drop into his hands like a ripe plum! Cleo could see it in his smile, the way he stood, the arrogant line of his chin. Well, he would see that she was not the sort of woman to fall for that sort of low charms Cleo Montague was not about to drop into his or anyone else's hands.

'Miss Montague, here you are.' He smiled as she came in, his eyes raking her quizzically. 'And I see you have... ah, straightened yourself out and fastened yourself down. Strange, but I prefer you a little dishevelled, myself.'

Cleo ignored this. He was opening a bottle of wine, and she looked at it with distaste.

He saw her look and gave her his mocking smile. 'You may leave after you have eaten,' he said, 'I promise. In the meantime... I would be most interested in finding out more about you. We seem destined to be thrown together, don't we?'

'Why should you wish to know about me?' Cleo retorted tartly, hoping he hadn't seen the colour come into her cheeks. She had never met a man like him before; her father had made very sure of that. He was not a man she would ever have been destined to meet, had not circumstance decreed otherwise.

'I've always been interested in beautiful women,' he said smoothly, 'although you try very hard to disguise your beauty, Miss Montague. But then, an expert like me is not fooled by such tricks as that.'

'Mr. Raines,' she said through gritted teeth, 'I am not beautiful, and certainly not trying to disguise anything. If you wish me to stay you must not speak so to me. It is...is improper.'

He laughed, pouring the wine into two glasses. He handed one to her, and for a moment she stared at the blood-red of it. But his eyes mocked her gaucheness, and she shot out her hand to take it when she knew very well she should refuse. It was vile, she decided, after one mouthful. But, other than spitting it back into the glass, she had to swallow it.

Jake Raines had seated himself on the couch, where Cleo had only lately reclined. After a moment, Cleo perched on the end furthest from him, cradling her glass in both hands. 'Come, Miss Montague, tell me,' he drawled, 'how do you find Nugget Gully?'

'Interesting, Mr. Raines. I believe you own most of it.'

He laughed softly. 'No, not quite all. The gold strike has done more for me than all the wheat and sheep I could grow in ten years. I worked like a slave to build up my property, and make something of it, and then along came the miners and I've made more money than I ever dreamt of, back in England.'

Cleo glanced at him under her lashes. The soft, well-sewn stuff of his coat, his white silk shirt and carelessly knotted necktie. He oozed assurance and wealth. He looked what he was: a dangerous, self-contained man. Cleo wondered how his wife dealt with him.

'But why are you in Nugget Gully?' he was asking her. 'The gold? Somehow I can't imagine you with a pick in hand. Or perhaps you mean to get rich some other way? Everyone who comes to the gold fields is in search of wealth, one way way or another.'

'My father meant to open a millinery shop,' she said softly, 'but he is dead. I have plans of my own.'

She met his eyes, and took another sip of the dreadful wine. 'Tell me, are you married, Mr. Raines?'

He let out a shout of laughter. 'No! You sound as though you have plans to propose to me, Miss Montague!' Cleo flushed angrily, feeling foolish to have allowed her curiosity to ask such a question.

The girl, Gertie, had returned. This time with a table, carried in by two men, and a tray set with their luncheon. The delicious smells made Cleo feel faint and she realised just how hungry she was. It tasted as good as it smelt, and she tucked in.

'Tell me, Miss Montague,' Jake Raines began at last, and then stopped. 'But it's such a mouthful, isn't it, "Miss Montague"! What is your first name?'

Cleo looked at him in astonishment. 'That is hardly proper, Mr. Raines. You cannot call me by my first name!'

'Can I not?' he said with a long, arrogant stare. 'I can call you whatever the devil I please. I would not object to your calling me Jake. Why can I not call you... whatever your name is?'

'I would not call you... *that,* even if you were my friend,' Cleo retorted furiously. 'It is not proper. If you think it is, you are no gentleman, sir.'

'I thought we were already agreed on that.'

Cleo was at the door before she knew it, but he reached her before she could open it. He was as lithe as a cat, and, spinning her around, pulled her against him. His grip hurt her arm, and she cried out with the pain of it. His breath on her temple was warm and gentle, and he said, 'Forgive me, I had not meant to hurt you or to anger you, and now it seems I have done both. Women like you stir up the devil in me, Miss Montague.'

'Like me?' Cleo whispered.

'Women who pretend at a propriety I very much doubt they feel. They've been brought up to be hypocrites, Miss Montague.'

Cleo felt she should be angry, but instead she felt weak. 'Please,' she said, and her voice was breathless. Something about his closeness was making her dizzy again, and at the same time so claustrophobic she wanted to run screaming down the stairs and out into the street. 'Please, you must let me go.'

'Must I, Miss Montague?' he mocked, and now, unbelievably, his lips brushed her temple, where before only his breath had been. She felt his hand on her hair, and then he was removing the pins she had so neatly placed there, one by one, until it cascaded over her shoulders in gleaming chestnut curls. 'What must I do?'

She looked up into his dark eyes, and saw something there that glittered and frightened her and was, she very much feared, desire. 'I cannot believe you would take advantage of a respectable woman, sir,' she whispered. 'You are not so wicked as that. In fact, you told me you would not.'

His smile was gentle, deceptively so. 'Did I say so? Perhaps we may strike a bargain. You will tell me your name, and I will let you go. What do you think of that?'

Cleo caught her breath. 'My name is Cleo—

Cleopatra,' she whispered. Then, in excuse, 'One of my mother's flights of fancy.'

Jake stared at her, and then he laughed. 'Cleopatra,' he said and let her go. 'Good God, no wonder you wouldn't tell me! How could any woman maintain a—a prim and proper front with a name like that? Cleopatra,' he said again, rolling it over his tongue until it sounded unlike it had ever sounded before. Cleo shivered, folding her arms about herself. He turned back to her and cocked his head to one side. 'It suits you,' he said at last, soft and dangerous again. 'Or it would, if you would let it.'

'What do you mean?' she whispered, and wished she hadn't.

'Well, if you were to dress the part, and let your hair curl about your shoulders...'

'How would I dress the part,' Cleo retorted caustically, 'when you ruined one of my gowns, and now this one too is soiled?'

He laughed. 'Well, you would have to find a gentleman of means to buy you suitable clothes and keep you in surrounds more suited to a Cleopatra.'

He was watching her now under his lashes, idly turning the stem of his glass. He was playing some deep game with her, and Cleo gave a shiver of apprehension.

'If you mean yourself, Mr. Raines, you should know that not even if you were the last man on earth would I consider such a proposal.'

His smile was mocking. 'Does this mean you do not wish to see me again, Cleopatra?'

Cleo turned and wrenched open the door. But he stopped her. 'Wait. Before you go, it may be wise to put your boots on, my dear.'

Humiliation brought colour flooding to her cheeks. She looked down at her stockinged feet, and then up at the boots he was holding out to her. In all the fuss she had forgotten he had removed them so long ago. For a moment she considered leaving them, but even as she thought it she knew she could not. Cleo swept forward with as much dignity as she could muster and snatched them from his hand.

'Goodbye, Cleopatra,' he murmured. She hurried from the room, down the stairs and, after pausing to pull on the boots, out into the street. His laughter seemed to follow her, like a knife in her back.

CHAPTER THREE

CLEO RETURNED TO her room at Mrs. Smith's, determined to forget all that had occurred. But it was not as simple as she had hoped. During the day she might fill her head with other matters—her future plans for one—but the night had other ideas, and she would wake in a cold sweat, thinking herself trapped in that gaudy room, with Jake Raines stalking ever closer.

Not that she saw him in the flesh, in the following week. She made sure of that. She was looking for the premises she would make into the millinery shop. She knew what she wanted, and was determined to find the best. If she was to be a success, it must all be the best—no pokey, hole-in-the-wall affair for Cleopatra Montague!

Mrs. Smith was enthusiastic, and confided Cleo's plans to one of her other boarders. This was the other female, a petite blonde woman with pale skin and fashionably tiny waist. She was also fashionably delicate—the sort of woman Cleo had always hoped to be. Mrs. Mulgrave was married to a police officer presently stationed on the gold fields at Ballarat.

'He's keeping an eye on the miners,' she said candidly, 'and is so hated by them that I refused to accompany him.'

Cleo smiled uncertainly. Mrs. Mulgrave might be delicate, but her languid air hid something sly—the green eyes, veiled by long, curling lashes, watched.

'I'm afraid I'm a very poor sort of wife,' she went on, 'not to go with him. But, really, the strain on my nerves would be too great. I would much rather the boredom of Nugget Gully.'

'Do you think it boring?' asked Cleo. 'There seems to be so much going on.'

Mrs. Mulgrave looked at her with sly interest. 'I think you very brave, Miss Montague, to have come out here alone. I wish I had your courage.'

Cleo bit her lip. 'I believe I am looked upon as being a little too impulsive sometimes, Mrs. Mulgrave. This is not exactly a quality sought in a lady, is it?'

'I must confess, I have heard the strangest story concerning you, my dear. You and the famous—or should I say infamous?—Jake Raines!'

Cleo flushed scarlet, and looked at her hands. The other woman eyed her speculatively for a moment, a smile flickering about her pink lips. Then she leaned forward, making her voice gentle, her manner that of a much older woman. 'I was quite shocked at the time, dear Miss Montague, and I think, I really do think, that I must take you under my wing. I would advise you against any such friendships with men such as Mr.

Raines. You know, a woman such as you, alone and unmarried, must be particularly careful as to your reputation.'

Cleo murmured some excuse and fled the parlour. But Mrs. Mulgrave seemed determined to be her friend, or, as she called it, take her 'under her wing', and Cleo was unable to dissuade her without being rude. In fact, she was not sure she didn't secretly welcome the friendship. She did not have many friends here, and even the overtures of Mrs. Mulgrave were comforting.

They were even more welcome when Mrs. Smith told her of Cleo's plans, and Mrs. Mulgrave became awash with enthusiasm. 'What a marvellous idea!' she cried. 'I can hardly wait until you open. There is so little in the way of sophistication in Nugget Gully. One has to travel to Melbourne for anything halfway decent.'

'I hope all the women, and men, feel like you... Mrs. Mulgrave.'

'Oh, Melissa, please. I'm sure they will, Cleo, my dear. The bank manager's wife, the reverend's wife, the doctor's wife... oh, and some of the landowners, would all be too delighted, I'm sure! I will make quite certain they hear of it when the time is right, I promise you.'

Cleo smiled back, pleased. Her friendship with Melissa Mulgrave was going to be more profitable than she had thought.

The only land-selling agent in Nugget Gully lived in a tiny office situated near the general store. Cleo had had little success with him so far—the only building he had informed her of was far too large and too far from the main street. But during her second visit he happened to mention what had been a liquor store. It was just off the main street, down a narrow lane. When they went to inspect it, Cleo found it dirty inside, and neat rather than small. She rather fancied it had been a sly grog shop, or drinking house, rather than a proper, licensed premises, and the smells which remained bore out her suspicions. But it was in a good position. People would be able to find her, once she made her name. The agent hovered near the door, glancing at his fob watch impatiently. But Cleo ignored him.

The front of the building was connected by a door to two rooms at the back. One had been a storeroom, the other a bedroom. Cleo looked about. She could turn one into a kitchen-cum-living area, and the other her bedroom. There was a tiny garden at the back, with some wild, overgrown daisies and a huge clump of lavender near the door. The delicious scent reminded her of home. She could see herself here; it felt like home despite the dirt and the work to be done. Yes, she thought in sudden decision, it would do. It would do very well. She turned to the man with such a bright pleased smile that he blinked.

'I see it has possibilities,' she said. 'What would the owner be asking, considering the... the state of the property?'

The little man cleared his throat, and ran a finger around his high, stiff collar. 'Well, considering it is so close to the main street, in the—er—commercial part of town, I think the price is reasonable.'

Cleo waited.

'Eight hundred and twenty pounds,' he said, and cleared his throat again.

His eyes told her he thought the price very *unreasonable*. Cleo turned away, shocked. She ran a finger tremblingly over the dust and grime on the table. 'You realise how much work will be needed if this building is to become anything like a decent establishment?' she asked finally, and turned back to face him.

The agent lifted his hands. 'I'm sorry. I don't make the prices, I only ask what my clients ask me to ask! That is the price he wants.'

'Is there no way we could come to some more fair arrangement?'

'Well...'

'Who is the owner?'

'A Melbourne man.' He shifted his eyes away. 'I can get in touch with him. But to be honest, ma'am, I doubt he will budge. Nugget Gully is a wealthy town and he believes the price will be matched, eventually.'

Cleo looked away. She had only five hundred pounds to spare for her premises, and even that was dangerously above what she had planned to pay. The rest she would need for redecorating and rebuilding, and buying her goods.

'You may tell him from me, sir,' she said at last, 'that I think he is grossly unfair.' She swept by the agent, with a dip of her head. Her anger made her face flame, and her disappointment made her feel sick. She had seen it all so clearly, and now that dream was to be taken away from her so cruelly, so unfairly. Eight hundred and twenty pounds! Even five hundred was ridiculous. Why hadn't she asked the price before she went to see it? Then she could have saved herself this misery.

She was walking so quickly she didn't see him until it was too late, and then, when she muttered some excuse and went to brush by him, he put out his hand and stopped her. It was a beautiful day, and despite her broad-brimmed hat she had to shade her eyes from the sun when she looked up at him. The sun seemed to be in his eyes, and they danced at her as if they knew all too well her discomfiture.

'Miss Montague—Cleo. You look a trifle flushed. Is the weather too warm for you?'

'Weather?' She looked about, still reeling from the shock of her dreams being snatched from under her nose, and now the shock of running into the very person she had no wish to meet: Jake Raines.

'Yes. Isn't that what people usually discuss in polite conversation?'

'What do you know about polite conversation?' she snapped, and then was ashamed at her outburst, and flushed when two passing elderly women looked at her in surprise.

But Jake laughed. 'You *are* in a bad mood. Whatever is the matter?'

'Why should anything be the matter?' she retorted, and yet, even as she said it, lifting her chin arrogantly, the tears stung her eyes. She knew then, to her horror, that she was about to disgrace herself as she had not done since she was a child, and her favourite puppy had been run over by the Bristol Mail Coach.

His hand was firm and warm about her arm, and before she could argue, or do more than disguise her face with an upheld gloved hand, he had led her into a quieter part of the street, and around a corner to what appeared to be the window of a repairer of clocks.

'Cleo, Cleo,' he said softly, and she sniffed and looked up, meeting his eyes' reflection in the rather dusty glass. They were dark, dark with concern and curiosity. They warmed her, and made her feel, ridiculous though she later found it, that she could confide in him.

'I beg your pardon,' she whispered huskily. 'I do not usually show my emotions to strangers.'

He shook his head gently at her. 'I hope we are more than that, Cleopatra. I feel by now we know each other intimately.'

'I...' She wiped her eyes with her gloved finger, and smiled a little wanly. 'I was disappointed, you see. It was so perfect that I was sure it was meant to be, just as my father would have wished it. And then, to be told... well, it is shocking, I don't care what anyone says! Quite shocking.'

Jake frowned at her. 'What is shocking? Did you see Annabel Lees? You shouldn't be shocked by her; she's just making her living, the same as us all. And the miners appreciate her... services.'

Cleo's puzzled expression made him laugh out loud. 'Not Annabel, then. Tell me, Cleo, what is the matter? It must be something *very* shocking to make *you* cry. You did not cry on either of the last two occasions we met, and they were enough to make any other woman howl!'

Cleo flushed. 'I always seem to run into you when I least wish to,' she murmured.

'I would have said when you most need me,' he retorted. 'Come, tell me what it is. I won't let you go until you do, you know.'

She realised then that he still held her arm, and jerked away as if she had been burned. 'It is none of your business, Mr. Raines, but I will tell you. You know I had intended to set up a millinery establishment. Well, I have been seeking a suitable premises, and had thought I had found it. A small building, in Hunter's Lane. Do you know it? Very dirty and in need of repair, but it had such possibilities…'

He nodded. 'I know it, Cleo. As you say, dirty, but …yes, I can see it would be the very place for you.'

Cleo looked away, the tears pricking her eyes again. 'I don't know if you can understand, but it seemed as if it were already mine. I had chosen the drapes, and the carpet. I had picked out the wallpaper, and where I would place my bonnets and my mirrors, for the customers, you know, and… but there…' she wiped her eyes again '… I am being foolish. I don't know why; I am rarely foolish and never tearful.'

Jake looked down at her pale face, and smiled. 'I know. And what was it about this perfect building which has made you both foolish and tearful?'

'The price. Eight hundred and twenty pounds.'

He blinked. 'Robbery.'

'That is what I said. But the agent told me it belongs to a man in Melbourne. I would offer five hundred, and that... that is still far too much, but I doubt it would satisfy him. I need the rest to do the work, and... oh, it is quite hopeless.'

They both looked into the window. One of the clocks had begun to strike. Cleo wondered why she had told him. He had seemed interested, and yet why should he be? Jake Raines was interested in no one but himself, and she was not the sort of woman to attract anything but mockery from him.

After a moment he spoke and his voice was quiet and somehow earnest. 'As I see it, you have three choices, Cleo. You can go to another town and find your shop there. Ballarat, perhaps, or Bendigo, although I would say there would already be milliners there by the dozen. Or you can give up your idea, and turn your talents to something else, although what, I can't say... barmaid, perhaps? No, I didn't think you'd like the idea! Or three, you could find yourself a partner in the business. Someone willing to help you purchase the building, as well as help you redecorate it, furnish it and so on. Someone who will leave all the business side of things to you, and be merely a silent partner.'

'And who would this fairy godmother be?'

He laughed. 'I wouldn't call myself that exactly, but I would come in as your partner. I feel it would be a good investment. You would be happy and I would be happy, and no one else need be the wiser. I will have the papers drawn up and you can sign them, and from then on you will run your millinery shop and no one in Nugget Gully will know that you do not own it lock, stock and barrel!'

It was ridiculous! No decent woman would go into partnership with a rake. Her reputation would be in shreds. If anyone ever found out... Cleo stopped. But what if no one found out? And why had she told him, if she had not hoped deep in her heart that he would help? Cleo felt suddenly ashamed. 'I cannot. It would not be right. I feel I have taken advantage of you, Mr. Raines.'

He laughed again. 'That is a novelty, then!' His eyes became candid. 'You have done no such thing, Cleo. It is to my advantage, as well as yours. I will be a richer man, and you will be able to do what your heart is set upon doing. I would offer the same deal to anyone, if I saw it as being profitable. Although I would not be as concerned about keeping it a secret. It would have to be secret, you know, at least at this stage. If it became known I was helping you it would be assumed, naturally, that you were as much my possession as your shop.'

'I am certainly neither your nor any man's possession!' Cleo snapped, flushing. She felt her heart beating with anger and embarrassment. A man with his reputation! How could she even consider for a moment...?

'Think of me as a father to you,' he added gently.

Now it was Cleo's turn to laugh, responding to the gleam in his eyes. 'Mr. Raines, really... I must think it over. You will understand?'

He shrugged. 'As you wish. But don't wait too long; I might change my mind.'

She left him there, walking quickly away. Her neat room was quiet and welcoming, and Cleo sank down on the bed, staring into space. Now she could think, and yet she felt confused.

A business deal, Jacob Raines had said. Was he to be trusted? But surely, if they signed legal documents... He was a rake, she reminded herself tartly. Don't weaken just because he showed you some sympathy! He is used to manipulating women. But why me?

Cleo clutched her head and moaned. It was not as if she was so beautiful he would want to pursue her. It must be as he said—he saw a chance to make a profit and being an astute businessman couldn't resist it.

But what of her reputation? He had said it must be a secret. Cleo imagined what her prospective customers would say, if it became known that she was a partner with the town's disreputable Jacob Raines. She would be ostracised, her reputation would be in tatters. They would believe the worst; she was not so innocent that she didn't realise how cruel and unfair Victorian society could be. One must be respectable at all costs, especially if one was a woman. A man may have his peccadilloes, as long as he was 'discreet', but a woman's virtue must be beyond reproach.

But, Cleo reminded herself, it would be a secret between only them. She would not reveal it, and why should he?

'You are very quiet tonight,' Mrs. Smith said at dinner, her blue eyes sharp.

'Am I? I was thinking of my shop.' She hesitated. 'I saw a place today which would be perfect. But I wanted to be sure...'

Mrs. Smith smiled. 'But that's fine.'

Melissa Mulgrave leaned forward. 'My dear Miss Montague, why hesitate?'

Why indeed? Cleo thought. Perhaps she was being impetuous again, as she had been when she rode alone from Bendigo, and yet then, as now, it seemed the *right* thing to do. The fear was that it could end just as disastrously.

'I have already been busy telling everyone you mean to make your hats,' Melissa went on. 'I was wondering if you could make me one—just so that I could wear it when I tell people, you know.'

'What a good idea!' Mrs. Smith cried.

Cleo agreed. 'I will do it now.' She gave Melissa a long look. 'I know just the thing that would suit you, Mrs. Mulgrave!'

Upstairs, Cleo unpacked the bits and pieces from her bag. There was green cloth and ribbons and some fine lace. Cleo began to cut and sew, bending close in the dim lamplight. Her fingers were quick and practised—she hardly needed to think as she sewed and fashioned the bonnet. It was something she did well, the only thing she really could do to make a living for herself in this new land.

Cleo decided then that she would agree to Jake Raines's proposal. She would find him tomorrow and tell him so herself.

The next morning Cleo hardly waited for Melissa's exclamations of pleasure over her bonnet. She made her way down Nugget Gully's busy street. Where would he be? Cleo hesitated opposite the hotel. She could hardly go in. A boy, playing marbles with his friends in the dust, came at her bidding.

'For a shilling,' he retorted slyly, when she asked him to take a message for her. Cleo grudgingly agreed, and watched the boy run across the road and disappear into the dim interior of the hotel.

The gaudy female was there again, laughing with her admiring group of miners. Was that the shocking Annabel Lees whom Jacob Raines had spoken of?

The boy returned. 'Says he'll meet you in Hunter's Lane,' he said in a conspirator's voice. 'And don't worry. He gave me a sovereign not to tell!'

Cleo hurried off, hoping no one had noticed. Hunter's Lane was deserted—well, once her shop had opened that would change! There was another house, back behind the shop, but the other side of the lane was taken up by a solid brick wall.

Quick footsteps. Cleo looked up. The dark eyes were alive with amusement. 'Have you called me to an assignation, Miss Montague?'

Cleo flushed angrily. 'This is business, Mr. Raines.'

'What a pity!' He laughed. 'Don't look so disapproving, Cleo! I am here; now what is it?'

Cleo was tempted to tell him to forget his deal and she would never have anything to do with such as he. But she bit her tongue on the words—it would be foolish to ruin her dreams for a momentary ascendancy over this man.

'Well?'

She met the dark, mocking gaze and watched his mouth quirk up in a half-smile. He had read her thoughts accurately from the expressions flitting across her face. Very well, then, she would do business with him, even if she never invited him into her home.

'Very well,' said Cleo. 'I accept.'

The black eyes were veiled. 'Very wise, Cleopatra. I will have everything attended to, and the papers drawn up. I would suggest you tell your cronies that you have already bought the place and set about choosing and ordering your little knick-knacks. Anything you fancy, now, no cost to be spared. I will lay out for the decorations and the repairs. Save your money for your hats.'

'Why? I want to pay equally in all things.'

Jake sighed. 'Cleo, if you want the place to look like class, then order the best and let me pay.'

Cleo fought with her pride for a moment, and then she shrugged. 'As you wish, Mr. Raines. We are partners.'

Jake was looking up at the building. 'It's sound enough,' he said. 'Just let go, somewhat.' He looked at her. 'Shall we shake hands on it, then?' He held out his hand. It was large and square and brown.

Cleo looked at it so suspiciously that he laughed. 'Come now, Cleo. Is it a deal?'

'I have said it is,' she murmured, but gave him her hand.

He squeezed it and then released it. His handsome face creased into a smile. 'Don't worry,' he said softly. 'No one will know. Your spotless reputation will be quite safe with me. And if, by some mischance, we are found out... I swear I will marry you and make an honest woman of you!'

'You are being ridiculous.' Cleo flushed angrily.

'I realise I am not exactly the most respectable of men in this town.'

Cleo glanced at him swiftly. He had sounded bitter. 'You are very rich,' she offered.

'Ah, then that's all right,' he said in mockery. 'Go, Cleo, before you make me angry. I'll see you again, no doubt, when the bills start coming in.'

Cleo still hesitated, feeling she had somehow hurt him and for some reason this made her uncomfortable. 'You said that you weren't, but you are, you know. My fairy godmother.'

He laughed, and the dark cloud was gone. But it was replaced in his eyes by something far more dangerous and Cleo took to her heels without further prompting.

Mrs. Smith was as pleased as Cleo when she was told. She hugged her as if she were her own daughter. Melissa Mulgrave came and looked at the place a little uncertainly. 'I'm sure it will all be as you say, Cleo, dear. You are so energetic, you will get everything done.'

The agent brought the deeds for Cleo to sign.

He seemed as shifty as ever, but said nothing about Jake Raines. Obviously he knew the truth; Jake was probably his biggest customer, and he wouldn't ruin that relationship.

Anyway, Cleo was enjoying herself too much to worry. She was ordering about the repair men, and picking out cloth and carpet, tables and chairs, lamps and lanterns. Everything would be just as she had imagined it, ready for opening day.

She saw Jake Raines twice during that busy time. The first time, she was striding down the street, in her usual brisk way, when she saw him handing a dainty woman up into a gig. The possessive manner in which he held her gloved fingers told its own story, and Cleo barely nodded at him when he lifted his hat as she passed. Well, it did not matter what his morals were, she told herself. They were business partners and nothing more.

The second time, a discreet note was sent around to Mrs. Smith's for Cleo to be present at Hunter's Lane the next morning. The door was open, and Cleo went into the cool interior. The workmen had finished, and it only remained for the room to be filled with Cleo's new purchases. She stood a moment, savouring the smell of fresh varnish and the clean, new paintwork. This had been her dream…her father's dream. She knew suddenly that it had all been worth it.

'Miss Montague.' He had come in so quietly that she hadn't heard him. There was another man behind him, a well-dressed little man with whiskers. 'This is Mr. Leopald. He has brought the papers for you to sign.'

The man bowed gravely and, flipping open a leather case, brought out a slim sheaf of papers. Cleo took it and glanced at the writing. As far as she could tell it stated they would be equal partners in the shop but she would have full control in making the decisions concerning the business, Jake Raines being merely a financial partner. When she looked up he was watching her, that quirk of a smile on his lips.

'Well, is it satisfactory?'

Mr. Leopald moved discreetly to the back of the shop. Cleo nodded. 'Yes.'

'When the bills come for all this,' he gestured about him, 'send them to me. I'll make sure they're paid by Leopald here, in such a way that they think him your man of business and not mine.'

'Thank you,' Cleo murmured.

'Oh, don't thank me. I expect you to pay me back tenfold.'

She looked at him a moment, wondering if he mocked her, but he merely smiled, and beckoned Leopald back.

'You'll have to sign now. Mr. Leopald will witness our signatures.'

Leopald produced a pen. Cleo took it and, before she could change her mind, signed. Jake took it from her and scribbled his name with a flourish.

Leopald slipped the papers back into his briefcase. It was done and there could be no turning back. She was partners with Jake Raines, and no one in Nugget Gully must ever know.

Jake was watching her, something in his eyes making her uncomfortable again. 'Regretting it already?' he asked softly.

Cleo lifted her chin. 'No, of course not.'

He took her arm, and led her over to the door. 'When is the big opening?'

'Soon. I shall let you know. Have you any orders for me?' She, too, could mock.

Jake raised an eyebrow. 'I have no need of fashionable hats, my dear!'

'I meant for your...friends, Mr. Raines. Perhaps the...lady I saw you with the other day? She would look ravishing in a blue bonnet.'

His dark eyes narrowed and Cleo knew she had said too much. But all he said was, 'That is my business, Miss Montague. I haven't become your partner so that you can pry into my private affairs. I am thirty-five years old. Would you have me live the life of a monk?'

Cleo wished the floor would open up. She had meant to be as mocking and world-wise as he, and instead had just been naïve and foolish. She turned her head away and bit her lip. Perhaps he would go and let her suffer her embarrassment alone?

But he didn't. She felt his fingertip on her averted cheek, tracing the line of her jaw around to her stubborn chin, then up to her closed, thinned mouth. His finger rested there, on her lips. 'Come, Cleo,' he murmured in a soft, deep voice. 'Are you really so disapproving of me? I know we're worlds apart, you and I. I can imagine the sort of life you've led—sheltered, secluded. You set great store by being *proper*, don't you? But not all proper people are good and honest people, or even *nice* people, Cleo. I judge my friends by things other than whether they would fit well into Nugget Gully's closed, hypocritical and oh, so proper society.'

Cleo turned to look at him in surprise. No one had ever said such a thing to her before. Her idea of the world had been black and white, until she met him. That he was not respectable, she knew, and she knew too that he would never be seen in the home of any 'decent' woman, and yet those same 'proper' people would feel free to take his money in business dealings with him. But she also knew that he had been kind to her, and he had even been a friend to her. Cleo was confused, her ideals turned topsy-turvy.

Perhaps he saw that, for he sighed and gently brushed the tip of her nose before dropping his hand to his side. 'Good luck, Cleo. No doubt I will see you again.'

'Thank you,' Cleo whispered, but he had already slipped out of the door. Mr. Leopald bowed and followed, and Cleo was alone to ponder her future.

CHAPTER FOUR

IT WAS SUNDAY. Cleo lay in her new bed, looking at her newly plastered and painted ceiling, and stretched luxuriously. The whole world was quiet; even the rumble of drays in the main street had ceased today. Only the birds in the pepper tree in the backyard disturbed the peace.

She had been here an entire week, and it was already her home. The first evening, she had put her clothing away and, after she had eaten her cold supper, tried to settle before the stove with a book. But she had been too restless, wandering around, touching the new green velvet drapes, the little table, the furnishings she had chosen with such care.

Out in the front of the house it had been cool, beyond the reach of her wood stove. In the light of the wavering candle Cleo had held, it was strange and empty. The mirrors had reflected back her ghostly face, the little tables and chairs, the rows of shelves and the hat boxes. Cleo had been working hard for weeks on new hats. She had felt inspired, and pored over the fashion journals she had had sent from Melbourne, copying some of their offerings, adapting others to her own design. She had something for everyone. Melissa had promised to be her very best customer.

'You're a magician, my dear,' she cried, trying on some of Cleo's creations. 'Now,' and the green eyes narrowed at her, 'I insist you allow me to make you as fashionable as your hats!'

Cleo protested, but Melissa persisted, and Cleo found herself with a new green gown with tight-fitting bodice and hundreds of shiny buttons. It suited her very well, and, when Melissa dressed her hair in a myriad ringlets, it looked even better.

'Now,' Melissa breathed a sigh of satisfaction, 'you look like a successful woman. You are very striking, you know, and although you are not beautiful in the usual way, you are...different. You should cultivate that difference, Cleo, not try to hide it.'

'Thank you, Melissa,' Cleo retorted, 'but I am very happy with the way I am. How can you make a silk purse out of a sow's ear? I am too tall, too... buxom, certainly too healthy, and I speak my mind instead of simpering!'

Melissa shook her head at her. 'Tell me, Cleo, don't you sometimes wish for the attentions of a handsome suitor? Even an ugly one? Have you ever had a suitor, my dear?'

Cleo flushed before Melissa's appraising glance. 'I hardly think that is any of—'

'Now, don't take that freezing tone with me.' The other woman tapped her on the hand with her fan. 'A woman can have success, but she needs more than that. One can become very lonely, Cleo. I think you should consider the idea.'

Cleo turned away, fussing with her hair to hide her annoyance. 'I am quite happy as I am, Melissa. Now, shall we get on with my hair?'

Melissa shrugged, but her eyes were sly and Cleo was glad when she had gone.

But Cleo took her advice about looking the part, and bought more plain but well-made gowns and tried to dress her hair less severely. There was no point in going too far, she told herself; she didn't want to intimidate her customers.

Melissa and Mrs. Smith had wanted to keep her company that first evening, but Cleo had wanted to be alone. There had been a bottle of champagne in the room when she arrived. No note, but she knew who had left it. She had put it away for the day she had someone to celebrate with.

It was still dark when Cleo had risen that first morning. She had been afraid and excited; this was her big adventure. She was going to be a success, she was going to be rich and famous—at least, in Nugget Gully!

From that morning until Sunday, when she woke in her bed, Cleo did not have time to think. It all went by in a blur. Everything she had made up was sold, and she had new orders for more. It was as if the whole town knew of her, and had come to buy her creations—Melissa Mulgrave had lived up to her promises. Even the notorious Annabel Lees had arrived and Cleo, schooling her rigid disapproval into a smile, sold her a straw chip hat to set on her hennaed curls.

Cleo had worked, ate and slept. And by the end of the week she knew she was a resounding success, and, though weary to the bone, she was triumphant. That she looked so striking in her new gowns did not occur to her, but in fact that was what most of her customers thought, and word spread about the hatmaker fresh from England as much as her hats.

Her pleasant thoughts came to an end. Cleo yawned, and eventually rose, pulling a wrap about her long nightgown. She wandered out into the little sitting-room to sip tea and glance idly through a *Ladies' Journal*. She planned to relax today, and perhaps later she might go for a walk in the sunshine before settling down to work on some of her orders.

The tap on the door came as a surprise, and Cleo frowned, wondering who could be calling on her when everyone knew she was taking a well-earned rest. A dissatisfied customer? But she rose, pushing her long hair back over one shoulder, and undid the shining new bolt, peeping out into the sunshine.

The day was full of warmth and glory, but it was not that at which she looked. For *he* stood there, Jake Raines, as well-dressed as ever, his smile a mocking gleam, and his eyes ran over her in the way she hated.

'Cleopatra,' he said. She met the dark, teasing eyes and felt as if she had opened the door to the devil.

'Mr. Raines.'

He met her hostile eyes, his own alive with laughter. 'Won't you invite your partner in?'

A chill went over her. 'No one is to know that,' she hissed, but stepped back hastily.

'And nobody does,' he retorted. 'I came to take you driving.' His eyes slid again over her long hair, her wrap, and the old, serviceable nightgown. 'Come as you are,' he invited.

For a moment she was tempted to push him out and slam the door in his face, but, even as the thought came into her mind, she knew she would not. He was her partner, and she was suddenly afraid of the rights that had given him. She had thought of herself, before, of her own future. And since then she had thought of nothing but her business and the success it seemed sure to become. But now she thought of Jake Raines and this hold she had given him over her, and she was chilled.

'You think a great deal of me, don't you?'

The quiet sarcasm made her jerk her chin up and meet his eyes. He had read her thoughts, and now was angry. Cleo turned away, flushing. She had forgotten. He was not interested in her as a woman. He had his pick of all the beauties; why should he find her the least bit attractive?

'I thought you might like to see my property,' he added after a moment, without expression. 'No ulterior motive. But evidently you are too grand to accept my simple invitation.'

Cleo frowned. 'I am not grand, Mr. Raines. I was planning to spend a quiet day alone.' She pulled her wrap closer about her, disliking his closeness in the small room. 'I have been so overwhelmed by the number of people coming to me! I am a great success.'

He threw back his head and laughed so loudly that Cleo was afraid the neighbours must hear. 'Never change, Cleo,' he said at last, and the gleam in his eyes was so warm and friendly that it took her off her guard.

She turned away, blushing, and said, 'I shall, of course, be sure you receive your share of the profits. I kept books for my father, you know, and am quite good at accounting.'

'I'm sure you are.'

Cleo dared another peek up at him. He was still smiling at her. 'Go and put on something pretty, Miss Montague. I'd like the pleasure of your company very much.' He reached up and brushed a tress of chestnut hair over her shoulder again, where it had fallen forward. The touch was almost a caress, and Cleo backed away nervously.

'I'll be ready in a moment. Please, sit down.'

Cleo closed her bedroom door and leaned against it with her eyes closed. She must be mad to agree to go with him. And as for letting him into her home, unchaperoned! What was wrong with her to behave like a hoyden, or worse? She seemed to lose all her level-headedness when it came to Jake Raines. She was constantly finding herself in questionable situations, and now she was risking her good name and her reputation. What if someone were to visit, some customer come to discuss a new hat?

Chilled again with fear, Cleo rushed about

the room, throwing off her clothes. She had a white summer gown she had not worn yet. It looked pretty and cool for the warm day, and as she brushed her hair, twisting it up with a tortoise-shell comb Melissa had given her, she thought she looked seventeen rather than a mature woman of twenty-five.

What did Jake Raines see in her? She sighed, and did not see the strength of her chin and jaw, the classical beauty in her straight little nose and wide-set slanting brown eyes. When she was an old woman, and others well past their best, Cleo would still be beautiful.

He was standing restlessly in the room, and turned quickly when he heard her enter. The quick glance was appreciative but all he said was, 'Ah, ready? Come on, then. It's about an hour's drive.'

His arm rested a moment about her waist, as she passed through the doorway, but it was gone almost immediately. But even that slight contact sent a tingle through her and Cleo wondered with annoyance how a man could manage such a thing with just a touch.

The sun was hot, and Cleo wondered if it might build up into a storm later on in the afternoon. But Jake was already ushering her into the gig and took up the reins. Cleo settled herself, and put up her parasol to shield her face and her identity.

The morning was clear and beautiful, if a little oppressive. Cleo settled her bonnet more firmly upon her head, and looked about at Nugget Gully from the protection of her sunshade. The streets were quiet and deserted, apart from the insistent ringing of a church bell. She sneaked a sideways glance at Jake's profile. Strong and handsome, his hat pulled forward to shade his eyes. Dark hair curled at his collar, and his shirt and waistcoat were without a wrinkle over the broad muscles of shoulder and back. His hands, holding the reins, were strong and capable, the sort of hands one could rely on. In fact, Cleo couldn't help but think that altogether he was a man you could rely on. If one needed a man, which Cleo didn't. Melissa was wrong; she was quite happy with her success and doubted she would ever feel lonely.

As if sensing her gaze, Jake turned and viewed her with a slow, lazy smile, black eyes dark and gleaming as oil on water. Cleo felt almost drowned in their depths, until she recollected herself and turned away, hoping he did not see the colour stealing into her pale cheeks.

'I would have thought Sunday was a morning you might lie in, Mr. Raines,' she said, with a hearty note in her voice. 'You must have much to do, Saturday night. With the hotel, and… and everything.'

He regarded her a moment before saying in a cool, conversational voice, 'It so happens that Sunday is my one free day. I have no commitments, no engagements. I do as I will. And today I want to take Cleopatra Montague for a drive in the country.'

There seemed little to reply to that, and Cleo sat back in silence and allowed herself to relax and enjoy the scenery.

The countryside was changing. They were on the outskirts of the town, and the tents and the buildings were soon left behind, giving way to softly undulating hills and bush. Birds fluttered in the branches, and a brief, fragrant breeze stirred Cleo's hair, where it lay damp against her neck in the heat. This was what it must have been like, before white men arrived in Nugget Gully and so changed the landscape. As the bush became denser about them, the heat become more oppressive, the air so still it seemed to shimmer on the track before them. The horse plodded on, tail swishing away the flies, and Cleo felt perspiration begin a slow trickle between her shoulder-blades. His voice came out of the long silence, startling her.

'How old are you, Miss Montague?'

Cleo looked up at him. 'I hardly see what business it is of yours, Mr. Raines. But I am not afraid to say I am twenty-five years old, and well and truly on the shelf, as they vulgarly call it. Not,' she added, eyeing him coldly, 'that I ever wanted to be married.'

'Oh, but why not?' He looked at her with interest.

Cleo looked for mockery, but he showed none, and after a moment she said, 'I kept house for my father for nearly twenty years, ever since my mother died. I have been my own mistress for too long to take lightly anyone—husband or no—telling me what I can and cannot do. I have seen my cousin submitting to her husband's whims and orders, foolish as they often are, and even seeming to enjoy her lack of power in her own destiny! I would not— could not allow such a thing to happen to me. Women are nothing in this world, once they are shackled to a man.'

She could not read the expression in his eyes, for he had turned away to click the reins, to hurry the horse on its journey.

'And what of Queen Victoria?' he asked at last. 'Not that I find her a terribly attractive specimen of womanhood, but she is powerful in her own right, and she is married with a great brood of children.'

Cleo was shocked, and turned to him impetuously. 'They are hardly the loyal words one would expect of an Englishman!'

But he laughed, giving her a cynical glance. 'England never treated me with anything other than indifference; why should I mouth words I do not believe or feel? I was merely pointing out an anomaly in your argument.'

Cleo bit her lip and forced herself to be as casual as he. 'Queen Victoria is hardly an ordinary woman. Come, Mr. Raines, you know what I say is true! Why, a woman cannot even spend her own money as she will without her husband agreeing. A woman loses her identity when she is married.'

'I do not agree, Miss Montague. I think it depends entirely upon the man, and the woman.'

Cleo shot him a sparkling look. 'Tell me, Mr. Raines, are you thinking of marrying? You seem a great advocate of it.'

Now he smiled. 'I have everything I could possibly want without tying myself irrevocably to any one woman,' he retorted. 'And as for so-called "love"...' and there was a sneer in his mouth '... that is a passing phase. It hits one like a gunshot, and then fades as swiftly, after one has sampled the... loved one's wares.'

Cleo felt her face flush a fiery red, and glared at him. 'I find your conversation distasteful, sir! You may think me an innocent, but even I know that what *you* speak of is not love.'

Jake laughed. 'You asked me. I thought you could stand the truth, but after all you are just a prim little miss.'

'I may be prim,' she snapped, 'but you are certainly not a gentleman. Your reputation may be in tatters, but I would have hoped you might try to mend your ways, in the presence of a decent woman!'

She sounded cold and unpleasant, like some ancient duchess full of her own importance. Cleo saw the gleam in his eyes and felt apprehension. 'Oh?' he murmured with dangerous softness.

'Sometimes, Cleo, I think you *are* the same as all the rest of them. Full of unspeakable correctness! Tied down with your rigid rules for living. One must not do this, a gentleman does not do that...' His voice was a savage imitation of her own. 'And then you do something outrageous, like riding alone through the bush at night, and I know I am not mistaken in you. Beneath all that primness, you are quite as improper as I!'

Disconcerted, Cleo looked away from those hard black eyes. Was she like him? Surely not! She had always prided herself on having the proper values, and never doing anything improper or unsuitable to her station. And yet she had on occasion behaved like the hoyden he described. Had not her father told her so? The silence lengthened, and, as Cleo had nothing to say, she allowed it to go on, until eventually Jake drew her attention to the river at their left. Cleo watched with interest as the bush began to grow thinner, and finally opened up on to Jake Raines's property, Belubula.

The house was a sprawling place with a veranda, set down in the valley, silhouetted against the side of one of the gentle hills. A green and peaceful place; the grass was being cropped by sheep and there were paddocks full of growing crops. Smoke drifted from the chimney, and birds sang in the orchard by the house. In the paddock beside the track, horses galloped full pelt before stopping, sweating in the sun, to nibble on the cool grass.

'Why, it's beautiful,' Cleo breathed, and missed the smile he gave her.

'You wouldn't think so if you came here a little later in the summer, with the grass dying... the sheep as well, and the water drying to a trickle. Nor would you think so in the flood, with the muddy water rushing through the valley and the dripping misery of the place. The land here is not kind, Miss Montague, but it seems to suit me, and I seem to suit it.'

'So you would not leave, even if you could live in...in Melbourne, or London?'

'No, I would not leave.'

'You were wrong,' she said suddenly, triumphantly, and he frowned at her. 'You said that love passes. Obviously, there is something you love, Mr. Raines, which is more than just a passing fancy!'

He laughed sharply. 'Minx! How have you managed to slip the bridal yoke for so many years Cleopatra? I can't understand it.'

'Men do not like tall women, or those who speak their minds. I have told you, I have no time for them.'

But she would not meet his gaze, and after a moment he laughed again, softly, this time, and turned away.

The homestead lay quiet, and the only thing which rose to greet them was an old brown dog. It thudded its tail on the veranda post and Jake pulled its tattered ears, before going around to hand Cleo down. She shook out her skirts, stepping into the cool of the veranda, and then the door was opened and a woman in a large white apron stepped out. She wiped her hands, and brushed back a truant strand of hair from her flushed, heated face.

'Mr. Raines!' She greeted him in a decidedly Irish accent. 'And a visitor! You never told me we were to have visitors, sir.'

But her blue eyes were kind, and she smiled at Cleo in a frank, friendly manner. Greying hair had escaped from the untidy bun on the back of her head, and the Australian climate had weathered her skin, but she had been a lovely woman and still was.

'Biddy, this is Miss Cleo Montague. She is making hats in Nugget Gully, and is a great success.

We are privileged to have her here to lunch. Miss Montague, this is Bridget, my housekeeper.'

Biddy raised an eyebrow. 'Is that so, sir? Well, welcome to you, Miss Montague. I'll go and make you both some tea. It's a dry journey. Excuse my untidiness, but I've been baking and I swear the temperature is one hundred degrees out in those kitchens.'

She bustled away, not, it seemed, at all fazed that her master had turned up with a woman as his guest. It must, Cleo thought sarcastically, happen all the time.

Jake bent down to the old dog again, patting its side. Cleo looked about her, breathing deeply of the still, warm air. The peace of the place was wonderful. She untied the strings of her bonnet, and with an unconscious movement lifted her face to sniff the scents of gum trees and Bridget's garden, full of herbs and wallflowers. Jake, watching her, said quietly, 'I was here before the miners all arrived at Nugget Gully, and I'll be here after they've gone.'

Cleo smiled. 'Has Bridget been here with you long?'

'About ten years. She was a widow, with one child.'

'And you took her under your wing; how commendable of you!'

The sarcasm in her voice surprised even Cleo. He gave her a long, cool look. 'We were of use to each other,' he said at last, and turned towards the doorway. Cleo, after a momentary pause, followed, wondering what could have possessed her to say such an unkind thing.

Inside the house it was cool and muted, and, surprisingly, a little shabby. Jake Raines, it seemed, had not used any of his new-won wealth in transforming his home. The parlour he led her to had long windows overlooking the sweep down to the river, and the furnishings looked as worn and shabby as the room itself. Cleo thought it a pity no one had done justice to it with some new drapes or wallpaper. Why hadn't Jake redecorated?

'You're not cold?' Jake enquired, for Cleo had shivered.

'No.' Cleo walked awkwardly to the window. 'I wondered... Why haven't you spent some of your infamous wealth on Belubula?'

He laughed. 'Trust a woman! I suppose there was no need; no one ever comes here but me. If I entertain, I do it at the hotel. Somehow I never get time to refurbish Belubula. When I come here it is to relax.'

Cleo frowned. 'But you've brought me here.' Outside, a butterfly was flitting about the garden. His hand on her shoulder made her jump and, as she turned, his warm lips came down on hers, surprising her so that she did not jump away as she knew she should have done.

'Cleopatra,' he murmured, and looked down at her with dark, dark eyes. She felt she could drown in them, and, as he bent down to kiss her again, her lips opened slightly. It was a gentle, warm caress, and Cleo closed her eyes on the wave of emotion which poured forth from inside her. His fingers brushed her cheek, then the damp tendrils of hair at her temple.

'Cleo,' he murmured. 'You're an untapped well. So proper on the outside, but beneath all that starch you're so alive. Why don't you let the sunlight inside you show? Melt the snow...'

Cleo wondered what would have happened then, if at that moment Biddy had not entered the room with a tray. Cleo felt the colour stain her cheeks like a scald, and moved to inspect the bookcase to hide it. Jake was smiling as if nothing had happened—perhaps to him it had not! But Cleo's heart seemed to be suffocating her and she tried desperately to steady it.

'Lunch will be in about an hour, sir,' Biddy was saying, 'if you want me to do justice to you and Miss Montague here. Will I fetch up some wine from the cellar?'

'Indeed, please do, Biddy!'

Cleo silently vowed that not a drop would pass her lips. She was wondering if Jake Raines's intentions in bringing her all this way were honourable. How could she have been so foolish as to trust him? He had lulled her into a sense of security and then struck. What a fool she had been to trust him.

'Come.' Biddy had gone. 'Let me show you the place.' Cleo turned at his voice, ready to let fly. 'I promise,' he added, smiling wryly at her expression,

'I will not come within a foot of you. In fact, I will not even offer you the assistance of my arm unless you expressly wish it!'

Cleo took a deep breath. 'I am glad you realise

that your action was reprehensible in the extreme. You must not... Mr. Raines, you cannot do such things. I should never have come here alone—'

'I beg your pardon, Miss Montague. I don't know what came over me. I can only promise again it will not happen a second time.'

Cleo unclenched her fists, looking uncertain. And then she nodded abruptly.

He looked suitably chastened, and yet...that smile played about his lips when he bowed his head and Cleo couldn't help but wonder whether she really could trust him.

The house was large, with a central hall and rooms leading off it. The kitchen was separate—which was the custom in case of fire—and joined to the house by a covered walkway. A veranda circled the house on three sides, and there was a garden for vegetables at the back as well as the usual stables and barns. The place seemed deserted but Cleo knew that on any other day of the week it would be a hive of activity, as Jake's employees went about their work.

Jake Raines knew about his property. Cleo had thought that perhaps he was one of those wealthy men who played at farming, relying entirely upon their foremen to do the real work. But he knew too much for her to doubt he had worked as hard, if not harder, than any of his labourers.

'How long have you had Belubula—and, I must ask you, what does the name mean?' Cleo asked, caught up again in the quiet beauty about her.

'It is a native word for stony river,' he answered her, 'and I have been here for a very long time. I came from England—or perhaps was sent from England is truer—with very little money. My father was a great believer in respectability, and even as a boy I showed little enough of that! When I was eighteen, I became involved in a "liaison", shall we say, with a very unsuitable woman.'

Cleo felt her mouth thin, but said nothing.

'Suffice it to say, I eloped with her, though there was never any marriage. After a week in her company I discovered enough about her to understand my father's disapproval. I came home.'

'You were wild,' Cleo said reprovingly. 'Did your father forgive you?'

Jake raised an eyebrow. 'No. I reminded him, he told me, of my mother's brother—another terrible black sheep—and he wanted to be rid of me. I was only the youngest son, you see, and of little importance to him or the family. So he gave me enough for my fare to Australia, told me that as far as he was concerned I was dead, and sent me on my way never to return. And, by God, I promised myself I never would!'

'But how did you survive?' Cleo murmured.

'I worked at whatever I could, and saved for as much land as I could afford. The wealth of the country is in the land, Cleo, not the gold. That will come and go, but the land will always be there to be worked. But until they found gold up at Nugget Gully I had little enough to show for my hard work.'

'So all you have now is because of your own hard work?'

'Oh, yes. I've had no help, nor do I need it. They

may have cast me off, but it was the best thing that could have happened to me. It made a man out of a milksop boy.'

He met her eyes, and his smile was almost bitter. 'Few enough famous actresses would have passed the time of day with me then. And as for the "proper" ladies, well, they didn't waste their time with me then, and nor do they now. I am not a fit person to grace their drawing-rooms or partake of their suppers. They call me a rake, and a black sheep, and all the other things they despise.'

Afterwards, Cleo wondered whether the bitterness was really there, like vinegar in his voice, or whether she had imagined it. Without thinking she put out her hand, and he took it, squeezing her fingers. 'Mr. Raines, I'm sure that if you were to sell your property...your hotel, in Nugget Gully, and become a little more concerned in community matters, you would soon be accepted into society, and your past sins forgotten.'

He laughed out loud.

Angry, Cleo pulled her hand away.

'I'm sorry,' he managed, raking his fingers back through his dark hair. 'But do you think I would really sell the things which have made me wealthy, merely to pander to their outmoded sense of what is right and what is wrong? If I am not as respectable as they would like me, then I will do my very best to be as infamous as I can possibly be!'

Cleo made an impatient movement. 'That is foolishness, sir. You are merely biting off your nose to spite your face. It is surely much wiser to...to pander, as you put it, a little, and be on good terms with your neighbours, than to make them dislike you even more? Perhaps, if you were to marry someone of their kind—'

'What I need is the love of a good woman to set me to rights,' he retorted, and laughed again at the expression on her face. 'Come, Cleo, is that not what you are saying? You who do not believe in marriage?'

Furious at having her words twisted, Cleo drew herself up to her full height, her face flaming, her heart pounding. 'I am not, sir! On second thoughts, I doubt a respectable or good woman would want to marry you. You seem to prefer the other sort. Now, if I am not mistaken, that is your housekeeper on the veranda waving us in. I will wish to leave immediately after lunch, and let me assure you I would leave before if it would not be grossly impolite to her!'

Lunch was delicious, and Cleo ate her fill, even forgetting to refuse the thick, syrupy wine which Biddy offered with a smile. She wondered what she thought of Jake bringing her back here, without warning. Did he always act so impetuously, or was he so selfish that he always did exactly as he pleased and expected others to fall in with his plans?

'Forgive me.'

The soft voice, the contrite look. Cleo glared at him suspiciously, and he bit his lip to stop that flicker of a smile.

'Forgive me, Cleo. I was unkind. Do not let that spoil your enjoyment of the day. I had meant to make it a day for you to remember.'

'Oh?' Cleo folded her napkin carefully beside her empty plate. 'It *has* been a day to remember. I thank you for some of it, but I feel it must be the *only* day I spend at Belubula. I think it would be safer and wiser to draw a halt to our friendship, if that's what it is, here and now.'

After a moment he bowed his head. 'If that is your wish. We shall be acquaintances only, then, Miss Montague. And you must forgo any plans you may have to reform me.'

Cleo's eyes flashed. 'I never held any such plans,' she snapped.

Biddy came in with coffee, and they went out on to the veranda to finish it. 'Looks like a storm,' the woman said, shading her eyes against the brilliant sky, now banked with dark clouds on the horizon. Then, seeing Cleo's face, 'But you will make it home first, I am sure, Miss Montague.' Then, with a glance at Jake, 'I hope you'll visit us again. It makes a change to have a *real* lady.'

Jake spluttered. 'You wretch, Biddy!' But she had whisked about and retreated into the house. Cleo pretended not to notice, but triumph was surging through her. Let that be a lesson to him, she thought smugly. She was a lady, a true lady, and she had been gracious indeed to come today to the home of such as he. Why, most ladies would not even set a toe over his threshold! But she, through the kindness of her heart and sweetness of her nature, had come today and he had treated her as if she had done him an injury!

Well, she would not come again. He did not want to be saved, so let him sink!

The heat had a sullen feel to it, and Cleo was anxious to get home before the coming storm broke. How terrible to be trapped at Belubula overnight. Nothing would save her reputation then. Jake listened to her fears, and agreed that perhaps they should get going.

'I have two bonnets to finish before tomorrow,' she went on, suddenly remembering all the work left undone at home. 'If I do not finish them, it will seem as if I do not care.'

Tell your customers you were out with Jake Raines,' he said, and laughed at her cold look. 'Come, then, Cleo, we'll get going, as you're so keen to be rid of me. But, tell the truth, didn't you enjoy yourself?'

'No,' she snapped, and ignored his laughter as he went to fetch the gig.

They drove in silence for some time. The sky was darkening with every passing minute and a sudden rumble of thunder sent Cleo's eyes anxiously up to the sky. 'Never fear, Miss Montague,' Jake said, misinterpreting her look, 'I'll get you home to finish your hats.'

The trees were enclosing them now, sullen and hot. Lightning jagged the sky and Cleo flinched, then thunder followed noisily. Her throat went dry. A sudden gust of wind set the leaves clacking against each other. Rain could not be far away. A bird flew overhead, crying a mournful warning. Cleo's fists clenched—she must not break down now. She must be calm and strong.

She must hang on to her composure until they were home, and then, alone, she could show her fear, her irrational terror of the storm.

Through the trees, Cleo suddenly saw an outcrop of great orange rocks set among the scrub and undergrowth. 'I think we must wait it out,' Jake shouted, above the thunder. The wind was gusting violently now. He reached out to take her arm. 'You're shaking,' he said, frowning at her white face and big eyes.

'Foolish,' Cleo said breathlessly, 'but I've never liked storms.'

Jake lifted his brows. 'I would not have thought anything frightened you, Cleopatra!'

She tried to smile, but another flash in the sky caused her to blanch and shriek, putting her hands up over her eyes. She felt Jake's arm come around her shoulders and despite herself allowed him to pull her against his side and the safety to be found there.

He helped her down from the gig, and she felt the fronds of the ferns, and the dry sticks littering the ground catching her skirts. She was reminded of the terrible night of the bushranger's attack, and shuddered, pressing closer to Jake and totally losing control of her cool head. Storms were Cleo's one terror. She remembered as a little girl holding desperately to her mother's skirts, while her mother tried to comfort her, and the black clouds rolled overhead. She remembered shaking, alone and terrified in her room, when her mother had gone, and lightning made the world seem like day outside. She had always been afraid of the storm, and, oh, why, why must one come now and show her up for what she was in front of the detestable Jake Raines?

The rain came in a rush, soaking the ground about them, deafening Cleo as it fell on the leaves above them. And then they reached the outcrop of rocks, and the dry, cool air of what was more a hollow than a cave. It smelt old, and there were branches neatly laid, as if someone had once had a camp here, and lit a fire. Jake still had his arms about her, sheltering her with his body, and Cleo pulled away, pushing him from her, shaking the rain from her hair. It came down from its pins, a chestnut cloud about her shoulders.

Jake slapped his hat against his leg, raking back damp dark hair with his fingers. His face was pale and strange in the muted light of the cave. Outside, the rain thundered down, and the horse stood, drenched, on the pathway.

'It should rain itself out in a little while,' he said at last, shouting above the downpour. 'Summer storms never last long.'

Cleo nodded to show she understood. Her eyes slid away from his, embarrassed, and when she felt his hand on her arm she jumped as though he had bitten her. His smile was wry.

'No need to be ashamed, Cleo,' he said. 'Everyone is afraid of something. It's not weakness. I myself must confess to a definite dislike of women with hennaed hair.'

Cleo smiled. 'You are very kind.'

'Kind? Me? You must be mistaken. I am never kind.'

She shook her head at him, almost shyly. 'I think you are kind, but you don't want anyone to know it. Perhaps *that* is your weakness, Mr. Raines.'

'I wish,' he said, softly, and came closer, 'you would call me Jake.' His kiss was as soft as a butterfly's wing, so gentle that at first Cleo saw no need to move away and stood, savouring it, judging it sweet as honey.

'You know, you are unlike any woman I have ever known,' he said, into her hair, and his breath sent shivers through her bones.

'That is because you only meet women who are not respectable,' she retorted shakily. He slid his fingers up through her hair, lifting it off her neck.

'Ah, but if you associate with me, are you still respectable?' he queried, and his mouth teased at hers, finally closing in a long, deep kiss. Cleo wondered if she were dreaming. She knew she should stop him, she had done so once already. But instead her hands came up around his neck in a clasp which was too firm to be ladylike. Was she respectable? It would seem not, indeed! She must have lost her senses entirely, to be kissing Jake Raines in the middle of a rain storm, and, worse still, enjoying it!

'Cleo,' he whispered, kissing her temple, his hands tangling in her hair so that he could draw her head back and stare straight down into the warm depths of her brown eyes. He looked into them for what seemed a long time, and then he let her go. He stepped to the edge of the cave and peered out, his back to her, and said coolly, 'It's blown over. Perhaps we should hurry on in case it comes back.'

Just as if, Cleo thought dizzily, they had never been, a moment before, clasped in such a lovers' embrace. She leaned against the cold rock, and felt her face flame. She felt foolish and embarrassed.

She had let him sample her wares, just as if she were some supper dish. And he had sampled, and perhaps enjoyed—who could tell?—and now he would move on to the next platter.

With a monumental effort, she straightened herself, and walked past him and out of the cave without a word. Down the now wet track to the bedraggled horse. It shook its head, snorting, and Cleo blinked back tears. Why? Why had she done such a thing? How utterly stupid she had been, after all she had told herself, after all she knew about him!

Jake was close behind her, and, before she could climb into the gig, he had her about the waist, and lifted her effortlessly up on to the damp seat. She met his dark eyes and could not look away. His mouth curled up into a half-smile, that mixture of mockery and amusement. 'What can I say this time?' he murmured. 'Sorry? I would be a hypocrite then, as well as a black sheep. You will say it was wrong, I suppose, but it didn't feel wrong to me. Life is too short to forgo its pleasures, Cleo. Don't try to be too perfect—let yourself be human. Remember *that*, even if you'd rather forget me.'

He turned away, and the spell of his eyes was broken. Cleo took a shaky breath, and began to repair the damage to her hair. The familiar action helped to calm her, and after a few miles she felt more in control of her emotions. So much so that she could start a conversation on the scenery without flinching when he turned a cool look on her.

He answered her, but she felt he wasn't really listening. His thoughts were elsewhere, and Cleo didn't dare to wonder where.

They reached Nugget Gully at last. The rain had come and gone, and now the sun was shining down on the wide main street. A few people straggled about, but it was quiet and mostly deserted. They turned down Hunter's Lane at last, and she took a breath to say the words she had been rehearsing for the last few miles. 'Thank you—' she began formally, but a voice behind her interrupted her.

'I'm sorry, my dear. I didn't realise you had a visitor.'

Cleo spun around, and met Melissa's feline eyes. Those eyes slid by her and rested with a certain amount of interest on Jake Raines.

Jake met her look, and it was as if he recognised a kindred spirit in Melissa. Cleo felt the tension between them, and felt herself go to ice. It was as if the blood stopped in her veins, as if she had died. All in a fraction of time. And then Melissa was saying archly, 'Aren't you going to introduce me?'

'Of course.' Cleo was surprised how cool and polite she sounded. 'Mr. Jake Raines, this is Mrs. Mulgrave, a friend from Mrs. Smith's boarding-house. Her husband is a—'

'I am staying at Nugget Gully while my husband kicks his heels in Ballarat in an... official capacity. So tedious.' But her eyes were anything but bored, and she continued to look at Jake, even though she now spoke to Cleo. 'I came to see how you were, my dear, and then the sky became too black, and it rained, and I could not leave. I had to shelter here on your tiny porch, as you see.'

'Would you like to come inside?' Cleo murmured. 'I will make some tea. We are rather wet, as you can see. Or perhaps Mr. Raines would prefer to return to his... his...'

Jake's smile mocked her. 'No, I'll come and drink tea with you. We sheltered until the worst of it was over,' he added to Melissa, as Cleo unlocked the door to her tiny sitting-room.

'Indeed,' she murmured, and Cleo heard the smile in her voice. 'Have you any of that excellent cake left, Cleo? She cooks like a dream, Mr. Raines.'

Cleo busied herself making the tea and arranging the cake on her best serving plate. But she could hear them behind her, talking and laughing, and the deep timbre of Jake's voice sent a shiver through her. It seemed madness, it seemed a nightmare. She had known it the moment he looked at Melissa in that way he must look at every woman, as he had first looked at Cleo. He played the game with everyone—Cleo was not special. And that was suddenly a dreadful shame, because Cleo knew that she had fallen in love with him. He might be a rake, a despicable, unfaithful rake, but she had fallen for him as totally as a ship's anchor dropping beneath the waves of the ocean. Even if he tore her apart, as it was clear he would do, she loved him and must bear it as well as she might.

The knowledge of it hurt like a body blow. Had she loved him all along? All those unselfish motives she had given herself for visiting Belubula, their partnership—had it all been a lie? Had she always loved him, and been trying to bind herself closer to him? Oh, he was right! She was no ice woman, she was only too human.

'Delicious cake,' Melissa said. 'Our Cleo is a marvel at cooking. At everything, really,' she went on to Jake, patting Cleo's hand as if she were ten years old. 'She is such a success, you know!'

'Cleo couldn't help but be a success,' Jake replied smoothly, and turned his dark smile on her. She looked away in confusion and misery, hiding it as best she could beneath a cold, stony indifference. To love the monster was bad enough, but if he should learn of it... She would rather die than give him that satisfaction.

'And have you heard from your husband?' she said, turning to Melissa. 'Is he returning this month after all?'

Melissa sighed, trying to look downcast, but her eyes were shining. 'No, I'm afraid not. Duty must keep him there at least another two months. He wishes me to join him, but... I shall see, I shall see.'

Suddenly Cleo could stand their smiles no more. She rose, almost upsetting the table. 'If you don't mind,' she said, 'I have a headache and much to do for tomorrow...' She turned to Jake and held out her hand, which was surprisingly steady.

'Thank you, Mr. Raines, for a lovely day. I very much enjoyed it.'

He stood up, searching her face, and for a moment she thought he was disconcerted. But his voice was as smooth and urbane as ever. 'I'm sorry you're unwell, Cleo. I enjoyed today, too.'

She looked away, and he moved towards the door. 'Cleo needs someone to take her out of herself,' Melissa said smugly. 'She's so...self-contained. Quite frightens me, with her efficiency!'

Jake smiled dutifully, but his eyes were on Cleo. 'Goodbye,' he said, and held out his hand again. She gave him her own briefly, forcing herself to smile in her usual cool, detached manner. 'Perhaps you will visit Belubula again?'

'Of course!' she said rallyingly. And they both knew she meant 'no'.

The door closed. His footsteps faded, and then the gig moved away. Cleo took a breath and turned to face Melissa. The latter was smiling oddly, watching her with narrowed, feline eyes. 'You really don't like him very much, do you?' she said quietly.

Cleo stared at her, wondering how she could be so stupid. Or perhaps she just saw what she wanted to see.

'I must say, I think he's quite delicious.'

'Melissa, how can you? What would your husband say?' Cleo cried, genuinely shocked.

'Douglas? My dear, he would laugh. We have an arrangement, you see. I do not play the clinging wife, and spoil his little...*affaires,* and he does not play the jealous husband and ruin my little, shall we say, friendships?'

Even more shocked, Cleo sat down and put her hand to her forehead. 'I am very tired, Melissa, really. I think I shall lie down.'

Melissa made soothing noises. She paused at the door. 'I must warn you, however, Cleo. For a woman like yourself, without the protective mantle of marriage, Jake Raines is a very different matter. You must not go out and about with him on your own. You really must not! If you wish to keep your good reputation. And I'm sure you do, mmm?' The door closed softly. Cleo wondered, miserably, if Jake was waiting for her around the corner, but decided that even he would not be so blatant. A tear trickled down under her lashes, and ran into her hair, followed by another. It was so unfair. Everything had been going along so well, and now...well, now everything was spoiled!

CHAPTER FIVE

FOR THE NEXT few weeks Cleo worked hard. The shop did well, and she seemed never to have a moment to herself. She was so tired at night that she fell into bed and slept deeply until the morning light woke her for another day. She did not see Jake, and, though she saw Melissa often, she did not mention him either. She meant to push all memory of him from her life. He had slipped past her cool guard as no other man had ever done, and Cleo knew if she was to preserve her composure she must not allow him to do more damage.

There was plenty for her to do during the days, and the evenings were full of work to catch up on, or often Mrs. Smith or Melissa would call. Cleo had built up quite a large clientele. Mrs. Morgan, the bank manager's wife, was very pleased with Cleo's efforts and sent along several new customers. Although she said something which worried Cleo a little.

The woman was chattering about Nugget Gully, when she mentioned that Jake Raines was out of town. 'Though you would know that already, Miss

Montague.'

Something in the other woman's arch look startled Cleo. What did she mean? But when she asked, Mrs Morgan said something even more puzzling.

'But you and he are close acquaintances! Or so I have been told.'

Cleo denied it, but something in Mrs. Morgan's bland smile frightened her. Had Melissa said something about their Sunday drive, or had some busy townsperson seen them together and been spreading gossip? Whichever it was, it was no good for Cleo's business or reputation!

At the other end of the scale, some of the miners' wives came to have modest bonnets made, and Cleo, feeling sorry for their plight, often took more off the price than she should. But she felt it was worth it when she watched them leave with such pleasure in their tired eyes.

'We've been working on the Lucky Strike for six months now, and found nought,' Mrs Trewin said in her lilting Cornish voice. 'My husband says we've dug down so deep we'll be bringing up Chinamen soon!'

Cleo smiled. 'Is that the mine just out of town? There are so many!'

'And likely to be many more! Mr. Raines says we'll give the Lucky Strike another month and then he's going to dig another shaft, to the east.'

It wasn't until Cleo met her own eyes in the mirror that she realised how white her face had become. She forced herself to straighten Mrs. Trewin's hat. 'Mr. Raines mines as well?' she asked at last.

'Oh, yes. He's a good boss to my Frank. Not like some of them. Come up from Melbourne, they do, and try and get as much work from their men as they can without paying more than they have to. Mr. Raines is always generous and always knows their names, even sent around a parcel when our youngest was born.'

Cleo didn't have time to ponder on this new, glowing side of Jake Raines; she was too busy. But it did surprise her, and, though she wouldn't admit it to herself, please her that the man she loved was thought of so well by his employees.

One night, the leading lights of Nugget Gully held a dance in the hall. Cleo went, at Melissa's bidding. She took great pains with her clothes, and, though it was very respectable, and although a number of men paid her compliments, Cleo was disappointed.

You fool, she whispered to herself. Of course *he* would not be here. Did you expect it? This is the sort of place you belong, not such as he. He is not considered respectable!

'Why do you not dance with Mr. Higgs?' Melissa murmured behind her fan. 'He admires you enormously, you know.'

'Why do you not dance with him yourself?'

Melissa smiled slyly. 'The man I favour is not here tonight.'

'Douglas? Your husband?'

Melissa's smile grew. 'No, not Douglas, you innocent! I mean quite another man altogether. I have been casting my net in his direction for weeks;

I am sure that, very soon, he must be caught. I will draw him in, ever so slowly...' Melissa shuddered with anticipation. Cleo felt sick. But Melissa didn't seem to notice. 'Now, *you* must dance with Mr. Higgs!'

'I have a headache. I think I shall go home.'

Melissa's fan snapped shut. 'You seem to have a great many headaches lately,' she said tartly. 'Dance with him, Cleo! Enjoy yourself! You grow very boring when you work all the time. Like some dreadful little Shylock.'

Melissa's green eyes glared, and yet there was worry in their depths. Cleo smiled wanly. 'You are my best friend,' she said. 'I would hate to lose you.' It was true. Melissa might be sly and rather shocking, and she might covet Cleo's hopeless love, but she had been a friend to Cleo. Melissa laughed.

'Well,' she said. 'You are the first woman who has ever said that!' Impulsively she squeezed Cleo's arm. 'Go and dance, my dear. You are young, you know, even though sometimes you act like a grandmother!'

Cleo did dance, and was surprised at how much she enjoyed herself. With her cheeks flushed and eyes sparkling, she felt young and free. Perhaps there was hope, still, that her heart would recover from this awful sickness.

So thinking, the next afternoon Cleo closed her shop for an hour, and set out for the emporium. She was tired of her everyday clothes—she wanted something with dash! She refused any longer to hide herself away and work herself to death while no doubt *he* went about carousing and didn't give Cleo a thought. She was a fool to continue this one-sided love-affair. She would cultivate Mr. Higgs—his compliments were good for her ego.

Out in the street it was hot and sunny. The brilliant blue of the sky made her blink, and the street had a warm, dusty smell. She had forgotten how pleasant it was beyond the door of her little shop.

People nodded to her, and smiled. Men dipped their hats. They knew her. She was a part of Nugget Gully, she had made her mark. Cleo felt pleased with herself, so pleased in fact that she did not see Jake in her path until she was upon him, and then it was too late to slip into a doorway, or turn the other way and…yes, and run! It seemed grossly unfair that her first moment of happiness in weeks should be spoiled.

'Cleo,' he said, and tipped his hat.

He was wearing a coat of brown cloth, and a white shirt, both fitted perfectly to his tall, strong frame. He was the same: the dark, rather long hair, the dark eyes. Those eyes were smiling now with every sign of pleasure. Cleo felt her pulse fluttering so badly she thought she might fall down in a fit, and her breath was coming so irregularly that she had to pretend to brush a speck from her sleeve, to catch it back.

'Mr. Raines!' So cool! It always surprised her that she could appear so calm and detached, while beneath her emotions were in turmoil. Thank God, it was so. She wouldn't be able to bear it if he knew.

'I'm sorry I haven't called,' he went on. 'I've been

in Melbourne on business.'

'Of course,' Cleo murmured, and forced a polite, bored smile to her lips. With a nod, she moved to brush by him, but his hand came out and grasped her arm like a vice. Dark eyes studied her face slowly, frowningly, oblivious to passers-by. 'What is it?' he asked quietly. 'You seem vexed. And, by God, you're paler and thinner than last time we met. What has happened to destroy your peace, Miss Montague?'

Cleo tried to shake off his hand, and when she couldn't said impatiently, 'I am very busy, Mr. Raines. If you will please release me, I will be on my way.'

But to her chagrin he ignored her, and repeated, 'Tell me what is wrong, Cleo, then I will let you go. Quickly, now, before your so good reputation is destroyed!'

She flushed, looking stonily past his handsome face. 'Nothing is wrong. I am very busy. Should there be something wrong? You have been in Melbourne, and I have been busy. There is nothing more to say, surely? Good day, sir.'

He released her, but now turned to walk beside her. Cleo swallowed, maintaining her cold exterior with difficulty. Go away, she thought, please, just go away. I will get over it. I must. If only he will go away!

'I thought we were friends,' he said, after a moment.

Cleo turned to look at him in disbelief, and something of her surprised anger must have shown on her face. 'Mr. Raines, you were never my friend. You must know that only too well. Perhaps once I imagined you had been kind to me. But you put an end to that. You know nothing of...of proper behaviour.'

His eyes narrowed at her, and there was a glint now in their black depths. 'You didn't complain of that once, if my memory serves me right. Or have you conveniently forgotten that?'

'Your words only prove what I say to be correct,' Cleo retorted through gritted teeth.

'I see. Is that it? I'm not up to your standards. I suppose Higgs is?'

Cleo stared in surprise. How did he know that?

Jake's mouth thinned in what might have been anger. 'I'd like to shake some of that starch out of you, Cleopatra! You like to pretend you're oh, so proper, but we both know you're a liar.'

'I never want to see you again,' Cleo said desperately. 'It doesn't do my reputation as a businesswoman any good to be seen with you, Mr. Raines! And,' she blundered on, 'as for your behaviour with my friend, flirting and... well, it is beyond speaking of.'

The anger came flaring into his dark eyes like fire, and his hand, on her arm again, pressed hard enough to leave bruises. 'Your friend, as you call her, would need only a flick of my fingers, and— like a cat—she'd be purring all over me. You know it, Cleo, but you won't admit it. And if you think I have done more than pass the time of day with her you are a fool.'

'Am I? I doubt you could pass the time of day with anyone as beautiful as Melissa and leave it at that!'

Her voice sounded high and shrewish, and suddenly Cleo was ashamed of it, and herself. Why was she doing this? To torture herself even more? He had liked her once, even seemed to enjoy her company. Now he would only despise her.

'I had thought better of you,' he said in an icy voice. 'As far as I'm concerned, the others may think what they wish, but I had thought better of you, Cleo. And, after all, you're just the same as the lot of them—self-righteous, full of your own importance and a bigger hypocrite than any I've ever met. If I'd wanted you in that cave, I could have had you. We both know it. Only you can't admit it, even to yourself, that the oh, so proper Miss Montague is capable of feeling like a woman. You're too bloody terrified!'

She stared into his eyes, colour draining from her face, feeling like a mouse fascinated by a large reptile. And then he had turned on his heel and vanished into the crowd.

'Cleo.'

Cleo looked up, startled, and smiled. Melissa stood there in the doorway, watching her curiously. 'You've been standing there staring into space for nearly five minutes!'

Cleo laughed, and started to sew again with her tiny, neat stitches. 'I was miles away; I'm sorry.'

'So it would seem. I have come to ask you to dinner. My husband has returned somewhat...

unexpectedly.'

Cleo frowned. Had he heard about Jake? But then, didn't they have an 'arrangement', as Melissa put it? Although Jake had told her he had not touched Melissa, Cleo was unconvinced. She had been careful in avoiding all mention of Jake since the night of the dance, and had often wondered if Melissa and he had become lovers. She suspected that if Melissa had anything to do with it they certainly were.

'Your husband? Of course.'

Melissa wandered about the sitting-room, touching ornaments idly. 'He says he missed me,' she said at last, and looked a little flushed. 'I think he must be getting sentimental in his old age.'

'He must have loved you, when he married you.'

Melissa shrugged, 'I had a background he approved of.'

It sounded a cold arrangement, but then weren't most marriages made for convenience? Cleo said nothing, knowing she had no right to criticise. And of what use was love, when it hurt one so?

'We're having a little party to celebrate his return,' Melissa went on. 'As my very best friend, I would dearly love you to come.' The green eyes slanted up at her, warm for once. Cleo smiled. 'Of course I shall come. I'll wear my best dress.'

'Best' was a new creation she had had made only a week ago, a deep plum colour with lace ruching and the lowest bodice she had ever dared wear. It suited her very well. She had told herself she had had it made to dazzle Mr. Higgs, but in truth it was not of him she had thought while she paid over the money.

'We've taken a room at the Nugget Gully Hotel,' Melissa went on, avoiding Cleo's eyes. 'You will have to come there. It will be quite respectable, you know. The Morgans will be there, and lots of others. Will you mind?'

After a moment, Cleo shrugged. 'Of course not. Why should I mind?' But she couldn't meet Melissa's eyes.

'He is really a very handsome man,' Melissa murmured softly, after a long pause. 'Any woman would be willing to give up much, to have him.'

'Your husband?' Cleo asked, surprised.

Melissa laughed, softly, but did not reply. Cleo changed the subject, but she felt as if a cloud had passed over the sun. Melissa and Jake, she thought, and knew she should not let it hurt her so much.

She remembered suddenly now she had once mistaken Jake for her 'dream'—the man who would love her for herself and be her companion, always. How foolish she had been! Better to marry Mr. Higgs and spend the rest of her life in comfortable boredom than to suffer as Jake Raines made her suffer. Or, better still, remain a spinster, making hats, for the rest of her days.

Douglas was not at all as Cleo had imagined: a tall, lean man, his face tanned by the sun, and his fair hair bleached by that same sun. His smile, though brisk and official, had warmth and something about him drew Cleo. He seemed to find her equally interesting. Melissa, beautiful in blue silk, a cashmere shawl artfully arranged about her shoulders, smiled under her long lashes, and yet there was a nervousness about her that Cleo had never seen before.

But Cleo was determined to enjoy herself; she felt daring tonight. Melissa had stated that she wanted Jake; what did it matter if Cleo flirted a little with Melissa's husband? She was aware that she looked, in her own opinion, tolerable. The plum colour suited her and her hair shone the colour of chestnuts under the oil lamps. The low neckline, the glow of her skin, the swish of her skirts, all pleased her. And she was surprised, when she caught a glimpse of herself in the mirror above the fireplace, at how mysterious she looked as she sipped her wine.

'A cool, alabaster goddess,' Douglas Mulgrave said, and Cleo met his eyes in the mirror, surprised.

He smiled. 'You remind me of a goddess, Miss Montague.'

'Am I so unattainable, Mr. Mulgrave?'

'You are majestic, Miss Montague!'

'I don't know whether that is a compliment or not, Captain Mulgrave. You make me sound like a ship in full sail!'

Across the room, Melissa moved her fan idly, listening to Mrs. Morgan chat, without seeming to feel the need to join in. She was like, Cleo thought mockingly, a cat waiting. The thought surprised her; for whom was she waiting? The room was already crowded with respectable citizens of Nugget Gully society. There would be no one else to come, surely? Even Mr. Higgs was there, trying to catch Cleo's eye. But she had no intention of leaving Douglas Mulgrave's side. Cleo liked him, and was enjoying listening to him talk about Ballarat and the gold fields.

'Melissa has told me you have had quite a few adventures yourself, Miss Montague,' he said, and his blue gaze dropped to her throat and shoulders.

The dress was very low cut, and yet Cleo read only admiration in his eyes and felt strangely elated.

'My father called me headstrong,' she said with a laugh, 'and I fear he was right. It was very unladylike of me to ride out alone like that.'

Douglas smiled. 'Sometimes I think Victoria is not a place for "ladies",' he replied thoughtfully. 'Life is too raw; there is little time for pretension.' He waved his hand generally about the room. 'But still they try!' His eyes met hers again. 'I think you are perfect just as you are, Miss Montague.'

Was it just the wine, or perhaps his smile? Cleo didn't know, but something about Melissa's husband was terribly attractive. She remembered what Melissa had said about their arrangement, and yet she could not help smiling back at him and even flirting with him. Perhaps it was the wine, melting away her inhibitions, but she felt a woman of the world, a woman who was capable of anything.

'Who is that? One of Melissa's many admirers?'

Cleo looked up, surprised at the bitter note in his voice, and then turned in the direction of his gaze. The door was open. It seemed as if everything stopped. *He* stood there, looking shatteringly handsome. Black coat and trousers, dark hair glowing in the dim light, and black eyes like oil as they slid over the guests.

'Jake, do come in.' Melissa went forward, taking his arm. She did it so easily, so familiarly. Cleo was even more certain that they were lovers, and felt sickness in her stomach. There was shock on Mrs. Morgan's face, dismay on her husband's. They all looked like chickens, suddenly noticing that someone had let a fox into the coop. Outraged, their plumage ruffled, and yet frightened too of what was to come...

'You know everyone,' Melissa was saying, and her smile dared them to make a fuss. 'And I'm sure you all know Mr. Raines! He is Nugget Gully's richest man, after all.'

There was a silence, and then Mrs. Morgan murmured something which could have been a greeting. No doubt she had remembered he was her husband's best customer.

Jake came forward, nodding to this person, shaking hands. He was as cool as ever—amused by their reactions at having to greet him as a social equal. Melissa, still holding his arm so possessively, drew him on until they reached Cleo and Douglas.

They appraised each other. Sizing each other up, Cleo thought, like tom-cats.

'Mr. Raines.' Douglas held out his hand. 'Tell me, was Lola Montez as shocking as they say?'

Jake laughed, and all the tension seemed to go

out of him. 'All that and more,' he retorted.

And then he looked at Cleo. She met his eyes as coolly as she dared. His smile was slow and appreciative as he took in her finery and her glowing beauty. 'Miss Montague,' he said, and bowed his head slightly. 'You are a golden girl tonight; a golden girl for a gold-rush town.'

Cleo was speechless but Melissa laughed oddly. 'Very poetical, Mr. Raines. A shame Cleo doesn't read poetry. Do you like Tennyson?'

'I prefer Anon,' Jake murmured.

Douglas laughed, and Melissa flushed angrily. Cleo felt sorry for her but when she moved to speak Melissa turned such a blistering look on her that she stopped.

The meal arrived, and they were seated at the long table. Cleo found herself between Douglas and Mr. Higgs, with Melissa beside Jake on the other side. The food was excellent and the evening passed quickly. Cleo was happy between Mr. Higgs's compliments and Douglas's warm glances. She felt heady with the excitement, and even the sight of Melissa's fingers always on Jake's sleeve did no more man cause a momentary twinge. And Jake? The only time she dared to look at him, he too was smiling, leaning back in a relaxed fashion. But his eyes, when her gaze finally reached them, were cool and hard as granite, and she looked quickly away, aware of a thrill of fear.

The lights were burning low by the time Cleo thought of leaving. Douglas was looking flushed and relaxed, sated with food and wine. Melissa made a languid movement. 'Must you?' she said, with so much insincerity in her voice Cleo was surprised.

'I must rise early tomorrow,' Cleo replied briskly.

'Ah, yes, our very own little captain of industry,' Melissa retorted. 'Or is it *captainess?* Quite the success, aren't you?'

'Melissa...' Douglas began warningly. The table had gone quiet—everyone was looking their way.

Melissa's green eyes sliced through him. *'Melissa,'* she mocked. 'Am I not to mind, then, if she tries to be equally successful with *my* husband?'

There was a gasp around the table; Mrs. Morgan clutched her hand to her throat in horror but her eyes shone with excitement. Douglas made a sound of disgust. 'You are a fine one to talk, madam!'

They glared at each other, and Melissa looked like an alley cat, claws out, teeth bared. Why had Cleo ever thought her delicate?

'Do you think I don't know what you've been up to while I've been away?' he went on, soft and yet hard. 'Whores do not only come from the gutter; they are born into fine houses, too, wife!'

'And I suppose you've been visiting Susan Lamont in Ballarat to take tea and discuss the weather?' Melissa spat. 'You see, I have my spies, too, *husband!'*

Jake made a movement. 'Perhaps we should all be leaving,' he said smoothly. 'It is late and perhaps we have dipped a little deep, mmm?'

Melissa turned on him, and her face seemed even thinner, her eyes even more feverish. For a moment she seemed to devour him with her eyes, but when she moved as if to touch him Jake stiffened in what anyone could see was disgust. Melissa's hand dropped to her side; she looked suddenly old. Cleo, pitying her, spoke without thinking. 'Melissa, you are tired. Come away, please.'

Slowly, Melissa's gaze turned to her. The green eyes gleamed in her white face, and Cleo felt the malevolence like acid.

'Ah, the lady,' Melissa whispered, and laughed. She was drunk, Cleo realised suddenly. They would never forgive, the citizens of Nugget Gully. She was ruined... 'Here she is,' Melissa went on. 'The *lady*. And yet is she really such a lady? Riding out to his property, chatting in the street, and he even comes to tea and cake in her home! I think they do more than chat, when the night falls. What do you say, Jake? Does she cling and squirm in your arms? Does that proper little mouth cry out for more?'

The shock held Cleo still as stone. And then colour rushed into her face like a tide. 'How could you?' she whispered. 'It is not so. You know it is not! Jake and I are partners. It is business only!'

'Cleo!' Jake said sharply, then swore.

Melissa's eyes positively gleamed, in the ensuing silence. 'Partners? You and him? My God, the lady and the rake. Did you hear? No wonder he wasn't interested in my charms, he already has a—a partner!'

Everyone seemed to start talking at once. Cleo closed her eyes. She felt as if the bottom had just fallen out of her world.

'Be quiet!' Douglas stood up. His blue eyes were apologetic as he looked down at Cleo. 'I'm sorry,' he said softly. 'She's ruined herself, but she's taken you with her.'

Cleo stared into his eyes and then pushed her way out of the room and into the passageway. She stood a moment with eyes closed, her heart hammering. The wine was strong; it had gone to her head. My God, what a tirade. Melissa, drunk and bitter, saying those things. Beyond the closed door, she heard them all talking, talking... about Cleo.

She put her hands up to her burning cheeks. What had she done? Why had she told them that she and Jake were partners? Melissa had jumped upon it with glee. They had all heard—they all knew. She thought Cleo had taken Jake from her, and she had lashed out like a wounded thing, blind with her hurt and anger. This was her revenge. Cleo was ruined; she knew it with sudden despair. None of the respectable people would come to her shop now. Douglas was right—Melissa had ruined herself but she had taken Cleo with her. How could they know it was a matter of business only? They would believe what Melissa had believed. It was the way of the world. No doubt, if she were Mrs. Morgan, she would believe the same.

Behind her, the door opened. A cold, controlled voice said, 'Are you drunk as well, to have said such a thing?'

Cleo turned on him in fury. 'How dare you? What right have you to criticise me? At least I have never stolen another man's wife!'

The flash in his eyes warned her, and she turned and fled down the passageway and down the stairs. There was no one about, and the night air was cold on her flushed face. For a moment, she swayed. What would she do? Cleo thought in despair. What could she do? Leave Nugget Gully? Melbourne, then. But she had grown to like and know this place, to start all over again would be a nightmare. And with what? She had no money to start again. Her profits had gone back into the shop.

Cleo wandered down the dark street, caught up in the horror of what had happened in that warm, stuffy room. She had gone there a successful, respected woman, she had been happy! And now it was all gone.

'Hello, there.'

The slurred voice startled Cleo. A man lurched out of the shadows, and the stink of beer made Cleo stumble back.

'Ah, give us a kiss,' he said, in a wavering, drunken voice. His outstretched hand fastened on Cleo's sleeve, and she saw his white face in the pale moonlight.

'Let me go,' she gasped, and pushed at his chest.

'Just one kiss,' the drunk whined, and pulled her closer with a strength born of desperation.

Cleo hammered at him, wondering if she was

in a nightmare. Then suddenly someone had wrenched the man away, sending him sprawling to the ground. Cleo, as suddenly released, staggered. An iron grip held her up, and a voice as hard said, 'You little fool.'

The drunk was struggling to get up. 'You wanna fight?' he shouted. 'Come an' fight.'

Jake made an impatient noise. 'Is that you, Tom Tredinnick? I know you, Tom. Go home to your wife, or go and find Annabel Lees. Go on.'

Tom blinked drunkenly up at them. 'Is that you, Mr. Raines? I'm sorry, Mr. Raines. I didn't know she was your woman.'

Jake laughed. 'Well, she is. Now go home, Tom, and sleep it off.'

The man hauled himself to his feet, and stumbled away, muttering to himself.

Cleo stood, breathing deeply.

Jake tightened his grip on her. 'You may think of me what you like, Cleo,' he said softly, 'but I am taking you home. If need be, over my shoulder.'

The anger had gone, and Cleo listlessly allowed him to take her arm. They walked in silence, the cool night breeze fanning their faces. Hunter's Lane was dark and deserted. Cleo fumbled for her key and opened the door. She could not believe that her life here was over. This room, which she had loved so well, decorated with such excitement and hope, seemed to mock her now. She would leave Nugget Gully a shadow of the woman who had arrived with such plans, such confidence. All gone.

'Cleo.' He had lit the lamp, its soft glow filled

the room. Cleo managed to stir enough to take off her gloves and lay them carefully on the table. She smoothed the fingers, one by one.

'Cleo!' Jake put his hand over hers, and she was forced to look up into his dark, serious eyes. 'I told you once that I would never lie to you,' he said softly.

'Did you? I forget.'

He stiffened, but controlled the anger she saw flash into his eyes. 'I don't think you forget,' he went on. 'About Melissa—'

'No!' Her voice startled them both. It was high and desperate. 'No,' she repeated, more calmly. 'I don't want to hear it. I don't want to know about Melissa, about anyone. I'm not interested. I just want to be left alone.'

'Is that what you really want, Cleopatra?' he asked softly.

'Yes! Haven't you done enough already?' She pulled away, stumbling to the window. Outside, the darkness was like coal dust, and her own eyes stared back at her like a trapped animal.

'Cleo, you remember what you said about making me respectable?'

'I remember. And you said you didn't want to be respectable.'

'I want to put a proposition to you. Think of it as another business partnership, if you wish.'

Cleo felt her body tighten in sudden terror. 'Oh, Lord, you're not going to make me an indecent proposal? I couldn't bear it!'

She saw his frowning, impatient expression behind her. 'Cleo, I'm asking you to marry me!'

Then, softly, 'I told you I would, remember, if we were ever found out.'

She turned and stared at him with big eyes, her face white as flour. 'You must be mad... or drunk. Or both.'

'I may be both, but I mean what I say. I know what Melissa has done. You're ruined. No woman can be a partner of mine and remain unsullied in the eyes of the citizens of Nugget Gully. I want you to marry me. You're the respectable wife I need. Help me back into the fold, Cleo.'

The mockery in his voice stung her. She went to turn away again, but he followed her, catching her arm. 'Say yes,' he said harshly.

'It is ridiculous, preposterous...' she began, but the tears were slipping down her cheeks. 'I'm not respectable any more. Melissa... She was my friend.' Her voice broke, and she covered her face with her hands, sobbing. He put his arms around her, and she felt his lips against her temple and shuddered. His chest was warm and so broad that she felt like a child again.

'You'll be respectable again,' he murmured. 'Once we're married, they will have no reason to slight you. I'll make you some tea,' he said gently, when her sobs had quietened. The kitchen fire glowed. Jake bent to stoke it, his profile silhouetted against the flames as they caught and danced. Cleo shivered, and tried to repair herself with her lacy handkerchief. He looked up, his dark eyes unreadable as he watched her. His voice was quiet and reasonable.

'Cleo, this is a disaster, and we both know it. But

we can turn our bad luck into good. No, don't argue! It is settled.'

'I can't,' she whispered, tears filling her eyes again. 'You can't ask such a thing. It is the sort of marriage I have always dreaded. A bargain. A business deal. Besides, I am a milliner. Your father is a wealthy man, back in England. A man who would not glance at me, if I passed him in the street, let alone approve of my marrying his son!'

He made an angry sound. 'Are you weighed down by such unimportant things? I have told you, I was cast off. My father is as dead to me as I am to him. Just because he is an earl does not mean—'

Cleo blanched. 'An earl!'

'Cleo, Cleo.' He grasped her hands. 'That is over. I do not speak of my past. I am what this country has made me. You are ruined. You must marry me. You have no choice. And as for bargains...perhaps love will come; it has been known to happen.'

The quirk of a smile stabbed her like a knife. How could he know that his offer of a loveless marriage, on this night of tragedy, had been the cruelest cut of all? He was being kind, perhaps. But his kindness hurt like a knife.

He turned away, as if he could no longer bear to face her. She heard him making the tea. What a terrible, terrible mess! And yet she could not believe it was over. Melissa might have betrayed her, but would everyone believe her? Surely it would blow over? A one-day wonder, soon forgotten.

Jake put the cup down beside her.

'They know I followed you out,' he was saying. 'They will be thinking the worst right now.'

'No,' Cleo whispered. 'How can they? Surely they will give me the benefit of the doubt?'

He frowned. 'You're deluding yourself.'

'But it's not true! I'm not your—'

'Mistress? No, we know that, but they don't, and besides …it's much more exciting to believe the worst of people.'

Cleo stood up impatiently. 'I've worked so hard to make this place a success. I won't be driven out by gossip.'

Jake looked at her for a long moment and then he sighed. 'I admire your determination, Cleo, and your courage. But I feel you are being foolish in prolonging the inevitable.'

The door closed behind him. Cleo stood, staring blankly after him. It would be all right. He was wrong, and everything would be all right. Her life depended upon it.

CHAPTER SIX

BUT IT WASN'T all right.

Cleo opened her shop as usual, but there were no customers. She worked on orders she had received, not allowing herself to believe they would not be collected. In the afternoon, she closed the shop and walked to the emporium. It was then she felt the full brunt of Nugget Gully's respectable citizens' disapproval and her changed status.

Whispers, all about her. Someone laughed, smothering it with a gloved hand. Cleo held her head high, her face flaming. If she had murdered someone it couldn't have been any worse.

Then, ahead of her, she saw Mr. Higgs striding along the street. Cleo took a breath. She would stop him, by force if necessary. He would understand, and take her arm and walk with her, and everyone would see that everything was all right. He would... He had seen her. For a moment he hesitated, and then he turned and hurried across the street like a frightened rabbit.

Cleo felt sick with anger and dismay. For a moment she thought of turning back, to the safety of her shop. But she was no coward. With a deep breath, she went on to the emporium.

It was full. Cleo heard the voices before she went in, but they stopped dead at her entry. After a moment, in which eyes avoided hers or stared viciously at her, Cleo came forward. Mrs. Hannah came forward with a disapproving expression.

'Yes?' she said sharply, and folded her arms.

Cleo tried to be calm. It would all go away. If only she stayed cool and seemingly unaware, it would all stop. 'I need some ribbon, thank you,' she said. 'Green ribbon. About a yard.'

'Is that all?' Mrs. Hannah hadn't moved.

'And some lace. That one there should do. A yard of that, too.'

Behind her, someone sniggered. 'Calls herself a hatmaker, does she? I know a better word for it!'

Laughter, quickly hushed. Cleo felt her face flame. Mrs. Hannah smirked, then straightened her already ramrod-straight back.

'I think it best if you don't come in here again,' she said. 'It upsets my customers.'

'Don't be ridiculous!' Cleo snapped. 'How am I expected to run my business without ribbon and...and...?'

'I don't know I'm sure,' Mrs. Hannah retorted self-righteously. 'But I can't have my customers upset!'

'And am I not your customer, too?' Cleo cried, her face getting redder.

'Brazen hussy, I'd call you!' someone said triumphantly.

Laughter and jeers. Cleo spun around. 'How can

you all be so cruel?' she whispered. 'You all speak as though you know the truth, but it's all lies. Lies!'

'We know your sort,' someone retorted.

'We'll have no wicked women among respectable folk,' said another.

'Please!' Cleo shouted, trying again to make them understand.

A male step at the door. They all looked up, and a deathly hush fell over the room. The women exchanged glances; Mrs. Hannah looked dismayed; Cleo went white.

'What is going on in here?' Jake Raines looked about him, his eyebrows raised. 'It sounded as if there were a miners' brawl going on.'

Mrs. Hannah bit her lip.

'Nothing to concern you,' Cleo managed. 'We were having a. . . a friendly argument.'

Jake looked skeptical. 'Oh? About what?'

Cleo hesitated. Someone said, 'About whether Mrs Hannah should serve your fancy woman, Mr. Raines.'

Some of the women looked uneasy now, and a little ashamed, but the others stood firm behind the speaker. Jake looked at her, and his face was cold and hard. 'I fear you are under a misapprehension,' he said at last. 'Miss Montague here is neither my nor any man's "fancy woman" as you put it so delightfully.'

There was a derisive sound. Cleo spun about. 'You're wrong,' she cried. 'Please, look into your hearts and see that you are wrong. Have you no Christian charity?'

Jake smiled coldly. 'I fear they have none, Cleo,'

he said softly into the long silence. 'Better marry me, after all.'

Cleo felt the tears stinging her eyes, but anger came to her rescue. 'Oh, go away!' she shouted, and ran past him to the door. 'You're only making it worse.'

Outside, Mrs. Morgan was about to enter the shop. At the sight of Cleo, she pulled back, drawing aside her skirts.

It was the last straw.

Cleo fled down the street back to her shop, not caring who saw her, only longing for the quiet safety of her home.

She should have known, then, that it was over. In her heart, she did. But she was determined to carry on, to win them all over, somehow. Every day she opened the shop, and no one came. And every night she closed it, and wondered what would become of her.

Jake came again.

'How long are you going to keep this up?' he asked her softly.

Cleo stared at him blankly, then bent again to her sewing. She had almost finished the orders, but no one had come to collect them.

'I want to help you, Cleopatra,' he said sharply.

'Then go away. You make things worse by coming here. What do you think people will say when they see you come here? That all the lies are true!'

Jake laughed abruptly. 'Will it make any difference? Cleo, have some sense. Do as I say.'

Cleo closed her lips stubbornly. She heard him sigh.

'Very well. Have it your own way. If you want me, you know where to find me.'

The door closed. Cleo put down her needle. Was she being foolish? But she had to try!

And try she did. She called on Mrs. Smith, her old landlady, but Mrs. Smith was away in Melbourne visiting relations. Melissa, she would not contact-Melissa was not her friend. She had no friends now.

At last a few customers came, but none who were serious about buying her wares. They came to linger and stare, and rush off to gossip to their friends. She had sold one bonnet in two weeks. As another evening stretched on, Cleo faced the fact that if she held out any longer she would go bankrupt—or starve. Perhaps, in time, the townspeople would come back to her, perhaps they would forget, but Cleo didn't have that sort of time.

Jake.

'No!' The whispered refusal came softly from her lips. Jake would marry her, but he didn't love her, while she loved him. Cleo closed her eyes. Her pride rebelled against it, but she knew deep in her heart she wanted to marry him. To say 'yes' and let him take her away from the terrible mess she was in.

Cleo bowed her head. She was beaten, and it was only a matter of time before he knew it.

The next day was Sunday. Cleo rose, wondering what she was going to do. At last, she dressed and wandered out into the town. Her steps drew her on towards the Nugget Gully Hotel, and when she realised it she stopped. But after a moment she knew she had lost. Jake had offered her a way out and now she must take it. He would not come to her, so she must go to him.

The hotel was closed, it being Sunday, but the door at the side was open, and Cleo stepped in. The place reeked of beer and spirits and cheap perfume—Cleo sniffed distastefully. There were the stairs, down which she had run from Jake that day long ago. She paused, clasping her hands.

'Can I help you?'

The voice startled her, and Cleo spun around to face the man who had come through the door into the bar. He was short and solidly built, and looked at her curiously.

'I want to see Mr. Raines,' she said as calmly as she could.

The man's face cleared, and something gleamed in his eye. Cleo moved uncomfortably, aware of the change in his manner.

'Miss Montague, is it?' he said.

Cleo nodded sharply, lifting her chin.

'You're wanting Mr. Raines?' Now the sneer in his voice was obvious. 'He's busy. Perhaps I'd do?'

Cleo's mouth went dry. 'You?' she gasped. 'I don't understand you.'

'Don't you?' The man took a step towards her. 'He'll get bored with you. He always does. But me... well, a fine woman like you would be all I'd ever want.'

Cleo stepped back, but before she could answer him another man appeared in the doorway. 'Tim,' he said sharply. 'What is it?'

Tim looked at Cleo a moment longer, then turned away. 'Lady says she wants to see Mr. Raines,' he muttered.

The second man was taller and looked tired. He nodded to Cleo, and his eyes, though curious, were kind. 'He's away,' he said. 'Should be back later today.' He glanced at Tim, and jerked his head towards the bar. 'There's glasses to wash,' he said. Tim, with a scowl, disappeared back into the bar. The other man shrugged. 'Sorry,' he said. 'He doesn't mean anything by what he says.' Then he added, 'It you want to wait for the boss, you can wait upstairs.'

Cleo shook her head hastily. 'No. I'll come back later, perhaps.'

Outside, she took a deep breath. She knew she wouldn't come back. If he wanted to see her, he could come to her. Cleo walked slowly back to the shop, enjoying the sunshine.

Why were people so cruel? So condemning, behind the safety of their respectable, ordered lives? But no one was safe, as she had discovered for herself.

The afternoon wore on, and then the evening came, and Cleo ate her small, lonely supper and sat stitching something no one would ever buy. The tap on the door startled her, and she rose quickly. Her hand on the latch, she paused. There had been a brick through the front window last week, and some dreadful letters she had burned. Why not a late-night caller spitting venom?

'Who is it?' Her voice was husky.

'Jake,' he said. 'Who are you expecting?'

Cleo opened the door. He stepped in, and, frowning at her, took off his coat. 'You wanted to see me,' he said, and looked hard at her. Cleo walked to the stove and warmed her hands at it— the night was chill.

'Yes,' she said, and turned to face him, taking a deep breath. 'I thought of going to Melbourne,' she told him. 'If you agreed to buy out my partnership.'

'Cleo,' he sighed. 'It would follow you, the whole sordid story. Do you think our respectable friends would not tell their friends? Will you change your name: skulk in some little faraway town? Always afraid of being found out?'

For a long time she met his eyes, and then her own dropped and she bowed her head in defeat. After a moment his hand rested on her shoulder and then brushed her throat. 'Say yes,' he insisted. 'It is a business deal, no more, no less. You will see, it will not be so terrible. There are advantages for us both.'

His finger, gentle as a moth's wing, brushed the swell of her breast above her gown. Cleo caught her breath. He met her eyes, unreadable in the lamplight, and smiled. Slowly, slowly, he took the pins from her hair, and it fell in a cloud about her pale, frightened face.

'Is it so difficult to agree?' he breathed, and stooping pressed his lips to hers.

Did love make one so foolish, or was it exhaustion? She had fought and fought, but she could fight no more. Cleo felt as if her bones melted in his embrace, the warmth flooded her, and her lips opened beneath his kiss. She felt his fingers undoing the fastenings of her bodice, as if he was used to such things. Slowly, slowly, her fingers crept up to his shoulders, and then, as he bent to kiss her rounded breast, barely covered by the lacy chemise, she clasped his head to her on a wave of feeling she had never known.

'Yes,' she said, her voice a ragged whisper. Her fingers ran through the dark hair, and she knew suddenly that she was as bad as any of them. As bad as Melissa, watching him with great longing eyes, willing to beg for his favours. She had fooled herself into thinking she was cool and detached, but she was not! She could give herself to him now, let him take her body without love, then discard her... Cleo made a sound like a sob, and pushed him violently away.

Startled, Jake blinked at her, his eyes all warm and blurred. 'Cleo?'

'I said yes, I'll marry you,' she spat, pulling her bodice together with shaking fingers. 'That does not mean you have any of the other rights to me which you seem to think you have. It is a business deal, and no more!'

Her furious white face shocked him back into sanity. Jake stood up, raking his fingers through his hair, 'Cleo—'

'No more, no more,' she cried, and stood up. 'Is it so difficult to believe I might find your advances repugnant? That I might feel tainted, when a man like you handles me as if…as if I were one of his cheap little singers?'

His face was grim and as white as hers now, his eyes black and gleaming. 'You've made your point,' he snarled. Turning, he made for the door. 'I won't sicken you by staying any longer, and God help me if I ever sully your purity, Cleo. You may surround yourself with respectability, and I hope you choke on it!'

Cleo held her breath, trembling as she stood and watched him. How could he know that anger had been her last defense? It had either been that, or to fall babbling into his arms, telling him how much she loved him. And then what? Laughter? Or his pity? It would destroy her, and she knew it. So, instead, she had made him so angry that now he probably would not even marry her.

But she was wrong.

At the door, Jake stopped and turned to face her. He filled the door-frame, and looked so wonderful in his rage that for a moment she was almost lost.

'You'll marry me, though, Cleo. I may be all you think, and more, but if you're ruined because of me, then I'll do what I can to repair your *good* name.' He swept an arm about him. 'I'll send someone tomorrow for your things. We can be married, quietly, at Belubula.'

If he expected more arguments he was disappointed. Drained, Cleo said nothing.

'And one more thing. My singers are never cheap!'

The door slammed.

He had gone.

If he expected Cleo to rant and rave, he was wrong. She was laughing, but the laughter soon turned to tears. She was lucky, she thought bitterly. She was to marry the man she loved. Oh, so, so lucky!

CHAPTER SEVEN

CLEO STOOD IN the doorway and looked at the empty room. Soon someone else would live here and dream here, as she had done. Soon someone else would open the shop, and perhaps the customers would come back. There had been few enough during the past weeks, mostly the curious, coming to see the brazen hussy—Jake Raines's woman.

And now it was closed. Her father's dream, her dream, ended. But at least she had made it happen—her father would have been proud of that.

Douglas Mulgrave had come to see her. 'I'm so sorry,' he said, blue eyes full of contrition. 'It all got out of hand, didn't it?'

'Where is... your wife?'

He sighed. 'I've sent her to friends in Melbourne. Until this mess blows over. If it's any consolation, she was sorry. She told me that her ...let us say, her obsession, made her foolish. She said if you wished to join her, if you had nowhere else to go...'

Cleo shook her head. 'I'm getting married.'

He looked so surprised that she laughed out loud.

'I'm sorry. I should congratulate you.'

But his face spoke of disappointment, which Cleo felt it best not to delve into. She was glad when he had gone. But at least he had cared enough to call.

Mrs. Trewin, the miner's wife, had also come. She was kind, so kind that Cleo felt her icy control slip a little and tears prick her eyes.

'We all think the world of Mr. Raines,' she was saying. 'It's a terrible thing when men like that are thought "not nice" just because they live the sort of life that suits *them* and not other people.'

It was only as she left that Mrs. Trewin asked shyly, 'Is it true that you and Mr. Raines are going to wed?'

Cleo nodded.

'I'm so glad! You will be just what he needs. I wish you both very happy.'

Mrs. Smith had been less enthusiastic. Back at last from Melbourne, she had come to bid Cleo goodbye, she said, as she heaved her rounded frame into one of the remaining chairs. The blue eyes were curious as they rested on Cleo. No doubt she had heard all the gossip.

'Could have knocked me down with a feather,' she said.

Cleo nodded, though she very much doubted a feather could perform such a feat.

'Hope you'll be happy,' Mrs. Smith went on. 'Seems a shame, though. A waste, really.'

Cleo felt her face flush. 'No doubt I'll find other

things to do, when I'm married.'

'No doubt.' Mrs. Smith laughed a little sourly. 'A child every second year and your looks soon go, dear. You don't have to tell me anything about being a wife!'

Cleo opened her mouth, and closed it again. There would be no children, but only she and Jake need know that. She would be the respectable wife he wanted, that was their deal. She would run Belubula as efficiently as she knew how. But there would be no love—he must never know that secret or it would be the end of her.

Sometimes, she wondered whether he was marrying her because he pitied her rather than because he felt such a responsibility for her predicament. He would pity her even more if he knew, and Cleo could not cope with that. Her pride, her self-esteem demanded she keep up a front and that was what she would do.

And Jake? She expected him to carry on as before. Why should he change? He owed her no loyalty. But he would be discreet, Cleo decided. He was a kind man, in his way, and he wouldn't want her humiliation to be too public.

There was still time to back out. But Cleo knew she wouldn't. She was weak, but even such a marriage as this was better than never seeing him again. There was always a flicker of hope that, in time, he might grow to love her. And so she would go willingly into this marriage, knowing what it would cost her.

Cleopatra blinked, and the empty room stared back at her. One of Jake's men would be here to collect her soon, and take her to Belubula. She would drive down the street with her head held high, ignoring the watching eyes. And all this would be forgotten.

Gently, Cleo closed the door and turned the key.

At Belubula, Bridget welcomed her, as warm and friendly as if she were truly the blushing bride. And Cleo unbent a little and admitted she was weary.

'You're thin and pale as a stripling!' Bridget declared. 'You'll need feeding up before Saturday.'

'Why before Saturday?' Cleo murmured, puzzled.

Biddy blinked at her. 'Why, it's your wedding-day!'

Cleo laughed abruptly. 'Is it? I had forgotten. Is…is Jake here?'

Bridget's eyes slipped away. 'No. He'll be here on Saturday, I believe. Wouldn't be proper before then, would it? So,' rallying, 'you've got four days to rest and eat.'

'You make me sound like a horse!' Cleo laughed, feeling cosseted despite herself.

Biddy smiled. Then, with a swift look, 'I'll tell you now, Miss Montague, I never believed the talk from Nugget Gully. I can see why Mr. Raines is marrying you, and for me that's an end to it.'

Cleo breathed a sigh of relief. She had been a little afraid of what Bridget might say. She should have realised that it would be only good.

'Now, come to your room. I've cleaned it from top to bottom, and made up some new curtains. But I expect you'll be planning lots of redecorating soon!'

Cleo followed her, wondering if Jake would give her free rein where Belubula was concerned. It might be fun, and she would have little enough else to do.

The room was small but pretty, with old, faded, flowery wallpaper, and creamy curtains and bedspread. There was a big mahogany wardrobe in one corner, and Bridget bustled over to it and flung open the door. 'Now, I'll need you to try it on,' she said, her voice muffled. 'There'll be tucks needed, and maybe the hem letting down.'

Cleo blinked. It was a dress. A beautiful ivory satin wedding dress, with fold upon fold of lace making up a train. 'But I cannot wear this!' she breathed. 'Where did it come from?'

Bridget smiled. 'Mr. Raines sent for it in Melbourne. Only the best, he said. And, seeing you don't have any family to bear the cost, he thought it was up to him.'

The dress was exquisite. Cleo touched it in wonder. Why had he done such a thing, after what she had said to him the last time she saw him? Cleo blushed at the memory. She could only think that his pride would not let him do otherwise.

'I'll leave you to rest now,' Bridget murmured. 'Dinner is usually at seven. You can eat in the parlour—the dining-room is too big and cold for one.'

Cleo looked up in surprise. 'But won't—I mean, will I be alone?'

'Yes, I told you. Mr. Raines will not be here until Saturday.'

'Oh, of course. Thank you, Biddy.'

'It just wouldn't be right, now, would it? The bride and the bridegroom here, together, before the weddin' day?'

'No,' Cleo said softly.

The door closed on Bridget's smile.

Cleo sat a moment, feeling confused, and then she rose and began to unpack her belongings.

Bridget had spoken the truth. She fed Cleo until she protested she would grow too fat to wear the dress, and that she wasn't allowed to do anything more strenuous than thread a needle.

'Mr. Raines said you was to rest,' she retorted. 'And rest you shall.'

It was so warm outside that Cleo found it more comfortable to stroll in the mornings or the evenings, with Jake's old dog for company. She felt better than she had for weeks—being looked after was new to her, but seemed to agree with her. She did not think too deeply of her future.

Belubula could have been an island, isolated as it was from Nugget Gully and the surrounding properties by time and distance. Everyone got on with their work, and the place hummed with a restful busyness, like a beehive. Bridget ran the house and kitchen in perfect harmony, and nothing was ever too much trouble for her. No wonder Jake had hung on to her all these years.

'Get on with you!' Bridget retorted, when Cleo told her so. 'Mr. Raines can work the pants off most men, if you'll pardon my language. He worked real hard in the early days. Wanted to make something of himself, and show that family of his that sent him away that he didn't need them. And he showed them all right. But it wasn't easy.'

'You'd think he'd spend more time here, if he's so fond of the place.'

Bridget sighed. 'Too busy in Nugget Gully these days. But he would never sell it. It's his home, and I think sometimes just knowing it's here is enough for him. He'll come back to it... maybe now he's marrying...'

Cleo tried to imagine Jake as he had been in the early days. A younger Jake, not so cynical, but bitter, ambition driving him to show that faraway family what he was made of. And he had done it, as Bridget had said, and what good had it done him? He was still a loner, still refusing to meet anyone halfway. Take me as I am, he said, or not at all!

The summer at Belubula steamed on. The hot, dusty days made Cleo tired, and the old dog puffed and panted in the shade of the veranda. She sat long into the evenings, enjoying the cool of the night and the clear, star-filled sky. It was beautiful but she felt restless, and alone. She needed someone here to share it with her, she needed that person she had dreamed of, she needed Jake.

But, even needing him, Saturday came all too soon.

She rose early, but even so Bridget seemed to have a hundred things for her to do. Bathing and washing her hair, while Bridget fussed and fidgeted about. She helped her to dress—she had taken in the wedding gown until it fitted like a glove. Cleo looked into the mirror. The dress was beautiful, and somehow it made her beautiful too. Bridget had brushed out her chestnut hair until it shone and then left it down her back beneath the veil. Cleo's eyes were huge in her white face, and Bridget had rubbed some colour into her pale cheeks.

'You'll look like a ghost, else,' she had retorted when Cleo, shocked, protested. 'There!'

Cleo thought the woman before her a stranger. A bride going to her wedding, to marry the man she loved but who did not love her. She had never thought of herself as a bride—she had pictured herself alone, always, doing exactly as she pleased. Well, she had done as she pleased, and look where it had got her!

Bridget mistook her sigh for nerves. 'Don't worry,' she whispered, squeezing Cleo's arm. 'You'll be all right. Mr. Raines can be a hard man to live with, but he's just and fair, and I've always thought that what he needed was a good woman to bring out the gentler side of him.'

A good woman, Cleo thought, slightly hysterical. That was not what they thought her in Nugget Gully.

Suddenly Cleo put her hands to her burning cheeks. 'I don't think I can go through with it,' she whispered.

'Don't you, indeed?'

The harsh voice made them both turn. He had come without either of them hearing him. Bridget, after one look at his face, scuttled away, leaving Cleo alone. Jake Raines shut the door on her. He looked as if he had just ridden hard from Nugget Gully.

'And why not?' he went on, still in that quiet, harsh voice. His usually mocking black eyes were hard as stone. Did he remember their last meeting as well as she did? 'You have no choice, I think. But don't worry. If you think I'm going to take you to bed as soon as the vows are made, you're mistaken. I have my own pleasures. You have no need to worry. But you'll marry me even if I have to drag you to the altar.' And with that he turned and slammed the door. His anger remained, and Cleo sank down on to the bed, confused. No doubt he was cross because he was being forced into wedlock with an ugly, tall female, shackling himself to her for life. Moreover, one who had insulted him as probably no woman had ever insulted him before...

Cleo remembered his kisses, his touch, and shuddered. She must not dwell on that, ever!

The minister, a bandy-legged little man, with the face of a terrier, made short work of the service. It went like a dream, and, before she knew it, Cleo was Mrs. Raines. It was still a dream. She sipped her sherry, while Jake had a quiet word with the minister. He was so handsome in his black jacket, so dark and unfamiliar. She had thought that she knew him, but she didn't. This stern, white-faced man was a stranger to her. And she was his property, something she had vowed she would never be to any man.

Bridget brought a plate of cake—wedding-cake—and Cleo smiled a little wanly and took a piece.

'For the Lord's sake, woman, cheer up!' Bridget muttered, before passing on to Jake and the minister. Jake met her eyes across the room, and Cleo felt their chill and turned away. What a terrible mess! What were they to do? Well, Cleo knew what she would do. She would play the contented wife to the end, she would smile and smile and never, never let anyone know, especially Jake, how desperately she was in love with him.

The minister left at last. Jake saw him off, and Cleo, standing by the long windows, watched him wave and then turn away. He stopped and then came towards the house, slowly, as though something unpleasant awaited him there. Carefully, she put down her glass and her cake. Carefully, she smoothed her skirts.

She heard his step in the doorway, and turned. He met her eyes, then looked away. 'As my wife,' he began in a cool voice, 'I'll expect you to take over the running of Belubula. You can do that?'

Cleo ran her hands over her skirts again. Her voice was as cool as his. 'I ran my father's house for nearly twenty years.'

'Belubula is hardly a little house in Plymouth with—what, one or two servants? There are many employees here on Belubula, and supplies to order and keep note of, stock to feed and water and take to market.'

'Surely you don't expect me to ride out and round up your sheep?' Cleo retorted.

His smile flickered and was gone. 'No. But you have to know what everyone's job is, even if you don't have to do it yourself. You will be paying them, remember. Do you think you can manage it, Cleo? You will need something to occupy your time.'

It sounded a tall order. And yet, she had run her little shop, and she was a woman of strong character. 'I can do it,' she said, with a calm she was far from feeling. 'But... won't you be here?'

He looked at her, and his eyes were dark and unfathomable. 'I have my own business, in Nugget Gully.' And his own... friends, thought Cleo unhappily. 'I'll stay overnight,' he went on, 'and leave first thing in the morning.'

Cleo turned away. 'Why not go immediately if your business is so pressing?' she said icily, to cover the hurt.

His hand on her shoulder was so unexpected that Cleo jumped and turned, startled, eyes wide, her lips slightly apart. His face was grim but, at her expression, softened. 'I'm staying for your sake,' he said. 'What do you think the gossips will say, if I leave before our wedding night?'

Cleo felt the colour sting her cheeks. His smile grew, and he flicked her cheek with his forefinger. 'Don't worry, Cleo,' he said drily. 'I meant what I said. We'll spend our night in separate beds, but no one else will know that, will they?'

Cleo felt suffocated by his closeness; his touch

sent tingles over her flesh. His smile made her breathless. If he should see... She wrenched away, her satin skirts swishing.

'I must change,' she said, and her voice was the exact opposite to how she felt—cool, calm and collected.

Bridget helped her to undress. She took the gown off and hung it up inside the wardrobe. It was a beautiful thing, the sort a beautiful bride, a bride in love, should have worn. Cleo thought about her childhood, and her mother and her father, and her great adventure to the new land. It all seemed a dream, something which had happened to another person. Perhaps it had; this Cleo seemed a long way from the clear-headed, confident Cleo of the past.

She rested during the afternoon, and, surprisingly, slept, waking almost refreshed. She dressed in the plum-coloured gown, at Bridget's insistence, and because she didn't want her to know that anything was terribly wrong with this union.

'I will find you a girl to help you dress and do your hair,' Bridget said. 'I think Clara will do. She is quick and neat, and quiet. She won't make your head spin with her chatter.'

'But I can dress myself! It is ridiculous—'

'You are Mrs. Raines now,' Bridget told her firmly. And that, evidently, was that.

Bridget had outdone herself. The supper was delicious, a study in intimacy. Candlelight and wine, cooled by the night air from the windows thrown wide to the darkness. The curtains fluttered, and the shadows danced, and it was so cosy that Cleo felt stifled. She forced herself to eat, although she was not hungry, and, because her throat was so dry and aching, forced herself to drink the sweet, thick wine.

Jake was as relaxed as ever. He spoke of what was happening in Nugget Gully, and how his mine, although following the reef of quartz, had yet to find gold. 'I know it is there,' he said, watching the light play on the crystal of his glass. 'And the men are confident. So we keep digging.'

After Bridget had taken their plates away and left them alone, Cleo went over to the long windows. Jake sat by the empty fireplace, sipping his brandy. He was watching her, she knew. She felt his eyes on her back, a stranger's eyes. What did he expect of her? She wished he would go, and release her from this charade he seemed determined to play out. For her 'honour'; or was it really to make her miserable?

Cleo rested her hot cheek against the glass. Her head was dizzy from the wine, and she longed to sit down beside Jake and drop her head on to his shoulder. How lovely, to feel his arm about her, his lips on her hair. Like a proper married couple, happy and in love…

'Are you ready to retire?'

Cleo turned nervously. He *was* watching her, his black eyes unreadable in the gloom. Her throat constricted so that she could not speak.

'What are you afraid of?' he asked softly. 'I won't touch you, if that's what makes you so white. I know that my touch is "repugnant" to you. Wasn't that how you so charmingly put it?'

Bitterness twisted his mouth. Cleo felt an ache in her chest. She started forward. 'There's really no need for this, Jake,' she said, and her voice was husky. 'I never meant to hurt you.'

His eyebrows lifted. 'Didn't you? I thought that was exactly what you meant to do.'

Cleo moved her arm impatiently. 'Has no woman ever refused you before, Jake?' she said, and her words stung.

He looked suddenly angry. 'What do you think I am, Cleo? Some disgusting gigolo, notching up each conquest on his belt... Cleo!'

She was laughing, the mirth bubbling out of her, and suddenly she couldn't stop. It had been a long, long day, and the wine and the emotions had made her dizzy and slightly hysterical. Jake stood and came to her. He grasped her arms, giving her a little shake. 'Cleo, stop it.'

She bit her lip, knowing she was losing her control. His hands slid down her arms, his fingers clasping her fingers and drawing them to his mouth. His lips burned, where they pressed, and Cleo gasped. Jake's eyes were as warm as the summer night, and she began to tremble. 'I said I wouldn't touch you,' he said. 'Unless you want me to...' Slowly, slowly he drew her into his arms, while Cleo stared, mesmerised by his eyes.

His mouth was gentle, but the kiss made her shake even more. Her arms clung, and, as his kiss deepened, she felt her insides begin to melt. As if all the fears and worries of the past weeks were so much butter, set too close before the fire.

She felt him taking the pins from her hair, and was powerless to stop him. His mouth closed over hers again, and then down over her arched throat, down to her bosom, where it spilled over the low-cut gown. Excitement gripped her, and she gasped, drawing his head closer. She was in a whirlpool, spinning down, down, out of control, and she didn't want to come out of it. Being in that whirlpool of passion, with Jake, was so nice that she didn't want to be set free of it.

'Cleo...' Dark eyes looking into hers, searching her face. 'Cleo?'

She closed her eyes.

He swung her up into his arms, light as thistledown. Cleo hid her face against his shoulder, breathing in his warmth. He is my husband, she told herself. He is my husband, and I love him, and it must be all right. Beyond that, she wouldn't allow her thoughts to wander.

The windows in her bedroom were open to the night air, and the moonlight. Still holding her, Jake began kissing her again. She felt the bed beneath them, her hair tangling about them like fine cord. He was undressing her impatiently, pulling the gown down to her waist, unlacing the chemise. He moved away from her and then, unbelievably, his bare flesh pressed to hers. The perspiration beaded between them.

'Jake,' she breathed, trying to clear her head, trying to make some sense of it all. 'No. Stop. Wait.' But even while she said it, her hands touched and smoothed and clung to his firm, strong muscles, her lips sought his in hot, passionate kisses.

'It's too late,' he groaned.

His hands slid down her long legs, clasping her against him so intimately that she was shocked from the hot madness which had held her enthralled. Her eyes met his in the moonlight streaming through the window. He was like a dream, with his handsome face, gleaming eyes and dark hair.

'Cleo,' he breathed, and covered her cry with his mouth as he made her in truth his wife. The kiss went on and on, and Cleo clung to him as if he were the only stable thing in a disintegrating world. And then he had freed her, and left her gasping still with pleasure.

After a moment she found the energy to sit up. He was standing by the window, looking out, dark against the moonlight.

'Jake?' she said, and her voice was nervous. Because now everything had changed, and she was afraid.

He turned and looked at her, and something in his look frightened her even more. 'It seems,' he said softly, 'I do not disgust you so very much after all.'

She felt as if he had struck her. No tender words, nothing of love. He had merely wanted to prove her a liar, and had done so completely and utterly.

After a moment, Cleo took a breath, and forced the hot tears back. And after a moment, she said, in her coolest voice, 'Don't expect me to be so obliging next time.'

He laughed sharply, and began to pick up his

clothes. 'I won't.' Then, at the door, 'The doubters should be convinced now, shouldn't they, Cleo? You'll be relieved to know that I'll be leaving for Nugget Gully first thing in the morning. Goodnight ... Mrs. Raines.'

He closed the door.

Cleo closed her eyes. He had taken her, and now she was to be left while he returned to more important pursuits. She had been a fool, and yet... in those moments it had seemed as if they were meant for each other. Cleo shivered, suddenly cold, and pulled up her sheet. Perhaps he would not go, perhaps it would be all right, after all?

Surprisingly, she slept, and woke to another hot, sunny day. Despite a faint throbbing in her head, she felt the same as she had done any other morning of her life. Or so she told herself. Bridget was busy in the kitchen.

'Good morning, Mrs. Raines. I've got your tea here, and your toast, just as you like it.'

Cleo smiled. She had thought maybe Bridget would resent her, think she meant to usurp her position. But Bridget was her greatest ally. 'Mr. Raines?' she asked at last, as casually as she dared.

'Gone into town, I expect,' Bridget murmured, and avoided Cleo's eyes. She would know about the wedding night, at least. Cleo felt too embarrassed to say more, and went into the breakfast-room to pick at her toast and sip her tea.

Outside the windows the sun was shining, and the birds were singing. She could hear men shouting down in the paddocks, and sheep bleating. A horse galloped past, dust flying up from flashing hooves. Belubula was alive; why did she feel so low?

'I was thinking maybe to show you the accounts today,' Bridget said, hovering about the sideboard. 'Mr. Raines says they're more properly your duty. And, Mrs. Raines, to tell the truth, I'd be grateful if you'd take them off me hands. I'm not a one for sums.'

Cleo smiled and agreed. At least it would be something to occupy her time. She rose, then hesitated. 'Why did Mr. Raines go back to town so soon, Biddy?'

Bridget glanced at her and away, probably thinking he should have told Cleo himself. 'Some famous singer was coming in to sing at the music hall, I think. He had to be there to welcome her. You know what they're like! Such a fuss must be made!'

'Oh, yes, I remember now...' Welcome her! Cleo could imagine the sort of welcome he would give his beautiful actress. She felt even more depressed, and found it hard to concentrate on the figures in their neat columns. But after a time she found herself becoming involved in the running of Belubula. Jake was thrifty, when it came to his property, but it didn't seem to be making much of a profit. Nothing went back into the place, although he must be making a tidy fortune from the hotel and music hall, and his mine, if it struck gold. Why was Belubula so neglected?

After lunch, Cleo went outside, wandering about the garden and the veranda. The hot day brought a waft of lavender scent from the bushes by the stairs, and she picked a purple sprig, twirling it in her fingers as she walked along. Bridget was sure that Jake would be home for dinner, and she was trying to think of what to say to him. Perhaps it would be best if she said nothing!

As the day waned, Cleo became more and more nervous. She dressed in her green gown, changed her mind, and then put it on again. She brushed her hair and plaited it up tight, and then redid it. She fidgeted and fiddled, and in the end threw the brush down in a fit of anger. It was all too ridiculous. He was her husband, yes, but that did not mean she must act as if she must please him. Why should she please him? He did not care for her.

The time ticked by. Cleo sat in the parlour, pretending to read. Bridget came finally, and with a sigh said, 'Seems I was wrong, Mrs. Raines. He isn't coming home for dinner. Shall I bring you a tray in here? Seems a bit lonely, in the big room, all by yourself.'

Cleo nodded, but hardly ate. When Bridget had cleared away, she rose and stood looking into the empty grate. So, that was the way of it. He had married her, and consummated the ceremony, but he would give nothing else of himself; did she really expect anything else? She must live her own life, and would begin straight away. They would go their separate ways, and no one would ever know the terrible unhappiness eating away at her soul.

CHAPTER EIGHT

'BUT MRS RAINES, I don't know if Mr. Raines will approve of your messin' around with his house. Lord, it will cost a fortune!'

Bridget was wringing her hands, looking worried. Cleo laughed. 'He has a fortune. Besides, what else am I to do? He's been away from home a month now, Bridget. Who knows, he may never see the place again!'

Cleo had thrown herself into a whirlwind of change. She had begun in the parlour, and moved on from room to room, making plans, poring through order books and journals, sending down to Melbourne, if what she wanted wasn't available in Nugget Gully or Bendigo. She had bought new material for curtains, new carpets, the latest in furniture, although some of the better pieces had merely to be refurbished. The house was beginning to look as smart and tasteful as befitted the home of a wealthy squatter. Cleo's taste was excellent. Nothing was too gaudy or too gloomy.

As the second month passed, Belubula was still a hive of activity. Although he must know what she was doing—the bills all went to him—Jake had not returned. And, although Cleo still smarted from his deliberate insult, she was so busy that every night it was all she could do to drag herself to her bed before she fell asleep. And yet in sleep her body remembered his, and she woke from shameful dreams, longing for him in a way she felt must be wrong. Bridget was still worried about what he would say, but she too was enjoying herself. 'I was always telling him he should do something about the place,' she said. 'It doesn't do for a man like him to have a house no one would invite a dog to!'

It was during the second month, with everybody busy with their allotted tasks, that Cleo decided it was time for her to visit her neighbours. Bridget was shifty.

'Well, there are the Barnets over to the west. They are old, but their sons run the property. They don't have time for visiting. Then, over the other way, there are the McDowells. They're too grand to come here. And a bit further on from them is a property owned by the Scotts. They're friends of the McDowells, and I don't need to say more than that!'

'I see. Then I shall start with the Barnets.'

'Mrs. Raines!' Bridget ran after her, and Cleo swung around, impatient to be gone. 'Mrs. Raines,' whispered Bridget, 'shouldn't you change? Your dress is all soiled, and your hair has cobwebs in it.' And, when Cleo turned back with a laugh, she added, 'And might I suggest your new gown? The grey one? It's ever so becoming.'

'Thank you, Biddy. You're a treasure. No wonder Mr. Raines has kept you here all these years, though it is a wonder to me that you have stayed with him!'

Bridget frowned. 'For some reason, you haven't got off to a good start, Mrs. Raines, but you wrong about him. He's a good man, deep down. A kind man. He would never hurt a living soul.'

Cleo met her eyes, and it was Bridget who looked away first.

The grey did suit her. While she had been ordering furniture and materials, Cleo had ordered a few dresses for herself. The skirt was full, with ribbons about the overskirt, looping up the cloth. She had a wide-brimmed bonnet to match, and a jaunty little parasol. With her chestnut curls piled up and her fresh complexion, Cleo looked a sight to behold.

The Barnets lived about five miles to the west, and the gig was not as fast as a lone horse. But Cleo persevered over the rough track until she sighted the homestead in the distance. It was not as grand as Belubula, but solid, and there was the usual veranda around it to keep out the heat of the sun. As she started up the track to the house, a horseman rode out to meet her.

He was a stocky man, with fair hair and blue eyes, and a face lined by harsh weather and hard work. 'Ma'am?' he said, plainly puzzled by this vision come to call. 'I'm Seth Barnet. Is there something you want?'

Cleo smiled and held out her gloved hand. 'How do you do? I am Cleo Raines. I live over at

Belubula. We haven't met, and I felt I should become acquainted with my closest neighbours.'

Seth took her hand, still looking amused. 'Mrs. Raines,' he murmured. 'Well, I have met Jake, your...your husband. But he doesn't often call here, and I don't think we've *ever* called on him.'

Cleo felt her smile becoming fixed. 'Well, now he's married, that will change, won't it? May I meet your—er—parents?'

Seth paused, and then smiled back. It lit up his face like a sunbeam, and suddenly Cleo felt less afraid. She followed him back to the house, and let him help her down. There was a neat garden at the front and, although plainly built, the house was tidy and well cared for. Mrs. Barnet came to the door, looking as amazed as her son.

'Mama,' he said, and Cleo could have sworn he winked, 'this is Mrs. Raines, from Belubula.'

'Mrs Raines,' Mrs Barnet, a little stooped and grey, took her hand, and her smile was as warm as her son's. Cleo was given tea and cake, and plied with questions. They were the nicest family she had ever met, but she could understand why Jake avoided them. They were as far removed from him and his lifestyle as lemon and sugar. Cleo was sure they would have had nothing to say to each other.

Mr. Barnet was grey, and rather worn, but as solid as Seth. Seth was the eldest, then there was Uriah, a taller lad with dark hair, and Luke, fair like his parents, with a sweet smile. The three young men admired Cleo, which amused her. They worked so hard that they obviously didn't have the chance to meet many women. They only visited Nugget Gully for their supplies, and never for entertainment. 'I don't think it's a very God-fearing place for young men,' Mrs. Barnet said confidingly, and then clapped her hand on her mouth. 'Oh, dear, I am sorry! I didn't mean your husband was... well...'

Cleo laughed. 'That's quite all right. You haven't offended me in the least. But I really must be going. It's been so lovely to meet you all. Will you visit me next time?'

They agreed to come as soon as they were able, and Seth rode with her to the gate. He waved until she disappeared around the bend in the trees, and Cleo only then realised how late it was. The sun was low on the horizon, making long, cool shadows of the trees. It reminded her, uncomfortably, of that night when she had first met Jake. The cicadas were making a wave of sound, and a moth brushed her cheek. Cleo waved it away impatiently, trying to hurry her horse into a trot when it clearly would rather have walked.

It was almost dark when she reached Belubula. The lights shone out a blaze of welcome, and Cleo felt the tension drain out of her. Joy surged like warm honey into her being, as she drew close. If nothing else, she had found herself a home she loved, and if Jake meant to stay away she could have it all to herself.

The old dog rose, wagging a tail in welcome. Bridget bustled to the door, and Cleo went past in a flurry, pulling off her gloves and tossing her parasol into the hallstand. 'Mrs. Raines,' hissed

Bridget.

'I know, I'm very late. I'm so sorry. They were so nice and friendly that I quite forgot the time.'

'Mrs Raines—' Bridget said in an agonized voice, twisting her fingers.

'I'm starving. Can I have dinner now? In the parlour will do.'

'Your husband is home!' Bridget cried, finally getting a word in. 'And he has guests with him. You will have to change...brush your hair, ma'am! There are twigs in it.'

'Jake?' whispered Cleo, and suddenly all the joy went out of her, to be replaced with trepidation. She felt weary. It had been a long day. 'Perhaps, if I sneak into my room, I could just have a tray,' she said.

Bridget frowned. 'He'll have heard you come in. He'll be waiting. We've already put dinner back for you. I think it would be best if you do as I say, Mrs. Raines.'

'Yes,' Cleo sighed. 'You're right. Quickly, then.'

She wore the plum-coloured gown, so low cut, which suited her so well. If it had bad memories for Jake, then too bad. Bridget brushed her hair, and somehow got it to fall into ringlets about her neck and shoulders, with a ridiculous little piece of lace and ribbon pinned on top. 'There,' she said, in satisfaction. 'You're as lovely as any of them.'

Clara, Cleo's maid, had finished putting away her discarded clothing, and went out. Cleo met Bridget's eyes in the glass. 'Tell me, Biddy, who are the guests? You did say there were guests?'

Bridget suddenly began fussing with the brush, but her back was rigid with disapproval. 'He's brought some singer with him, and her manager. At least that's what he *calls* himself.'

'I see.' Did she? Cleo thought she did. He meant to humiliate her. Well, he wouldn't. She would not let him see how much he could hurt her. She had been amusing herself very well without him, thank you, and if he thought she would play the neglected or wronged wife, he would soon see he was quite mistaken! She would be serene and unruffled; she would act as if he had only left her this morning.

They were in the parlour. They didn't at first look up as Cleo entered, and she had a chance to study at her leisure the tableau they made. There was a tall dark man, a glass in his hand, leaning negligently against the mantel. His face was lined—from hard living, Cleo supposed—and he had an amused smirk on his lips as he viewed the other two occupants. One, a beautiful woman with dark, glossy hair and a white bosom almost spilling from a yellow gown, was examining one of the knick-knacks on the side-table. And leaning close to her, his arm brushing hers oh, so proprietorially, was Jake. He hadn't changed; he looked as dark and handsome as ever. They made a handsome couple, and they were obviously old, old friends.

'Jake, I think your wife is home.' The tall man by the mantelpiece had seen her, and his dark eyes were quizzical. Did you notice them? he seemed to be saying. Don't you mind?

'Mrs. Raines! Cleo...may I call you that? I've heard so much about you.' She was enveloped in a scented embrace. 'I am Molly Mulligan. I'm appearing in Nugget Gully... ah, but then Jake must have told you that.'

Molly's eyes were as blue as the sea, and as cold. Cleo forced herself to smile. 'I've heard of you, of course. You are very famous.'

Molly smiled again, smoothing her hair. 'Well, and much of that is due to Jake.'

'I'm sure it is,' Cleo murmured sweetly. Jake was standing still by the table. There was no welcome in his eyes. He had changed, after all—his eyes had never been so bleak before. Was this the man who had held her in his arms, who had kissed her mouth and claimed her trembling body? He was a stranger, this husband of hers.

Cleo forced herself forward until she reached his side. Then, she boldly stretched up and brushed her lips to his cheek. She felt a tremor go through him, and his arms came up involuntarily to hold her, but she had already stepped away. 'Jake,' she said sweetly, and smiled coolly into his eyes. 'So sorry to be late. I was at the Barnets'. So nice. They've promised to come over soon. I'm sure you and Seth will have lots to talk about.'

Something in his black eyes, which had been so cold and so dark, like a stranger's, changed. They narrowed. Cleo knew she had angered him, and nervously gestured to the other gentleman. 'I don't know your name, I'm afraid...'

'*Mr.* Mulligan, ma'am, at your service.' He bent, setting his lips to her hand. He had the eyes and face of a libertine, and Cleo felt herself shiver with revulsion—if this man was a rake, what was Jake? And yet she feigned friendship, and took his arm as they went through to dinner.

'You are so lucky to have such a beautiful and talented wife,' she said. Better lay it on thick!

He laughed. 'I could say the same to Jake. He did not tell us just how lovely you were, my dear, and I can see why. Does he always keep you hidden away here? All to himself? Is he afraid someone might whisk you away?'

Cleo laughed. 'I doubt he's thought of it,' she retorted.

'Ah, but you are magnificent,' he murmured, and squeezed her arm.

Cleo escaped to her chair, avoiding Jake's eyes as Bridget came fussing in, serving the meal and the wine. Jake and Molly were talking, heads close together. They did indeed make a lovely couple. Cleo thought of what they must have been up to over the past weeks, and felt a chill, like cold steel entering her heart.

'You are a very forbearing wife, I think,' Mulligan murmured.

Cleo smiled and said nothing, sipping her wine.

He leaned closer, and Cleo wished she could lean away. His breath smelt of cloves and brandy, and his hair hung lank over his brow. She disliked him heartily. How could she like him, after the wholesome Barnets? *They* were the sort of people Jake should cultivate, not this ageing libertine and his pretty wife. They were not worth tuppence, the pair of them.

'I beg your pardon?' Cleo started. Jake had spoken to her, and she had not heard a word. Mulligan laughed, thinking it was he who had flustered her.

'Frederick, you must not flirt so with Mrs. Raines... Cleo,' Molly chided, with her big smile and cold blue eyes. 'She is not used to such attentions.'

Frederick sighed and winked. 'I wish I had time to tutor her further,' he said softly. 'I believe it would not take me long, and she would be begging for my *attentions*.'

Cleo felt herself go to ice. To have such a man make such a suggestion to her, in the company of his wife and her husband. She looked at Jake—he was twirling his glass around, but his eyes were glittering. Was he angry at Frederick, or her? Cleo took a breath.

'I did not hear what you said,' she whispered again.

'I said... you were very late tonight. I thought you would have learnt better than that.'

Cleo clenched her hands under the cover of the table. 'If I had known you were to arrive with guests, I would not have been late.'

'You should know better than to expect me to advise you of my every move.'

'I would never presume to ask such a thing.'

There was a cool silence. The Mulligans were lapping it up. Jake met her eyes, and she couldn't look away. They were dark with anger—she knew that anger well. The indifference was gone; they were Jake's eyes again, Jake's angry eyes.

'Jake, your wife has a right to go out calling. What was his name, my dear? Seth?' Mulligan winked again. 'Well, no doubt he is a very handsome young man, and Jake is away so often. Who can blame you?'

'You are quite wrong,' Cleo snapped, her face on fire. 'You don't know what you're talking about.' But her anger only made her look more guilty, and Frederick laughed softly, his finger brushing her scorching cheek, and then, slowly, sliding down to her throat, where the pulse beat so quickly.

'A beautiful woman should be admired,' he murmured. 'It is a crime to shut her away. Jake should bring you in to Nugget Gully more often. Were you never on the stage, my dear? You would make a stunning actress! You would set the town alight!'

Cleo dared not look up, and was glad when Bridget came to clear away and she was able to rise with Molly Mulligan and go into the drawing-room. 'Your home is beautiful,' Molly said, looking around, and Cleo was surprised to realise that she had never been to Belubula before. 'I wish I had a home like this. But I seem to move from place to place so often, there is no time to settle down.'

'But eventually you must retire, must you not?' Cleo retorted.

Molly patted her hair in the gilded mirror over the mantel, and admired her gown. 'Not for a time yet. Frederick is certain we can go on another ten years, at least. We may even travel to

America.'

'How exciting for you,' Cleo murmured. She opened the french windows, and felt the cool evening air on her hot cheeks.

'How on earth did you and Jake meet?' Molly asked, and smiled in the mirror. 'You are such an... unlikely couple, aren't you?'

Stung, Cleo turned to face her. 'In what way?'

'Well, you're rather proper for Jake. You must know it. He prefers women to be... oh,' and she waved her arms in the air, obviously thinking of herself, 'to be a little *improper,* if that does not shock you.'

'It doesn't shock me. I think you are wrong. Jake and I are very much in love.'

But though Molly smiled, it was the sly smile of one who thought she knew better.

The men came soon after that, and Frederick moved straight to Cleo's side. He smelt even more strongly of brandy, and even Bridget's disapproving look at him when she brought coffee did not seem to do more than amuse him.

'I am so sorry we will be leaving town on Friday,' he was saying. 'I wish we could stay for another week, at least. A year, let's be frank!'

Molly laughed in a high-pitched voice. She rested her hand on Jake's sleeve. 'So do I.'

Cleo slipped away, to pour the coffee, and then went out to speak to Bridget. The little woman was indignant. 'What has got into him?' she demanded. 'I've never seen him like this. He's usually so...well, he's usually the life and soul! It's as if someone's died.'

'Well, hopefully our guests will be leaving before too long.'

Bridget bit her lip and shook her head at Cleo. 'I'm afraid they're staying overnight, ma'am.'

Cleo's eyes widened. 'Oh, no. I had hoped to be rid of them. They are so awful, Biddy!'

'I know. Why do you think I was so pleased when he brought *you* home for lunch, ma'am?'

Cleo had to laugh, as she went back into the passage. Frederick was waiting. He made some excuse that he had been to his room, but she knew it was a lie. He slid his arms about her waist, and his breath was hot on her cheek. 'What a beauty you are,' he said. 'No wonder Jake has decided to keep you hidden!'

'Please,' she muttered, struggling. 'Let me go.'

But he only tightened his grip. 'You don't mean that,' he retorted, and planted a kiss on her cheek when she twisted her face away.

'I do mean it.'

'But you can see how well Molly and Jake get on. Why be the odd one out? I know under that cool exterior you're burning for me.'

'Will you let me go?'

'I think you'd better do as she says,' a voice said drily. Frederick went still, and then with a laugh dropped his arms. Jake was standing behind them, in the shadows, and his face was hard. 'My wife is not up to your games, Freddy,' he said after a moment. 'Perhaps you'd better stick to chorus girls. They're more your thing.'

'Of course. If you say so, old chap.' But his smile was bland, and he sauntered past and back into the drawing-room as if nothing had happened. Shaking, Cleo leaned against the wall, and wiped her mouth with the back of her hand.

'Are you all right?' Jake was polite again.

'No, I am not all right!' Suddenly, she was so angry she didn't care what she said. 'You stay away for months, and then... How dare you bring those dreadful people into my house?'

'Your house?' he whispered, and his anger answered hers. Gone was the stranger. She was almost glad. 'Your house? How the hell is it your house? I'll invite who I want to *my* house. And if you don't like it, then you can go to your room and let us get on with it.' Mockery twisted his mouth. 'Can't you pretend to like them? Can't you laugh a bit, flirt a bit?'

'Like Molly, you mean?' she said, and her face showed him her disgust. 'Shriek with laughter and paw him at every opportunity, as she does you? Is that what they do, your friends? It's hardly polite society, then, is it?'

'Who ever said it was? But at least the people are alive, not weighed down with their rules and regulations, not all pretending to be something they are not! Half of your so-called gentlemen have women like Molly tucked away in some house somewhere, and their wives only pretend they don't know.'

'You're disgusting! Would you prefer I had let him maul me, here in your house, just because he is your friend? Do you want me to go in there now, and simper at his crude remarks, and pretend I'm enjoying being made the butt of his jokes, while his wife makes it so obvious she is your mistress?'

They stared at each other, and Cleo watched his face go white. 'At least she doesn't turn to ice, when I kiss her, and when I take her to bed she opens her arms to me in welcome.'

Cleo felt a pain, deep inside. She turned away, as though to run, but he caught her arm. 'Cleo,' he said harshly. 'That was all over long ago. Before I married you.'

'Was it?' She wouldn't look at him, her throat ached with unshed tears. 'Should I care what you do? Just as long as it is a secret from my friends, then you can do what you like!'

His fingers bit into her flesh. 'Oh, yes, you hate me, don't you? But we'll be gone soon enough. Then you can ask your Seth Barnet over. He's more your type, I can see that. Salt of the earth, eh? Full of pap about hard work and good living. But I bet, when it comes down to it, he and Frederick both have the same thing in mind for you, oh, so proper Mrs. Raines.'

Cleo didn't realise until she felt the stinging pain in her wrist that she had raised her hand to strike him. 'You may not like the Mulligans,' he went on furiously, 'but they make money for me, and you. Don't tell me you haven't enjoyed spending my money these last months. So be polite, play the hostess, and beyond that do as you please!'

Cleo pulled away, rubbing her wrist. 'I thought you were better than that,' she whispered. 'I had some idea that you were a good man, a decent man—even Bridget believes that, poor Bridget—

but I was wrong. You're just like Frederick, and nothing can change you.'

Cleo brushed past, into the drawing-room. Molly and Frederick were looking through the music on the piano. It wasn't long before they began to play and sing, and Cleo was able to slip away and leave them to it. She felt exhausted, hurt and angry. All the happiness she had brought home had drained out of her. That was Jake's doing.

Bridget came with a glass of warm milk. To help her to sleep, she said, but Cleo saw sympathy in her eyes and was grateful for one friend. She brushed her hair and, tired, didn't bother plaiting it. Her bed looked inviting—it had been a busy day—and soon she was asleep. It seemed only minutes later that she was awake again.

For a moment she could not understand what had woken her, and lay still, confused in the darkness. Then it came again. A stealthy footfall by the bed, the rustle of clothing. And then someone's soft breath—the smell of brandy. Cleo sat up in a flash, not knowing what she was going to do, only knowing she must get away. She couldn't bear the thought of Frederick touching her, kissing her...

She opened her mouth to scream, but a hand closed over it, pushing her back down on to the mattress. Her hair was everywhere, blinding her as she arched and struggled, and then the intruder was pressing her even further into the mattress with the weight of his body. Cleo twisted her face, and then bit down on the hand covering her mouth. She tasted blood. The hand was jerked away. A voice uttered an oath.

Confused, she half sat up, pushing back her hair. He was sitting up too, nursing his hand. 'Jake?' she whispered. She could see the outline of him now. It was the brandy which had confused her, and the memory of Frederick. 'Jake?' she whispered again. 'What are you doing here?'

'What the hell did you think *you* were doing?' he muttered. 'You've bitten me to the bone.'

'I thought you were Frederick...' she began, and tried to clear her head.

She heard him sigh. 'That's why I came in,' he said at last, sounding more like the Jake she remembered. 'I know Freddy. He's quite capable of a midnight visit, even though I plied him with as much brandy as he would take. So I thought I'd better be here, just in case. I hadn't counted on being attacked by the victim.'

Cleo felt the giggles rising up inside her, and covered her mouth with her hand.

But he knew. 'It's not bloody funny!'

'I'm sorry.' Searching on the table she found the flint and lit the lamp. A soft glow illuminated the room. Jake looked tired to death, with lines cutting into his face, and purple shadows under his eyes. His clothes were untidy and his hair messy. Cleo felt suddenly almost maternal, looking at him, and knelt beside him on the bed to look at his hand. It was bleeding but not badly.

'I'm sorry,' she said again, and, pushing her hair back over her shoulder, gently touched the bruised flesh. 'I'd best bathe it.' There was water in the ewer, still warm, and she wet a cloth and, stooping, bathed the wound. There, it's all better,' she said, and looking up with a smile met his eyes. Something there made her pause. They were dark and intent, and though he returned the smile he was not really smiling. She felt the danger, and went to move back, but he had already clasped her waist, pulling her on to his knees as he sat on the bed. Her long white nightdress made her look like a young girl, and her long hair spilled about her face and shoulders.

'You look tired,' she managed, in a strained voice. 'I'll be all right, I'm sure. Frederick must be asleep. You'd best go to bed if you have to travel back with them tomorrow.'

'I was tired—that is, I thought I was,' he said, and he smiled that quirk of a smile. Cleo's heart began to beat faster.

'You said—' she began.

'I said far too many things.' But though his voice was mocking, his arms were tense and serious. She found herself held against his body. It was different from Frederick, so nice that she didn't pull away. She felt his warmth through his clothes, and her hands, after a moment, came to rest on his broad shoulders.

'What you said,' she whispered, feeling as unsure as a child. 'About Molly and you...'

'I told you the truth. It was over long before we married.'

His mouth closed on hers, teasing and warm. When he drew back, the lamplight caught his eyes and made them shine. She knew she should push him away, remembering their biting words, but she could do nothing, and when he kissed her again she let him smooth her long hair from her shoulders and pull undone the ribbons which held her nightgown gathered at the throat.

It slipped down over her shoulders, catching at her wrists, and she was bare to the waist. Jake caught his breath. 'He was quite right. You are beautiful,' he said, and, bending his head, began to kiss her breasts.

Cleo pressed closer, dizzy with desire, her body starved of him for so long. She would never have believed one man could throw all her prized good sense into chaos, but Jake could. She lifted his head, and as he bent to kiss her again, said, 'Am I really so cold, so unwelcoming?'

His fingers closed on her nape, and he kissed her long and hard, while her arms held him fast against her, and her head spun with longing for him. When he lifted his head again, his black eyes gleamed.

'You want me,' he said. 'I know that much. Why don't you admit it, Cleo? What are you afraid of?'

Being hurt, she could have told him.

Behind them, the door clicked.

Cleo spun around, her arms about her nakedness. Jake cursed. Frederick stood there, as startled as they, his eyes going from Cleo to Jake and back again. Then he muttered an apology, 'Sorry, wrong room...' and, backing out, closed the door again.

Cleo bit her lip on hysterical giggles. Jake laughed softly. 'The fool,' he said. 'Did he think I'd let him cuckold me in my own home?'

Cleo tried to pull away, but he held her fast. Her

voice was breathless. 'You said we had a bargain, Jake. But you broke it. You said you wouldn't touch me. But you did.'

He frowned. 'It took two of us to break our bargain, Cleo, and you know it.'

'You lied, Jake,' she retorted.

'So did you,' he said, and he suddenly pushed her off his knee and on to the bed. 'Admit you want me as much as I want you, my oh, so proper wife. Admit you think about me, at night, in the darkness. Admit you dream about—'

'No,' she gasped. 'No! Get out of here. You said—'

'All right,' he said. He stood up, and he was angry, as angry as she. 'But at least I'm honest enough to tell you the truth. I want you, Cleo. I want you all the time, and if I stayed here at Belubula I'd take you. And because I'm trying, God help me, to stand by my promise, then I have to stay away. But if you're willing to forget that bargain we made, then I'll come back here, and I'll be faithful to you for as long as I'm able. And if that sounds like the words of a cad, then I'm sorry, but I've never been tested before, on faithfulness, and I'm not sure of my limits. But I can say this much, Cleo. Since we married, and before that... there's been only one woman I've bedded, and that is you.'

'And that's all it is to you, isn't it? Bed? Cleo whispered, her bitterness like acid in her throat.

He laughed, his face in the shadow of the room beyond the lamp. 'What else would it be? Don't tell me you feel more for me, Cleo, or I'll know you're lying. I doubt you *could* feel more. You're like ice, and fire. Will you tell me now that you love me, as a wife is supposed to love a husband?'

His voice was harsh with mockery, and Cleo knew she could not tell him that she did indeed love him. He would laugh in her face. He had given her his truth, as he saw it, but it was far from what she had wanted to hear. She was not Molly Mulligan. She needed love, she needed to give love.

Jake's smile quirked and was gone. 'So,' he said softly, 'we are not to be honest tonight? Well, I will not stay where I am not wanted. Goodnight, Cleo.'

The door closed. Cleo let the scalding tears fall. He was hateful. He hurt her with his words and she let him. She was a fool to fall for his kisses, and yet... she loved him still, heart and soul. He was right. She did want him, and she was no more 'proper' than Molly when it came to that. But should she release him from his promise, without admitting her love for him? And how could she admit her love, in the face of what he had told her? He would pity her, or laugh at her, and so destroy her.

CHAPTER NINE

THE NEXT MORNING Jake and his visitors were gone. Cleo hadn't been able to sleep after Jake had left. Her mind had spun around and around, remembering what he had said and trying to make sense of it. He wanted her, he had said, and because he had made a promise he stayed away. It seemed so amazing that it should be so, that Jake should want her, Cleo. All this time she had thought he stayed away through dislike or indifference, and instead... But he had said it was so, and it must be so.

And yet he had not said he loved her, and when he spoke of it, it was in a harsh, angry way that frightened her. As though he dared her to admit there was such a thing. But he wanted her, and if she would agree to release him from his promise he would live with her like a husband, as far as he was able. Without love.

Cleo twisted and turned, trying to escape her thoughts. Wouldn't that be better than nothing? But if she said 'yes', and then found he couldn't be faithful, and left her, it would be far, far worse than being alone. How could she choose? She finally fell into a sleep of exhaustion at about three o'clock, still without coming to a decision. She slept late, and did not see them at breakfast, something for which she was grateful.

The house was quiet again, and Jake's old dog followed Cleo around. He seemed to have transferred his affections to Cleo now that his master spent so little time at home. But then, Nugget Gully was home to Jake; the hotel was *his* home.

Cleo spent some time choosing new curtains for the drawing-room, but she was bored with decorating today. After lunch, she decided to visit her other neighbours, the McDowells, and set out in the gig.

The McDowells were, as Bridget had said, rather grand. But Cleo was not about to be fazed by them, and their initial frostiness soon thawed. She listened politely to Mrs. McDowell's talk of Melbourne and her 'dear friends' in high places; she smiled at Mr. McDowell's long jokes and agreed they were letting too much 'riff-raff' into the country.

'We need more families to work on the land,' he went on, encouraged by Cleo's interest. 'Not the sort that only come to make a fortune and then leave.'

'My husband said the same thing only the other day,' Cleo murmured.

The McDowells looked uncomfortable.

'In fact,' Cleo went on, flushing a little, 'it was he who thought it would be a good idea to meet our neighbours. He's so busy, you see, that he has been rather negligent in that department.'

'Well, yes.' Mr. McDowell cleared his throat and twisted his magnificent moustache. He was a big man, running to fat, while his wife was a thin sparrow of a woman with darting eyes.

'Neil is very busy too,' she put in now, smiling frostily. 'The church in Nugget Gully is quite dilapidated, and we really need a new one. Neil is president of a committee to raise funds, you know.'

Cleo didn't, but she could lie like the best of Jake's actresses. 'What a coincidence! *My* husband was just saying the other day that it was a disgrace. I'm sure he would be more than happy to make a donation.'

She smiled at them. They didn't believe her for a moment, but they couldn't accuse her of lying if they wanted the money. And everyone knew that Jake was very rich.

'Well, most decent of you,' Mr. McDowell murmured. 'Most decent.'

Cleo left, feeling that her short visit had been a great success. The Scotts were not so successful. They were less grand than the McDowells, but a great deal more self-important. Cleo felt they looked upon her as they might upon a slug which had come in from the garden. Jake's money meant little to them—it could not buy good 'breeding'.

'We are related to the Earl of Buccleigh, of course,' Mrs. Scott announced, over her teacup.

Cleo, awash with tea, bravely sipped from hers. 'I wonder if Jake's father knows him?' she said thoughtfully. 'I shall ask him.'

The Scotts didn't know whether to be impressed or sceptical. Their long faces reminded Cleo of horses. Strangely, their daughter was ravishingly attractive, with blonde curls and big doll eyes.

Peggy had just had her first visit to Melbourne and had evidently created a great deal of interest. Mrs. Scott was hoping for a great marriage. 'Although she's too young yet,' she added.

Peggy, listening to this, simpered. 'Mama, stop, you are embarrassing me,' she said, agog for more.

Cleo smiled at the girl. 'But she is charming,' she lied.

Peggy took the compliment as her due. 'We hear so much about your husband,' she said slyly. 'Is he as wicked as they say?'

'Peggy!' Mrs. Scott reprimanded, but only adoration shone in her eyes.

Cleo set her cup down a little sharply. 'I doubt anyone could be quite that wicked,' she laughed. 'Now, I really must be going. Thank you so much for your hospitality.'

It was a lie. They had received her politely because it would be beneath their dignity to turn her from their door, but they had not really welcomed her.

The perspiration was trickling down between her shoulder-blades, as Cleo drove back to Belubula. The heat seemed to go on day after day without respite. The green paddocks had dried to brown, and the river was a trickle, and always the burning sun shone out of a clear blue sky.

Cleo felt as if the dry, hot air were drawing the very moisture from her skin. She pitied Bridget, working in her kitchen with the wood stove constantly blazing. And she felt sorry for the sheep, and the horses, standing still beneath the feeble shade of the trees.

Well, she had done her best. She had played the dutiful wife to the best of her ability, and even lied. She could do no more. It was up to Jake—she supposed he would laugh at her efforts. But surely he could not begrudge her making her own friends? He had his, after all. The dreadful Molly and Freddy—what were they all up to now? She dreaded to think.

Belubula lay sweltering in the heat. Cleo stepped into the cool hall and untied her bonnet, wiping the dust and sweat off her face with the back of her hand.

'Mrs. Raines,' Bridge hissed, and Cleo looked up in surprise.

'Biddy, what is it? Not—not Molly again?'

But before Bridget could answer someone stepped out of the door to the parlour, and a familiar voice said, 'Cleo, how lovely to see you.'

Melissa.

Cleo viewed her with shocked eyes. Melissa, looking as delicate as ever. The memories came back in a flash, and Cleo felt sick. But the green eyes meeting hers were not vicious—the thwarted fury had gone. This Melissa was pale, and there were new lines about her mouth; perhaps she had suffered too.

'Come, Cleo, why be unfriendly?' she said quietly, and Cleo was astonished at the note of desperation which had crept into her voice. 'You have what you wanted, haven't you? I realise that now, but like a fool I thought you disliked Jake. I should have known he was just the sort of man you would fall for.'

'I hardly think—' Cleo began.

'I know, I know. It's not *proper* to discuss such things. Douglas thought you were very lovely, you know. You made a great hit with him.'

'I don't know how you can talk so to me,' Cleo whispered, 'after what you've done. Or how you can come back here—are you staying in Nugget Gully?'

Melissa laughed at the disbelief in her face. 'Yes, for the moment. Douglas is stationed there and he wants me by him—some sort of trouble with the miners, you know. He says he wants us to pretend we are newly weds again. Isn't that sweet?'

But her smile was strained.

'Not that it's been much fun,' she went on. 'Being cut in the street by one's so-called "friends" and "acquaintances". So, of course, I thought of you, Cleo. Come now, we used to be friends, didn't we? If Douglas can forgive me, surely you can?'

There was a strange look in her eyes, and Cleo's heart went out to her despite all that had happened. Should she turn Melissa away? They had once been friends, as she said, and now they were both rather short of friends.

Cleo smiled. 'Poor Melissa. Have you come alone, or is Douglas with you?'

Without waiting for a reply, she passed into the parlour. Bridget appeared with cool lemonade, and Cleo took the glass with a smile of gratitude.

'He is in Nugget Gully,' Melissa went on, and

now her smile was less taut, more genuine. 'As I said, trouble with the miners. They want more money, I believe, and the mine owners are not keen to give it to them.'

Jake was a mine owner. Cleo sipped thoughtfully at the cool drink. Bridget had said something the other day about a new mine, a new shaft being dug.

Melissa wandered around the room. 'I believe you have transformed this place,' she said. 'And now you are out sweetening up the neighbours. Does Jake appreciate your efforts, my dear?'

Cleo shrugged. 'I'm not doing it for him.'

'Oh, no?' Melissa's eyes narrowed. 'I want to say something,' she said seriously, and Cleo frowned. 'You probably think me a bitch, and I suppose I was. But I know what you feel, Cleo—I've been through it all before. You think you can change him, make him...suitable. You never will. You can never hold him if you try to change him, you know. You do know that, I suppose? Or are you fooling yourself into thinking he will reform for love of you? No!' as Cleo went to rise. 'Wait and listen; I am your friend, if only you will listen to me. You must accept him as he is. If you love him, then forget all the rest. What does it matter what some people think of him? It is what *you* think that counts. And what does it matter if, occasionally, he strays? Turn away, pretend not to notice. Take him as he is, Cleo, or not at all.'

There was a long silence. Melissa turned away, and went to the window. She stood there a long time, her hands clenched upon the sill.

'There,' she said at last. 'I have said my piece. Or should I say *peace*. I will go. Douglas sent one of his faithful troopers with me. He is somewhere about.'

Cleo swallowed, and rose. The surprising thing was that she did not resent Melissa's words. 'Thank you,' she said. 'I know you mean well.'

Melissa laughed sharply. 'But you will go on as you please,' she retorted. 'Well, don't say I didn't warn you. Goodbye, Cleo.'

But Cleo stopped her. 'Wait. I'm intending to hold a... I suppose, a dinner party, soon. If I send you an invitation, will you come?'

Melissa looked astounded, and then she smiled. 'Will I come? When I am dying of boredom? Of course I will come!'

'And Douglas, too.'

'Oh, Douglas will come, when he knows it's your dinner party.'

Cleo wondered, when she had gone, if she had done the right thing. But Melissa had seemed so tortured; she just hoped Jake would be kind.

After dinner, she sat in the parlour, in her new splendour, and planned her first dinner party. There were invitations to write, and a date to set, and menus to plan. Bridget was thrilled, and promised to get in some help for the big day. Cleo knew she must have a new dress, and decided to go into Nugget Gully for the material, at the end of the week. And Jake *must* be there. It would all be pointless, if Jake was not there. She thought of his words, again, that night. It was *all* pointless, if Jake was not there. Could she tell him so? Did she dare? Must she, as Melissa said, take him exactly as he was, or not at all? It seemed a cruel decision to make, but perhaps she had no choice.

***

The day of the journey dawned hot and still, and Cleo set out with Bridget. Nugget Gully sweltered in the summer heat. Cleo ignored the looks from some of the people, and smiled at those who smiled at her. Bridget had some supplies to order, and hadn't finished when Cleo returned from the emporium. So Cleo turned to the hotel. It wouldn't, she thought, be a party without the host, and if she didn't tell him Jake was unlikely to turn up.

The hotel was as gaudy as ever. She was directed, with curious looks, into the back office. Jake was bent over his desk. Cleo, pausing in the doorway, was relieved. She hadn't admitted it to herself, but despite what he had said she had been afraid she might catch him in the arms of one such as Molly Mulligan.

'Jake.'

He looked up, surprised, and then smiled in genuine pleasure. He was so handsome, his eyes were so weary, her heart turned over in love for him. Suddenly, she remembered what he had said, about wanting her. The colour stained her cheeks, but her voice when she spoke was as cool as ice water.

'I am arranging a dinner party for next Saturday night. Will you be there? Only, with—er—seating and so on, I need to know.'

His smile had gone, and he looked down at his papers. 'Must I be there? If it's what I think it is, I'd much rather not.'

His smile was wry when he looked up at her again. Cleo made an exasperated sound. 'Jake, please. You must come. I have told them all you will be there. What will they think if you are not?'

He laughed in surprise. 'It hardly matters to me what they think. But, as it seems to concern you, then I'll come.'

Cleo sighed with relief. 'Thank you,' she said stiffly. Then, 'Oh, you will need to make a donation to the new church committee. Mr. McDowell is the president. I said you were very keen.'

The smile was still there, mocking her. 'Oh? So that they can damn me from their pulpit? What else have you told them?'

'Nothing, really. Only that your father knows the Earl of Buccleigh.'

Jake raised his eyebrows. 'He probably does!' He laughed at her face. 'Cleo,' he said, serious again, 'may I suggest that you speak to me before you attribute any more of your imaginings to my name?'

Cleo flushed to the roots of her hair. 'I'm sorry,' she said. 'It just seemed the thing to do. I wanted them to see the best side of you, not be blinded by their prejudices.'

He looked surprised. 'I suppose I'm grateful but. . . if you think I mean to change to please old Mr. McDowell, and that dreadful Mrs. Scott—'

'I don't want you to change,' Cleo retorted,

Melissa's words fresh in her mind. 'At least, not in that way. I just think it foolish to be on bad terms with your neighbours, just because you're too stubborn to do anything about it. They could do a lot for you, and you could show them you're not the black-hearted villain you like to pretend you are.'

Had she gone too far? But he was smiling his mocking smile. 'You always manage to surprise me, Cleopatra,' he said. 'You have good reason to hate me, and yet you don't, do you?'

She met his dark eyes, and shook her head. 'No,' she whispered. 'I don't hate you, Jake.'

Now, now was the time to tell him! But he had looked away, down at the papers on his desk. He sighed. 'I've been too busy lately to pretend to be anything much.'

'Busy?' she whispered, surprised, and received a sharp look.

'Did you think I was cavorting with my 'cheap little singers", as you once called them? Sorry to disappoint you, my dear. The new mine looks hopeful. We've struck a quartz reef. Only thing is we're having trouble with the miners. More money. I can understand some of the poor beggars complaining, when you see what they're paid. But mine have always had a fair deal. Discontent is like a disease—it spreads.'

'Will there be trouble?' Cleo asked.

Jake shrugged. 'Perhaps. If the owners give them what they want it could all blow over, but if not... strikes, maybe. The troopers will be called in.'

Cleo felt her breath stifle. To hide her fears for his safety, she said, 'The mine, what is it called?'

Jake shuffled his papers. 'The Queen of Egypt,' he said, and laughed at the look on her face.

'I hope,' Cleo said stiffly, 'she is not as big a disappointment to you as I am.'

His eyebrows lifted. 'Oh, I have high hopes!' The dark eyes teased, forcing her to remember less formal times. Cleo looked away, and knew now she would not speak. She was too afraid to reveal any weakness to him. If once he found out how vulnerable she was beneath her self-possessed exterior, he could hurt her unbearably.

'I'd best be going.'

Jake looked out of the window. 'Looks like a storm brewing. Is Biddy with you?'

'Yes.'

'Until Saturday, then.'

She forced herself to smile, and closed the door. And closed her eyes. She had had her chance, and failed.

Bridget was ready, and they set off. They reached home safely, but as the day drew on the sky darkened, and by dinnertime there was a deathly hush in the air. Cleo sat alone, reading, but was too restless to settle, and stalked the room, peering out of the window. The faint throbbing in her head told her there was a storm gathering.

Bridge brought her warm milk, and Cleo went to bed. She lay in the darkness, listening to her own heartbeat and feeling the perspiration gather on her body, making her stick uncomfortably to the sheets and her nightgown. There was no breeze from the window. Only a terrible still waiting.

The thunder came first, rumbling from far away, the lightning not even visible at this distance. And then, a swirling wind that clacked the leaves on the trees and tossed her curtains into the room like a bride's veils. Cleo rose to close the windows, the breeze drying the sweat on her body. The flash of lightning caught her by surprise, and she jumped, crying out, and then again as the thunder burst like cannon fire overhead.

The storm seemed to engulf the house. Thunder rolled and lightning made the night into day. Cleo shuddered, feeling the power of the storm in the air. She pulled the sheets over her head, cringing and whimpering, like a puppy. She thought of going to Bridget, but felt too humiliated by her own weakness to show it to others. She was a grown woman, not a child! Why could she not overcome this irrational fear?

The touch on her shoulder nearly sent her through the roof. And then Jake was there, his arms holding her safe against his big body. His hair was wet, and Cleo clung to him, knowing he had come home in the storm. For her? She didn't dare hope.

'Poor Cleo,' he mocked, but his hands were gentle as they caressed her. 'It will soon pass. Hush, now.'

And he held her, and rocked her, smoothing her hair and murmuring reassurance.

Gradually, the rumbling drew away, and only the rain was left, falling at a soft, steady rate. Jake's breath fanned her cheek. 'I'm soaked,' he said in a strange voice. 'And I've soaked you too.'

'It doesn't matter,' she murmured. She didn't want him to go. She felt him rise, and bit her lip on words begging him to stay. His silhouette against the window, and the rustle of clothing being removed.

'Cleo? Do you want me to stay? You know what it will mean, if I do?'

She took a breath. 'Yes,' she whispered. 'I know what it will mean.' There, it was done. No turning back. And yet she felt that it was the right thing to have said. 'I do want you, Jake,' she breathed. It was a night for giving up secrets.

His hand reached out and found her. His lips teased her mouth, hesitant at first, then closing on hers in a deep kiss. Cleo shuddered, her body pressing closer to his. He was naked, and everywhere she touched was smooth, hard flesh. His hand cupped her breast, then slid down to her trim waist. He kissed her bare shoulder, slowly untying the ribbons of her nightgown. Cleo's heart was thumping, and when she felt his lips on her breast she gasped with the sheer pleasure of it.

'Cleo?' He stilled. 'Do you release me from my promise?'

'Yes,' she said. 'Yes.' And her arms came around him, pulling him close to her, as she abandoned herself to his love.

He was so gentle; perhaps that was what made him the perfect lover. And yet he could be demanding too, when passion had its grip on him. He said her name, at the end, and then, in a sighing breath, what she thought was 'darling...'

Afterwards, they lay together in perfect peace, Cleo's body moulded trustingly to his. Jake kissed her temple, stroking back the damp curls. It was perfect. She loved him so much that she couldn't believe he did not love her, a little. And so thinking, she fell asleep.

When Cleo awoke, Jake was gone. She hastened to dress and wash, but he was not in the breakfast-room. Bridget, avoiding her eyes, said he had left very early, but that there was a letter for her. It was in the parlour, on the mantel. It was very simple.

Cleo.
Promise I'll be back on Saturday, and on my best behaviour.
Jake.

She sat down on the chair, crumpling the paper into a ball.

What had she expected? She was a fool to think he would change—Melissa had told her so. And she couldn't really blame him, because she had asked him to stay, hadn't she, knowing all it would mean?

He had her in the cruelest trap of all—unrequited love. She was here for him at Belubula, whenever he visited, but he still led his own life in Nugget Gully. It seemed his talk of living with her like a proper husband was nothing more than that—talk. Somehow she got through the day, and later there were the preparations to be made, and so many things to be decided that she didn't have time to think. She made sure of it.

Seth came to call during the week. He was flatteringly pleased to see her, and smiled so often that Cleo felt as if she must be the most amusing woman in the world. But he was sweet, and so unlike Jake's 'friend' Freddy that she was grateful for his company. 'Have you met with your other neighbours yet?' he wanted to know.

Cleo darted him a look as she poured the tea. They were sitting on the verandah, the day being so fine and sunny, and Jake's old dog sprawled at her feet.

'I have. They will all be here on Saturday night. Rather fine, aren't they?'

He laughed. 'They're fine, all right. And with the right connections. I wonder that they agreed to come at such short notice.' And then he bit his lip. 'Sorry, I didn't mean... that is...'

Cleo touched his arm soothingly. 'I know what you mean, Mr. Barnet, and I am not at all offended. You wonder they would come to the home of the owner of the Nugget Gully Hotel and Music Hall? Well, maybe they're curious to see the man himself. Or maybe they want to see what Mrs. Raines has done to the house. But if they think Jake is vulgar, then they will be disappointed. He is as well-bred as any of them, only more so!'

Seth watched her a moment in silence, noting her flushed face and glittering, angry eyes. 'It means a lot to you, doesn't it? Jake being accepted? I hope he appreciates what you're doing.'

Cleo shrugged her shoulder. 'I think it foolish not to be on good terms with one's neighbours. Especially when they are as nice as you.'

Seth flushed in turn, looking pleased. Even his ears were pink, Cleo thought in amusement. 'Oh, we're on good terms, Jake and I,' he said. 'I helped him out a few years ago, during the floods. He's just been busy with other things—he uses Belubula as a retreat rather than a home. If he wanted to, he could do a lot more here. There's plenty of land lying idle, or not being worked to full capacity.'

'Is there? I didn't realise.' Cleo narrowed her eyes thoughtfully and bent to pat the old dog. It thudded its tail. 'Perhaps you could advise him about that, Mr. Barnet.'

'I don't think he would take kindly to my interference, Mrs. Raines. Besides, he knows as well as I what can be done. He just doesn't want to do it. He's too busy elsewhere.'

When he had gone, Cleo sat thoughtfully for a while. It seemed a shame that Jake did not spend more time at Belubula. Perhaps it bored him; perhaps in time *she* would bore him. Perhaps she already did. With a sigh, she rose and went inside.

Saturday evening, and everything was going to plan. There were flowers arranged in the rooms, and the table was set in the dining-room, with all the best silver and crystal and crockery laid out. The food was being prepared—Bridget, like a general, ordering about her temporary labour. Cleo had bathed, and dressed in her new gown, and was brushing out her hair. She looked wan, she had lost weight, and yet the new hollow of her cheeks only added to her classic beauty. The gown, of apricot satin, suited her well, and she had fashioned a feather to go into her piled curls.

The knock on the door startled her, and she was even more startled when Jake entered. He was dressed in black jacket and trousers, and looked so dark and handsome that her heart turned over. His dark eyes met hers and slid away, as if he were nervous. The thought seemed so ridiculous that Cleo dismissed it. She had not seen him since the night of the storm, and now she didn't know what to say.

'You made it, then,' she managed, and sounded stiff and cool with nerves.

'Yes.' He ran his eyes over her gown. 'You look beautiful. I've brought you something. Think of it as a peace-offering.'

'There is really no need …oh!'

Jake had opened his hand, and in it sparkled a necklace. But what a necklace! It caught the light and flashed in a hundred facets. Diamonds. He went around her, and slipped them about her throat. They were cold, but in the mirror looked so fine that she could hardly bring herself to touch them. 'I've earrings here somewhere,' he said, searching in his pocket. 'Ah, here they are.'

Cleo fixed them on her ears, her hands shaking.

That he should bring such a gift, for her. She wanted to throw her arms about his neck and kiss his mouth and tell him they were beautiful, and she loved him. But all she did was meet his eyes in the glass, cool as a cucumber, and say, 'Thank you, Jake. They're lovely. How thoughtful of you.'

He smiled, a quirk of his mouth. 'Glad you like them.'

He was so close that she felt the warmth of his body behind her. Was this the man who had held her, and caressed her, discovering all her secrets? The memories surged forward, threatening to overwhelm her. And when he slipped his arms about her waist, she could not move away. There was a gleam in his eyes now which had nothing to do with laughter.

'Mrs. Raines—oh, Lord, I am sorry.' Bridget peeped around the door, and then shut it again. Cleo felt the spell broken. Jake dropped his arms and moved away, avoiding her eyes.

'I'd better go and greet your—sorry—our guests.'

He was gone. Cleo sank down on the bed, and cursed herself in unladylike terms for betraying herself. Why make a fool of herself, when he didn't love her? He treated her, no doubt, as he would treat any pretty girl. It meant nothing more than that. She must be cool; it was her only defence.

Melissa and Douglas were first to arrive. Douglas was as handsome as ever in his uniform, and Melissa beautiful and petite beside him. Jake bent attentively over her as he poured her a glass of Madeira, and Cleo smiled at Douglas's compliments. 'What a beautiful house,' Melissa whispered. 'Why do you not entertain more often, Jake? You should not spend so many nights at that hotel of yours wining and dining your lovely actresses.'

Cleo pretended not to hear. Douglas began to talk about the fine weather.

'Good for mining,' Jake replied. 'We're down sixty feet at the new mine. Looks promising.'

Melissa moved impatiently. 'You're a Midas, Jake. Do you need any more money? Do you count the gold and gloat over it?'

She seemed to hate, where once she had loved. Perhaps she did hate him; she had certainly made a fool of herself over him. And Melissa could never do anything by half-measures.

Cleo met his eyes, and she wondered if he read the thoughts in them, for suddenly he smiled, and it was the old mocking look of long ago.

'I don't have time to count my money,' he said quietly. 'And I leave the spending of it to my wife. As you can see, she has done wonders for Belubula. I am thinking of asking her to redecorate the Nugget Gully Hotel.'

'Oh, I couldn't,' Cleo retorted. 'It's so wonderfully gaudy as it is, Jake.'

He laughed. 'You're right. I wouldn't want it to become too respectable. No one would go there!'

'Oh, I don't know,' Douglas murmured. 'There's something very exciting about respectability. One can't help but be suspicious of it, and wonder what dark secrets lie hidden.'

Melissa made a sound of disgust. 'Cleo is respectable,' she said. 'Do you mean to tell me she has dark secrets?'

Cleo was glad when the Barnets arrived. They were wearing their best, and Cleo was so pleased to see their friendly faces that she couldn't contain her warmth. Jake was more sardonic, and, when Seth told her how beautiful she looked, raised an eyebrow in mock surprise.

'And your necklace, my dear,' Mrs. Barnet said. 'So...big. An heirloom, perhaps?'

'A token of my fond regard,' Jake replied, and let his finger rest on the necklace, warm as it was cold, then slid it down over the swell of her breast. Even that single touch brought the blood stinging to her cheeks. Cleo heard Melissa catch her breath, and turned away, trying to cover her agitation with formalities.

The McDowells and the Scotts arrived together, very polite and withdrawn—apart from Peggy Scott, who was agog to see wicked Jake Raines. But Cleo worked to win them over, and Jake was so charming and so handsome that Mrs. McDowell even condescended to compliment him on his home and his sweet wife.

'Why should she compliment you on me?' Cleo asked, later, when they had a moment alone in the chatter of the room. 'You didn't make me!'

'But a wife is the property of her husband. He has to school her in ways to please himself and his friends. Didn't you know that?'

The gleam in his eye mocked Cleo, and she had to swallow her retort. 'You know what I think of that. If the evening is a success it will be entirely due to Bridget and me. You had nothing to do with it.'

'Very true, my love,' he murmured and, bending, kissed her palm.

Thrown into confusion, Cleo muttered about mingling, and escaped.

The meal was perfect; everything went off as planned. Cleo had a bad moment when she heard Mr. McDowell talking about the new church, but Jake had such an interested and concerned look on his face that she felt able to relax again.

Later, the women retired to the drawing-room, and were soon joined by the men. Peggy tried to be vivacious, but Cleo just thought her silly. The young girl couldn't keep her eyes off Jake, but the only time he spoke to her Cleo could not detect anything but polite boredom in his eyes.

Melissa was drinking too much. Why had she invited her? Douglas steered her away from the others and, catching Cleo's eye, said in a low voice, 'We'd best be going, I think, Cleo. It's been a lovely evening.'

The McDowells and Scotts decided to leave too.

'She is very unhappy,' Douglas said quietly, when they were outside, waiting for the carriages to be brought around. 'She hasn't been well for some time. I've very grateful, Cleo, that you have stood by her. You are a true friend.'

Cleo looked up, startled.

Douglas smiled gently. 'She was a little obsessed

with Jake, I know. But Jake was never anything but a gentleman. There was nothing between them, Cleo. I know that. If she now dislikes him, it is partly because he wouldn't have anything to do with her, and partly because she blames him, unfairly, for what has happened.' He sighed. 'I'll be glad when my time in Nugget Gully is up and we can return to Melbourne.'

'Will there really be trouble?' Cleo asked gently.

Douglas met her eyes. 'I hope not, I truly hope not.'

When Cleo returned to the drawing-room, Jake and Seth were deep in conversation. Mrs. Barnet came to chat with her, and it was late when they all left. The night was cool, and Cleo stood a moment on the veranda, drinking in the still, clear night. The stars shone like her diamond necklace in the black velvet of the sky. She didn't want to go inside, to be alone with Jake. She was too afraid of herself, and suddenly she was tired, too tired to keep up her pretence of being his cool wife. What if it should slip and the truth spill out? Like milk on the floor. Would he be revolted? Would he back away, and leave at once for Nugget Gully? Or would he laugh, and be sorry for her, and make love to her just to please himself, and then be gone again in the morning?

When she finally re-entered the drawing-room, Cleo thought it was empty. With a sigh, she went to warm her hands by the embers. His voice startled her. 'Cleo? I thought you'd gone to bed.'

He was sitting in the chair by the window, a glass

of brandy in his hand. He had been smoking; the lingering scent of tobacco filled the air. 'Do you mind?' he said, holding up the thin cigar.

'I'm too tired to care, although Bridget may have something to say about the curtains in the morning.'

He grimaced, and after a moment said, 'I was speaking with Seth just now, about Belubula.'

Cleo, wary, watched as he swirled the brandy in his glass, his handsome face intent. He looked tired—she did not remember him looking so tired before he married. Was it such a strain? And now Seth had no doubt told him about the unused land and made him angry at her interference. 'Oh,' she said as carelessly as she could. 'What did he say?'

'That he wished it were his, and that I neglected it.' He looked up with his half-smile. 'He's right, I do. I've been so caught up in the hotel, and Nugget Gully, that I've put Belubula to one side. But I never meant it to be neglected. It's my home. Nugget Gully was to be a passing fancy, something to make the money I needed for Belubula. And now I've turned it into a rod for my back.'

'What about Molly Mulligan?' It slipped out, and even Cleo was shocked by the sarcasm in her voice.

There was a long silence, then Jake met her eyes. There was anger in them, and danger. 'Molly and I go back a long way. Too long for details, nor do I intend to excuse my past to you. It doesn't concern you, just as yours doesn't concern me.'

Cleo moved her hand dismissively. 'That's like

saying the discovery of Botany Bay is past history and need not concern us, when past history plainly does concern us very much!'

'Must you forever argue with me, woman?'

'Why not?'

He set the glass down and stared moodily into the fire.

'God knows, you're hardly ever here to argue with,' Cleo went on, unable to stop herself. 'What do you plan to do with Belubula? Employ a manager while you play with your actresses and your singers and gallivant with...? Stop laughing!'

'Cleo, Cleo,' he gasped. 'If you will be silent for a moment I might tell you. I mean to sell the music hall, and the hotel. I mean to sell the lot. I don't need them. I want to make Belubula into the place I always used to dream I would, before I got rich and forgot my dreams.'

Cleo frowned. 'You'll be bored.'

'Why should I be bored? I never was before. Do you expect me to be off for the Melbourne fleshpots within a month? What a charming fellow you must think me, if you believe I would be bored so easily. What the hell do you think I was doing here all those years before the gold-rush?'

Cleo sighed. 'I suppose so. I just thought.... But what of me?'

The dark eyes narrowed. 'What of you? You're happy enough, aren't you? Are you bored?'

Cleo turned away, clasping her hands. 'No,' she whispered. 'Only, sometimes, a little lonely.'

He was so quiet that Cleo wondered if he had heard her. Then he said, his voice as soft as a breath, 'Come here.' Turning, she looked at him suspiciously, but he was smiling, his eyes like black velvet. 'Come here. I won't hurt you.'

Cleo came, slowly, and stood before him. 'It's late,' she said icily, terrified of betraying herself.

But he laughed again, and, abruptly taking her wrist, pulled her down on to his knees. Cleo sat up straight and stiff as a poker, and glared at him.

'I don't know what you think you're doing,' she began.

The dark eyes teased her. 'I know exactly what I'm doing,' he retorted. His mouth came down on hers, hard and demanding. Cleo tried to remain detached, but the passion in him fired her own, and she began to weaken. His arms were strong and warm, and when she leaned against his chest she could feel his heart thud.

His hands were busy pulling out her pins, until her hair tumbled down, gleaming with red lights like the embers. 'God, I've wanted to do this all evening,' he groaned. His fingers tangled in her hair. 'Cleo, Cleo...'

I love you, she thought. The words rose to her lips, but before she could utter them he said, 'You're so cold, like an ice queen. You make me long to melt you to fire. And I can, can't I? I can.'

Cleo closed her eyes tight, knowing she would not now speak. He liked her to be what she was pretending to be, his 'ice queen'. If she became his warm and loving wife, what then? Surely, disaster?

He lifted her up in his arms, and carried her out into the corridor. His room was cool, and the window wide open to the night. Cleo lay, watching him undress. No wonder Melissa had loved him, and probably Molly still did. And when he came to her Cleo was far from the ice woman he had called her. They clung in the darkness, and he turned her to fire, as he had said he would.

The next morning, she woke in the strange room, alone. Outside, the sun was well up in the sky. It felt as if it had been a dream. Trembling with trepidation, Cleo went to the breakfast-room. It was empty—he was gone.

Cleo stood, feeling cold and empty, against the jamb. Would there be a note this time? She felt bitter, and very like tears. Then, behind her, footsteps. A warm hand closed on her nape, caressing the soft flesh.

'Good morning,' he said quietly, and, turning her slowly about, looked deep into her eyes. 'Did you think I'd gone?' he teased. 'I told you, Belubula is my home now.'

Her lips opened gently beneath his long kiss. Then he laughed.

'Let's have our breakfast, woman, before I turn around and take you back to bed!'

CHAPTER TEN

EVERYTHING CHANGED. JAKE was at Belubula most of the time, though there were still his mining interests. But he set about selling the Nugget Gully Hotel and Music Hall. People flocked to the auction, and it was a Melbourne man who finally bought it. The sale price was so astounding that Cleo wondered if Jake would still be satisfied to remain at Belubula, and wouldn't want to take a whirlwind trip around the world.

But he stayed.

'Where's Jake?'

Seth had come upon her in the garden, busy in the flower-bed. Cleo looked up, shading her eyes as he stood against the brilliant sunshine. 'I think out in the south paddock. Why?'

Seth squatted down beside her. 'He said something about needing a hand with clearing some logs. He was over yesterday. My mother has fallen in love with him—he brought her peaches from your orchard.'

Cleo laughed. 'Did he, now? Oh, he can be charming enough, it's in his nature. He can't help himself.'

Seth smiled. 'He's certainly done wonders for Belubula. I thought, when you told me what he planned... well . . .' He looked a little nonplussed.

'I know,' Cleo said, and bent to pull another weed. Her arm brushed a thick clump of rosemary and the sweet scent filled the air. 'But he is happy, really he is.'

The words sounded a little desperate, even to herself. Seth said nothing.

But he had been happy. Tired, but happy. 'I'd forgotten what hard physical work was,' he said that night over dinner. 'I'm used to sitting in my office, using my mind, or flattering already spoiled darlings of the stage. I'd forgotten how satisfying life on Belubula could be.'

Cleo sipped her drink and smiled. The low lamplight caught the red colours of her hair, and flashed on the crystal glass in her hand. 'You have been here almost a month,' she said, softly. There had been those of her acquaintance who had given him much less. Melissa had called, full of negative talk.

'He'll be bored within a week,' she had said. 'Bored with farming, bored with being a faithful husband, and bored with the one face over dinner every night. See if I'm wrong.'

Melissa and Douglas were still in Nugget Gully. There had been no great trouble, though Douglas had put down a small skirmish at one of the mines.

With Jake at home, the mine seemed far away. And though he still went regularly to Nugget

Gully to oversee operations, Cleo did not think greatly of it.

'Is it a month?' Jake seemed surprised now, and then laughed. 'Didn't you think I'd last so long?' And, when she didn't answer, his eyes narrowed in mockery. 'Oh, Cleo, you of so little faith!'

She rose restlessly, and went to the window. The stars were as brilliant as the diamonds in the necklace he had given her. Her reflection in the glass stared back at her. She was looking pampered and expensive. She had fine clothes and fine food, and everything she wanted; she need only ask. Jake was generous to a fault. And yet the only thing she really wanted from him was the one thing he could not give.

Jake's reflection appeared behind her. She felt his arms about her waist, and he bent his head to kiss her bare shoulder above the lace of her gown. 'Are you tired of having me around already?' he murmured, and knew before she shook her head that she was not. He laughed softly, and began to unpin her hair.

'Jake...' she began, trailing off. What could she say? Will you tire of me? Will you break my heart by leaving me? I could not bear it. I was wrong when I thought any happiness would be worth it; it would be better never to have known such joy if it is to be taken away from me.

'Jake,' she said, 'we're to go to the McDowells' next week, you remember?'

'Hell, must we?' he sighed, continuing his kisses. Her hair tumbled down, and he raked his fingers through it, feeling the soft tresses. 'I'd rather spend the evening here, with you, alone.'

Cleo turned, searching his eyes rather desperately. 'Would you?' she asked. 'Jake?'

But he only smiled, drawing her into his arms. 'Stop talking and kiss me. I want to save my strength for... other things.'

Cleo looked up. The horse's hoofs which had hammered up to the front door had skidded to a halt. She had been busy with her accounts, but now threw down the pen and hurried outside.

Bridget was already there, and beside her a sweating man and horse, held by a groom. 'Mrs. Raines,' she cried, 'where is your husband?'

'Out at the stables, I think. What is it?'

Bridget jerked her head at the groom, and he ran off towards the stables. The man took off his dusty hat, and with a shock Cleo recognised Tom Tredinnick. But clearly, by his wide smile, he did not remember her.

'Mrs. Raines, great news,' he cried. 'Great news!'

Footsteps behind her, and Jake arrived. 'Tom? What is it?'

But instead of answering, Tom searched into his pocket and drew out a greenish-looking rock. Jake took it and carefully turned it over. And then he shouted, frightening Cleo out of her wits, and threw the rock into the air. Tom was laughing. Then Jake grasped Cleo around the waist and swung her round and round while she shrieked for him to put her down. He did, and gave her a great, smacking kiss on the mouth. 'Gold!' he cried. 'They've finally struck gold.'

Bridget clapped her hands, laughing.

Cleo whispered, 'Gold?' And then began to laugh as Jake hugged her again. 'Jake! You're breaking my ribs!'

He put her away ruefully. 'Sorry. Tom, go in and have a drink. I'll come back to Nugget Gully with you.'

Bridget hustled Tom inside, and left Jake and Cleo alone. The groom had taken the horse to give it water, and Jake had ordered his own animal to be brought around.

'Jake, what will happen now?' Cleo asked. He smiled, and his black eyes fairly gleamed.

'Now? There will be another rush of miners, looking for their fortunes. They'll buy claims, hoping the same reef we've struck goes under their patch of ground! The Queen of Egypt will make us a fortune, Cleo.'

Cleo raised her eyebrows. 'Another one?'

'Where is your sense of adventure, my dear? Ah, here comes Tom. I must go.'

'Jake!' He was already leaving. 'When will you be back?'

'As soon as I can.' He stooped down and kissed her, hard, on the mouth. 'Don't forget me,' he said.

And he was gone. Cleo shaded her eyes and watched him go with a sinking heart. She was not sure if this gold was a good thing. Jake had been happy at Belubula, and now he was rushing off again, leaving her. She had become used to him beside her during the day, and at night.

It would be doubly hard now, if he were ever to leave her.

He was gone for two days, and when he came back was tired but excited, and full of talk of the gold. 'It's pouring out,' he said over dinner. 'It's like the first rush all over again.'

'How is Nugget Gully?'

'Getting larger. People are flooding in. Our friend Morgan and some of his cronies have bought up the land in the north and the west, but I think they'll be disappointed. The gold reef seems to be going due south—and that's *our* land.'

'What about the trouble, with the miners?' Cleo murmured.

'All gone, it seems. Douglas Mulgrave is talking of leaving. Melissa sent you her love.' His tone was ironic. 'She accused me of treating you badly,' he went on. '"She's there, alone?" she said. I explained there were about ten other permanent employees at Belubula, so you weren't exactly alone.'

Cleo frowned, and set down her knife and fork. 'She is my friend,' she retorted.

He laughed mockingly. 'There was a time when that woman nearly destroyed you. Do you remember?'

'That is over.'

But he mocked her. 'I wish I could inspire as much loyalty in you as she does.'

Cleo looked surprised. 'You know I missed you!'

'Did you?' The quirky smile played over his lips.

'Yes,' she admitted grudgingly. 'I've grown used to you, like a... a child's old toy.'

He laughed. 'And is that so bad?'

She looked down at her half-eaten food. She felt little hunger lately, and in fact found it hard to keep the food down. But, as was her way, she told no one, keeping her fears to herself. Hiding her thoughts behind a cool exterior. Only, gradually, Jake was chipping away at her detachment, and exposing the vulnerability underneath.

'No, I suppose not,' she answered the question.

The black eyes narrowed. 'Still don't trust me, do you, Cleo? You really expect to wake up one morning and find me gone, don't you?'

She couldn't deny it. But later, in the privacy of their bedroom, Cleo showed him what she could not say.

'You are my delight,' he breathed against her lips. 'I would never leave you, Cleo. Don't you know that yet?'

'Not even if they found gold in your other mine?' she mocked.

Jake laughed and kissed her. 'Not even then,' he told her.

Cleo woke alone the next morning. Outside, a gusting wind rattled the window-panes, and wilted the leaves with its hot breath. She stirred, and went to rise. But as she did so her stomach lurched queasily, and she sank back again with a groan. It was not like her to be ill, and she frowned.

'Cleo?' Jake closed the door after him. He smiled

down at her. 'Lazy,' he said. 'You'll have to get up. I mean to show you your namesake today.'

'The mine?' cried Cleo, and sat up, forgetting her stomach. 'Oh, Jake, really?'

He laughed. 'If you hurry up, lazy-bones.'

It was a blustery day, as they drove through Nugget Gully. The people were hurrying about their business. A few nodded, and raised their hats to Jake and Cleo. The mines were beyond the town, their poppet heads and chimneys dark against the skyline. They passed the Lucky Strike, with its noise and clatter and busy men. The landscape was weird, the earth bare and pitted from early alluvial mining, which had uprooted trees and brought the soil from beneath the surface to the top. It looked as if giant ants had been at work, a nightmare.

The new quartz reef mines were even more destructive. They left great mounds of powdery tailings, which the wind caught and blew as fine dust across the land. It stung Cleo's eyes, and she shaded her face, choking. There were a number of new shafts being sunk, and furious building was in progress. Timber was being sawn up for shoring the shafts, building the poppet heads, and fueling the gold batteries and boilers. Smoke belched, and the forest was receding further and further from the area of the quartz reefs. Mines, it seemed, had an insatiable need for wood.

The Queen of Egypt was on a rise. The great mountain of tailings lifted to the sky, dust rising with each gust of wind. The mine machinery was dark against it, the poppet head with its pulley on top, the engine house, and the battery. The noise was deafening, a great thundering, pounding sound that Cleo could feel to her very fingertips.

'How can you bear it?' she shouted to Jake. 'Does it ever stop?'

He laughed. 'On Sundays. You get used to it. The men who work in there hardly even notice it.'

Another swirl of dust, and Cleo put her handkerchief to her face. 'Why is the rock so fine?' she said. 'It's like sand.'

'Once it goes into the battery, the iron stampers crush it to powder. That is mixed with water, washed down on to tables covered with quicksilver on copper plates. The quicksilver attracts the gold, and what is left goes out on to the mullock heap. You should see the place when it's really blowing! It's like a storm in the desert.'

There were a number of rough wood and bark buildings a little way from the mine, further up the rise. There were men everywhere—some had just come from below ground, their clothes filthy, their faces pale and drawn.

Jake pulled the carriage to a halt, and someone came to help Cleo down, as the wind tossed her skirts, and tugged at her hat. Dust stung her lips and eyes, and she put her hand up to her face, as Jake came to take her arm. 'This way,' he said above the pounding of the battery, and led her towards the nearest hut.

Inside, it had been made comfortable, with a desk and chairs, a day-bed, and maps and notices covering the walls. The noise was lessened slightly here, and without the hot, choking wind Cleo felt better. A small man rose from behind the desk, and Jake introduced him as Daniels, the mine foreman.

Cleo accepted his offer of water, while Jake asked some sharp questions concerning the mine. Afterwards, they went out again into the dusty, blustering wind, and Jake led her down towards the thunderous noise of the battery.

'The gold's doubled in the past two days,' Daniels was saying, as if he hardly noticed the noise. 'This is the richest gold-bearing reef I've ever seen, Mr. Raines.'

'We'll just have to hope it doesn't go too deep,' Jake replied. Then, to Cleo, he explained, 'The deeper you go the more problems you get, with water seeping in, maybe flooding and foul air, because of lack of ventilation. If it gets too bad down there, you just have to close the mine down altogether.'

There was a shelter at the base of the poppet head, which rose like a laddered tower above them—sixty feet high, Jake told her. Here was the pulley system which could lower equipment, even horses, down into the depths of the mine. There was a sort of cage, which carried a couple of miners at a time, or else they climbed the ladders.

'Once you find a gold-bearing reef like ours,' Jake was saying, 'you follow it along as far as you can. You sink more shafts. And you just pray to God that the reef doesn't leave your land!'

'Is that why Mr. Morgan is building a mine? To try and find the same reef?'

'That's right. He's hoping it runs under his land. We're hoping it goes on southwards. Of course, it could just vanish altogether. Maybe this is just one rich pocket in the quartz. It has been known to happen.'

Cleo looked down the shaft. There was a ladder, going down, down into the darkness. She tried to imagine what it would be like, climbing down, down into the bowels of the earth, with only candles and lanterns for light. Digging and tunneling, and blasting the rock, drilling into the quartz, choking on dust, all in the dark depths of the earth. Mrs. Trewin had told her once, in the millinery shop, that they called the quartz drill the 'widow maker' because it killed miners so regularly. The fine dust got into their lungs, and took their breath away.

Daniels was talking to Jake, and she tried to concentrate. 'There's been some talk of using cyanide to extract the gold. It's cheaper, but more dangerous.'

The noise of the mine, the smell of dust and damp and sweat. Cleo swallowed, and with a shaking hand pushed back a tendril of hair. Daniels's voice droned on.

'They put potassium cyanide through the flotation tanks, over zinc. Takes out the gold. But the stuff is deadly, if anyone swallows it. And I've heard it turns cuts bad; men lose their fingers and their hands. But it saves pounds, Mr. Raines. Morgan is talking of using it, if he finds gold.'

Jake frowned. 'Sounds like trouble to me.' He nodded to a couple of men as they went by—he knew them by name. 'What's Morgan calling his mine, by the way?'

The St George, so I heard. There's another three

going up beyond that. Melbourne companies. They throw all their money together in the hope that they'll strike it rich, and if they don't then they go broke.'

'Are all the miners Cornish?' Cleo asked, to take her mind off the shaft.

Jake smiled, and shook his head. 'We've some from America, and some from China. Men from all over the world. They're willing to risk life and limb, to go after the gold. Miners are a tough lot, they work hard and live hard, but not very long.'

Cleo shuddered. 'I think, if they want more money, they should have it!'

Daniels looked shocked, but Jake only laughed.

'Things have changed since the early days,' he said. 'Then a man paid his thirty shillings for a licence, and dug. Sometimes he found gold only a few inches below the surface, sometimes he had to dig thirty feet. The gold fields were so crowded that you couldn't walk a step without falling into a hole, or over a tent! But those days are almost gone, Cleo. A man could make a fortune then, just by hard work and a bit of luck. Now it's the day of the quartz mines, the deep mines, and only men with money can afford to run them.'

Daniels cleared his throat, evidently thinking this conversation frivolous. 'About Trewin, Mr. Raines...'

'How is he?' Jake was instantly serious.

'The arm had to come off. The rock-fall mangled it too badly. It was touch and go, but he seems to be recovering. No gangrene, as yet, and he's in good spirits.'

Trewin? Little Mrs. Trewin's husband? Cleo put her hand to her brow again, and felt the perspiration beading it.

Jake was nodding. 'Give him all the help you can,' he said. 'And when he's well enough, a job here on the surface. A miner with one arm is no use underground.'

'But, sir—'

'Find him something, Daniels,' Jake snapped. 'He's a good man, and he has six children.'

Trewin with a mangled arm, Cleo thought, and her head began to spin. She closed her eyes and suddenly she was down in the mine, choking on the dust, the acrid scent of the explosives burning her nostrils, and the rocks falling, burying her, smothering her...

Cleo swayed. 'Jake,' and her voice was far away. 'I think I am going to faint...'

His arm came around her waist, tight. 'Hold on, darling,' he said, and she clung to him. Outside, the wind caught her skirts, swirling them about, and blew off her hat. Daniels ran after it, while her hair whipped about her, and she lifted her face to the sky, trying to find some clean air to breath. Jake's arm squeezed her waist.

'Are you all right?'

She met his narrowed eyes, dark with concern, and tried to smile. 'I think so.'

He smoothed a curl back off her brow. 'You can lie down for a moment in Daniels's hut, if you think—'

'No, no, I'm fine now. Really.'

'What was it?'

Cleo looked down at her gloved hands. Cleo Montague fainting! She, who never succumbed to physical weakness, who rarely even caught a cold! 'The noise, I think,' she said, her voice controlled again. 'And the shaft …so far down. I was dizzy.'

He laughed. 'You're lucky you're not a miner!'

'Jake.' She looked up at him almost shyly. 'Mrs. Trewin used to come to my shop. She was so nice. Is it her husband?'

He sighed. 'Yes. An accident. We're as careful as we can be, but they happen. I'll do what I can for her, and her family.'

'I know you will,' she murmured. He was a good man, this Jake Raines. He cared for people. He was an admirable man. She blinked and realised he was smiling at her broadly.

'Cleo, Cleo,' he said softly. 'Be careful. I can see what you're thinking. Are you beginning to like me a little, after all?'

She flushed, fiddling with the fastening of her glove. 'You know I like you. How can you say such a thing?'

But he only laughed and flicked her cheek with his finger. She hardly dared to speak to him on the way home, in case she betrayed herself again.

The night of the McDowells' invitation arrived. They had invited all their influential friends. Jake was charm itself, and if Cleo noticed him flirting with pretty Peggy Scott she pretended she didn't.

It was in his nature, she told herself; he meant nothing by it. Besides, she felt unwell and it took all her concentration to hide it.

Mrs. McDowell presided over the dinner like a maestro over her orchestra—everything ran along in smooth, syncopated time.

Cleo found herself between Mr. Barnet and a Mr. Jong from Melbourne. Jake was far away, or so it seemed, between the pretty daughter and Mrs. Jong, and half hidden by a great towering arrangement of fruit and flowers. Cleo tried to enjoy herself, but somehow the sound of the girl's laughter jarred her and her queasy stomach balked over the rich food. She found her smiles growing more and more wooden.

Mr. Barnet chatted about the farm, but it was Mr. Jong who would not leave her alone. 'Your husband is making an absolute fortune with his mine,' he said, his tiny eyes bright with greed. 'Even in Melbourne we've heard of Jake Raines.'

Cleo smiled. 'Really? At one time no one wanted to know him, and now everyone does. Strange, isn't it?'

Mr. Jong didn't notice the sarcasm. 'What's he call it? The Queen of Egypt?' His mouth smiled unpleasantly. 'I wonder who she was? Some dashing actress he once knew?'

Cleo felt her heart begin to beat faster, but controlled her voice. 'Actually he called it after me. My name is Cleopatra. It was a joke.'

He smiled again, but she could tell he didn't believe her. Her hands clenched under the table.

'Nugget Gully must have been a wild place,

during the first years of the rush,' he went on, oblivious to her seething emotions.

'I wouldn't know. I wasn't here.'

'I believe Lola Montez was here at one time—and what glowing things she had to say about Jake Raines! And all the others, the famous from Europe, passed through. I'll have to have a talk with him later. I've an idea for a book on the subject, and I'm sure Jake could tell me a thing or two.' He tapped his nose and winked. Cleo felt the colour flushing her cheeks. The anger came like a hot wave, and she knew if he didn't soon stop she would say something she would later wish unsaid.

'That is in the past,' she managed. 'Jake has sold his property in Nugget Gully.'

'Ah, but he'll buy elsewhere,' Jong said with certainty. 'A man like that, the business is in his blood, don't try and tell me differently! You'll have to live with it, my dear Mrs. Raines.'

Cleo opened her mouth. Across the table she caught Seth's eyes, and he winked at her. What is the use of saying anything to such a bore? he seemed to say. Cleo managed a smile, and turned again to Mr. Barnet, pretending interest in the plight of his pigs.

Thankfully, the ladies soon withdrew, and Cleo escaped the stuffy, overheated dining-room for the cooler drawing-room. She fanned her hot face, wishing the sickness would leave her. She found herself with Mrs. McDowell. 'I see dear Peggy has made quite a hit with your husband, Mrs. Raines,' she said, smiling falsely. 'Such a sweet, unaffected child. I always thought she would make a fine marriage.'

Cleo blinked. 'Indeed.' Her fan moved more quickly.

'She would grace any table.'

'Perhaps my husband is thinking more of her gracing the stage,' Cleo murmured sweetly.

Mrs. McDowell looked surprised, and after a moment moved away. Cleo knew she had been rude, but couldn't care. How could Jake make such a fool of her? For one pretty face. And after all he had said to her. 'My delight', he had called her.

And now he tormented her with jealousy when she was feeling so vulnerable.

She was so unsure of her hold on him... what hold on him? She had none. He enjoyed her body, but that surely would not last. He would begin to look around for other entertainment, and she must be prepared for it.

'Mrs. Raines, are you quite well?'

Cleo looked up and smiled wanly. Mrs. Barnet, always so kind. 'A little tired,' she admitted.

Mrs. Barnet patted her hand. 'Shall I ask your husband to take you home?'

'There's no need,' Cleo said breathlessly. 'I'll be all right in a moment.'

But she wasn't. When the men joined them in the drawing-room, Peggy Scott again sought out Jake, fluttering her lashes at him. Cleo gritted her teeth. And what must Mrs. McDowell do but insist the girl sing to them!

Her voice was pleasant, but Cleo could not enjoy the pretty picture she made, singing at the piano. Jake turned the pages of her music, his dark eyes veiled—admiring, Cleo thought. Her fan moved quickly. All along, she had been right to be afraid. To keep her feelings to herself. But, even so, she had given much to him, and now he was hurting her with a sharp, agonising pain which would not go away.

'Mrs. Raines... Cleo.' Seth sat down beside her. 'I see you were impressed by our Mr. Jong.'

She laughed despite her discomfort.

The french windows were open, and a breeze came into the room from the veranda. Mrs. McDowell's potted plants stirred, rustling.

'He was asking Jake about Lola Montez, over brandy,' Seth went on. 'I don't think he got much joy.'

'He said he was writing a book,' Cleo retorted. 'What do you think he will call it? *Secrets I Heard Over Dinner?*'

Seth laughed. 'Or *Things Which May Or May Not Be True, But They Make A Good Story?*'

Cleo giggled, feeling suddenly better. 'What a horrible little man he is,' she sighed. 'If you had not winked at me, I think I should have said things that would shock you.'

Seth grinned. 'Nothing can shock me. Besides, Jake told him to mind his own business, and that didn't seem to deter him in the least!'

Cleo looked over at Jake. Peggy Scott was rattling on, her pretty face alive with excitement. But Jake was watching Cleo, and the look in his eyes made her go cold. Anger and—could it be?—jealousy. Shocked, Cleo found it hard to believe

Jake could feel about her and Seth as she did about him and Peggy. It must be that she was his wife, his property and possession, and he didn't want anyone but himself monopolising her.

Suddenly, she felt the queasiness in her stomach grow until it threatened to overcome her. Her face blanched. 'I must get some air,' she gasped, and, rising, escaped on to the veranda. The cool dark night brushed her flushed face, like healing hands. She breathed deeply, and the sickness began to pass.

'Cleo?'

Jake. His arm slipped about her waist. 'Are you all right?'

'Tired,' she said, and forced a smile. 'It was so stuffy in there.'

'I'll take you home.'

There's no need—'

'Don't argue.'

She laughed despite herself, and, when he went back into the room to order the carriage around, shivered. The thing she had been refusing to admit to herself came like a shadow into her mind. She was with child, Jake's child. And how would he feel about that? Trapped, probably. Cleo shivered again. No doubt he would stay for a while, because he would feel obliged to—he was a kind man. But he would feel trapped, and gradually he would begin to hate her.

Cleo remembered her cousin, back in Plymouth, heavy with her child. A great, flushing mound, puffy face and hands and feet, moving slowly about the room. Jake desired her now, but it was unlikely that he would desire what she would soon become. Without love, and all the caring tenderness that went with it, what man would stay? It was logical that, if he felt only physical attraction for her, when that was gone so would he.

'Cleo?'

'Seth. Sorry, I was miles away. I must say goodbye to everyone...'

'Are you unwell? You should have told me, I would have fetched Jake earlier. Here, lean on my arm.'

'If she needs an arm to lean on, then she has mine,' Jake said coolly, behind them. Seth's face closed up, and he stepped back. Jake held out his arm, and Cleo was forced to take it, and with as much dignity as she could swept into the drawing-room to say her goodbyes.

Out in the carriage, Jake settled her. She looked back as they drove away, and almost laughed to see Peggy's pretty face, pouting at the window.

'Didn't you enjoy yourself?' Jake asked. The carriage rocked on the well-used track to Belubula, and the warm night air caressed her upturned face.

'No.'

He laughed sharply. 'Why not? You were the one who wanted to cultivate our neighbours.'

'I wanted you to be friends with them... No, I wanted them to see you weren't the terrible ogre they thought you, that was all. They know that now. You were right. They're silly and pretentious, and their opinions don't matter a bit.'

'Cleo, what is it? Has someone said something

to hurt you?'

The sudden concern in his voice made tears prick at her eyes, but she blinked them away. Her laugh was cold and brittle. 'Nothing different from usual. I hope you enjoyed your little flirtation with Peggy—everyone else did.'

There was a silence. She wished the words unsaid, but it was too late. After a moment he said, his voice as cool as Mrs. McDowell's ices, 'If you believe what you hear about me, then you're a fool. I can tell you it meant nothing. You can believe me or not. What are you afraid of? That I'll run off with some other woman? That I'll bring in someone else to take your place at Belubula?'

She said nothing.

'I see,' he murmured, soft and dangerous.

'Jake, I...' Cleo bit her lip. She couldn't say it. He would laugh in her face. 'I'm not saying I am unhappy with the way that things are,' she managed. 'For I am happy. But things change, people change. How can you know that one day you will not be tired of me, that I may even...disgust you, and you will wish to leave me?'

'Very reasonable,' he said, but his voice was furious. 'So when this day comes, when I decide to leave you, where will *you* go? Across the paddock to Seth Barnet, I suppose. Very cosy. And thoughtful of you to think of me. Do you think I haven't noticed the way you stare into each other's eyes over dinner? The secret smiles? You must think me a fool indeed!'

'You're wrong about Seth,' she whispered. 'I would go to Melbourne, I suppose, and open another shop.'

'Or sell your memoirs to the scandal-hungry public? Mr. Jong would be very interested, you must keep him in mind.'

'How can you think such a thing?'

'Easily. You think worse of me.'

'Jake, please—'

'Leave it, Cleo. Just be quiet!'

'But you're wrong—'

'Leave it! I'll say something I'll really regret, if we go on. Let's just pretend none of this happened.'

He didn't come near her that night, nor the next, and she lay awake, her mind going around and around, wondering what she would do. She would have to tell him about the child, and yet it would mean the end of the attention he had lavished on her. Or perhaps he would still be kind, the gentlest of husbands, only he would go into Nugget Gully every night, and never do more again than chastely kiss her lips.

But she could not blame the baby for that. Cleo put her hand to her trim waist and sighed. It was Jake's baby, the only part of him that could truly be hers. She would keep it her secret a little longer. Just a little longer.

CHAPTER ELEVEN

'WHO IS IT?'

Bridget had come to fetch her, and Cleo sat up, pushing back her untidy hair. She had been lying down—it seemed to help banish the sickness which afflicted her.

'Mulligan,' Bridget repeated, and rolled her eyes. 'Both of 'em.'

'Oh, no, not them!' Cleo closed her eyes. Then she sighed. 'I suppose I must offer them a drink, and some luncheon, and let them wait for Jake if they don't wish to go out to the mine.'

'It would be the polite thing to do,' Bridget agreed. 'I'll send Clara to set you to rights.'

Cleo put on her grey dress, and, after Clara had tidied her hair, went to the parlour. Molly came and hugged her, as cold and glittering as a jewel. Frederick ogled her and pinched her palm when he took her hand in greeting.

'Molly is appearing in Nugget Gully,' he said, 'and we had to call. It is her "farewell appearance". We're going to America next month.'

'Congratulations!' Cleo said.

Molly smiled. 'Well, it is very exciting. But we

thought you and Jake would like to come and see me perform. As it is the last time for a long time.'

'Well, I... Of course we will come. Thank you so much.'

Frederick touched her arm. 'Best seats in the house,' he declared. 'Where is Jake, anyway?'

Cleo explained about the mine. 'He'll be back soon, I'm sure. Will you stay for luncheon?'

They agreed so readily that Cleo's heart sank, but she rallied, and even began to enjoy hearing of Molly's exploits. And Freddy's looks and sighs, instead of angering her, began to amuse her. She must be mellowing, she thought. Was that Jake's doing?

She heard the horse returning just as she was pouring a second cup of tea, and excusing herself went out on to the veranda. Jake, climbing the steps, looked up at her in surprise.

'Jake.' Her voice was breathless. 'Your friends are here. The Mulligans.'

His eyebrows lifted. 'Oh?'

'They're staying to luncheon. And... and they want us to go to Molly's performance.'

He looked at her out of cold dark eyes. 'Do you want to go?'

She glanced away. 'I... oh, why not?'

If he was surprised, he didn't show it. 'Then we will,' was all he said to her.

In the parlour, Molly rushed to embrace him. Freddy seemed totally unembarrassed by what had happened last time they were at Belubula. 'It doesn't seem the same without you,' he said.

'How could you sell up, Jake?'

Cleo hardly dared to look at him, but after all it was all right. Jake laughed. 'I was tired of staying up late,' he said. 'I wanted to go to bed early for a change.'

Frederick thought this was very funny. 'And you found an excellent reason for that!' he cried.

Cleo looked at him, and for a moment she was tempted to tell him exactly what she thought of him. But somehow the memory of his face intruded into her mind, that night when he came to her room. His shocked expression, when he had realised Jake was there, committing the ultimate sin—a husband in his own wife's bed! And the memory made Cleo smile.

She smiled a lot during their luncheon, and when Freddy whispered that she was 'as pretty as a pearl', she laughed and told him he had a 'silver tongue'. Cleo was getting on so well with the obnoxious Freddy that she was sure Jake would be pleased. But when she looked up and met his eyes, they were gleaming black and angry.

Surprised, Cleo looked away. Was there no pleasing the man? She was glad when the meal was over, and Molly and Freddy left with much noise and excitement.

'Until tonight,' Freddy murmured in Cleo's ear, and climbed into the carriage, leaving her flustered and cross.

The vehicle was hardly out of earshot, before Jake gripped her arm and said, 'You certainly enjoyed yourself.'

Cleo pulled away. 'Wasn't that what you told me

to do, last time? Smile and flirt?'

His eyes narrowed. 'If I'd wanted Molly, I would have married her.'

Cleo stamped her foot. 'There's no pleasing you, is there? If you ever make up your mind exactly what you do want, tell me!'

'I know I don't want to come home and find Freddy in my bed,' he said, and his voice stung like nettles.

She stared at him, and suddenly tears pricked her eyes. 'Why not?' she whispered. *'You* don't seem to want to be there any more.'

The eyes narrowed.

'Perhaps you mean to keep me locked up here for the rest of my life, as if you were a selfish little boy,' she went on, the bitter words spilling out as if they would not be stopped. 'You don't want me, but no one else shall have me either! Wouldn't it be fairer to give me away to Freddy? At least he seems keen to have me.'

'And how long do you think that would last?' he said, his voice like a whip. 'A night, or two. Is that what you want? Does that sort of life excite you? Cleo, you know nothing! You would be destroyed.'

'Is that what you want?' she cried, and now the tears spilled over. She turned and ran, back towards the house. But he caught her as she reached the door, and swung her about and into his arms.

'Cleo,' he whispered. 'Oh, Cleo, I'm sorry. You're right. I don't know what I want. But I know what I don't want—not another Molly, or any of her kind. Forgive me?'

She met his eyes, and laughed shakily through her tears. He looked contrite, and worried, and dear. 'Jake,' she said, and suddenly stretched up to kiss his cheek. 'Let's enjoy ourselves tonight,' she said. 'Let's not argue. Let's pretend... let's pretend we're in love, just for tonight.'

Had she said too much? He looked at her for a long time, his dark eyes unreadable, and then he smoothed back her hair, and smiled into her eyes. 'Why not?' he said, and he mocked, 'We can stay overnight at Nugget Gully. Save us the journey back. You know I always wanted you to spend the night there with me.'

His look warmed her. It would be all right, she thought. It really would be all right. Perhaps she could even tell him about the baby? Perhaps the terror that had gripped her since she found out, that he would find her ugly, that he would leave her, was unfounded. Perhaps he would be pleased? Perhaps the physical attraction he seemed to feel for her would be strong enough to overcome the changes the baby would make to her body?

Their seat at the music hall was the best, overlooking the stage and the rest of the audience. It was reserved for mayors and foreign princes, Jake told her with a laugh. The crowd below was a mixture of motley miners and couples in their 'best', all determined to have a good time. Cleo felt like a queen, perched above them, in the opulence and glitter of the place. She wore her apricot-coloured gown, and felt at her best. It had tiny pearl buttons, running down the bodice, and Jake had come upon her when she was dressing, and startled Clara so that she had fled the room.

'Jake,' Cleo had whispered, 'I must get ready, if we are to be on time.'

'There's plenty of time,' he retorted, and slid his hands over the tight-fitting bodice. 'A kiss for every button,' he murmured against her lips. She gasped beneath his touch, and arched her throat as his mouth ran down, his hands tangling in her long hair. 'It's all right,' he went on. 'We're pretending to be in love, remember? Your idea.'

She met his eyes, gleaming between dark lashes, and then closed her own. His mouth closed on hers in a deep, passionate kiss.

'If you loved me,' he went on, 'what would you do, Cleo?'

Her heart was thudding, but she felt suddenly as if she had nothing to lose. Cleo placed her hands on his shoulders, and then slowly, slowly slid them down to his chest, and began to undo his shirt. He watched her so intently that she was nervous, and wondered what game he played with her now. But it was too late to back out. His chest was smooth and brown, the muscles like rope beneath his flesh. She placed her lips to that warm flesh, and he groaned, and, lifting her in his arms, carried her to the bed. His face swooped down to hers, and they lost themselves to the moment.

And so they had been a little late, and Cleo's gown was creased, and her hair messy, and both had to be repaired, but she felt so happy that none of that mattered.

'Cleo?' Jake was watching her, while the audience

chattered noisily below. His dark eyes were mocking her, and she flushed. 'You're very quiet,' he murmured. 'What are you thinking of?'

'I was thinking that it is very grand, your music hall,' she said, looking about with shining eyes.

'What did you expect?' he retorted. 'You know my taste runs to grand things.'

'I just didn't think it would be so sophisticated.'

'Or so respectable?' he corrected her, and laughed when she gave him an uncertain look. 'It's all right. I've given up trying to make you see that "respectable" doesn't mean one man is any better or any worse than another.'

Cleo looked away, down on the heads of the rowdy audience, calling now impatiently for Molly. 'I do believe it,' she said, with difficulty. 'I can hardly believe I spoke those words. I was a child.'

After a moment she dared to look at him, but the expression on his face told her nothing.

'Hey, Jake!'

A loud voice called up from below. A man with a wild beard and straggling hair, and a long coat.

'Keep the gold comin', Jake! You're a good bloke...'

They all cheered, and Jake bowed his head, and smiled. Cleo felt her heart bursting with pride. What did 'respectable' matter, when a man was liked as much as Jake Raines?

'If you don't stop looking at me like that, I'll not be responsible for my actions,' he said, without turning from the noisy crowd below.

Blushing, Cleo turned away, just as Molly came on to the stage. She wore a bright green gown, which only just reached her knees. The crowd roared. From then on, she held them in the palm of her hand. Teasing, wooing the audience, making them laugh and cry. She was wonderful, and Cleo was spellbound.

She sang of the miners, and danced and kicked her legs. She answered their shouts, and laughed back at them. At the end, she sang a sad song of a young man, on the gold fields, yearning for his home and the woman left behind. The miners went mad, throwing money and flowers, even a few nuggets. Molly collected them, with her big flashing smile.

'Oh, Jake,' Cleo cried, turning to clasp his arm. 'You didn't tell me!'

His face swooped down close to hers. 'She's wonderful, isn't she?' he said. 'Whatever you might think of her off the stage, on it she is magic!'

Cleo searched his eyes, her excitement plummeting. The fierce light in them turned dark, and he put his hand up to touch her cheek. 'Cleo,' he breathed, 'trust me.'

Her eyes flickered and fell. 'I want to,' she whispered. 'But if I did, and...for whatever reason you left, there'd be nothing left, Jake. You'd have drained me dry.'

He laughed softly. 'I'm not leaving you, Cleopatra. Freddy can wait all he wants, and Seth Barnet can grow old and grey. I'll be with you as long as there's life in me.'

Did he mean it? Cleo tried to read truth in

his eyes, and then, when he kissed her, no longer even tried.

'Oh, Jake... Cleo.' Freddy stood in the doorway to the box, half hidden by the curtain. Cleo broke away, straightening herself. Jake rose leisurely, not at all put out at being caught yet again kissing his wife.

'We've arranged a supper, at the hotel,' Freddy went on, smirking. 'That is, if you can tear yourself away, Jake.'

'Lead on,' Jake said, and tucked Cleo's hand firmly into his arm.

The supper was a crush, the room stifling. People shouted and laughed, and Molly was surrounded by an adoring group. Freddy was in his element, oiling his way around the room. Cleo stood it as long as she was able, smiling and smiling until her face hurt. Jake seemed to know everybody—it only reinforced Cleo's realisation that he was a popular man.

The room was so stuffy. Cleo began to feel dizzy, and forced her way to the door. She could see Jake's head above the others, and he was laughing. Molly was there, clinging to his arm, her pretty face flushed with happiness. Cleo slipped out into the corridor. The cool air fanned her, and she breathed deeply. The dizziness began to pass.

She would have to tell him. She could not keep it secret for much longer. But the fear was still with her, that he would not stay with her once he knew.

Their room looked over the Nugget Gully main street. Cleo could hear the noise floating up from the supper below, and a group of drunken revelers added to the variety of sounds. She undressed, and brushed her long hair before the big mirror. It was a sumptuous room, with velvet and lace drapes, and brass fittings. Could Jake really be satisfied at Belubula, after living such a life? He had been so relaxed tonight, so...at home. He belonged with those people, not here with her. They were a part of him.

The bed, with its canopy, was like a little world in itself. Cleo sank down under the covers with a sigh, and fell asleep. He woke her with kisses, tasting of brandy and cigars, and she responded sleepily. He pulled her on top of him, rolling her over and over in the big bed, until she cried out in protest.

'Jake, stop it! You're making me ill.' She half sat up, looking down on him in the faint light from the windows. 'Have they finished? I thought they would be going on until dawn.'

'They probably will,' he retorted. He began to wind her long hair around his fist, drawing her face closer to his.

'You could have stayed. I wouldn't have minded.'

'But I did. I'd rather be with you. You know that. And if you don't, then you should.' He kissed her, long and hard, while a voice in the street outside started to sing a mournful ballad. He rolled over again, pinning her to the mattress, and went on kissing her while his hands made her burn. He tugged off her nightgown, and ran a finger over the fullness of her breast, down to her waist, and paused over the swell of her stomach.

He paused for so long that Cleo stiffened with fright, thinking he must know after all, and how could he? But she could not see his expression in the shadows, and after a moment his fingers moved on, so that she let out her breath in relief before passion claimed her in earnest.

'Good God!'

'What is it?' Cleo came forward into the breakfast-room, where Jake stood by the window, an open letter in his hand. He waved it at her. 'The Scotts,' he said, 'want our attendance at one of their dreadful dinners.'

'Jake!' She took the letter from him. 'But this is wonderful for you. They must think you are a respectable person after all,' she teased, and looked up at him with a smile.

'Do you really want to go?' he asked, eyebrows raised. 'You're still not well, are you?'

Cleo moved away, making a show of straightening her skirts. He had sounded ironic. She made her voice cool. 'I'm perfectly well. And, yes, we must go.'

Behind her, she heard him sigh. And yet when she turned he was smiling in a mocking way. 'Then I rely on you to stay by my side the entire evening,' he said. 'And dance every dance with me.'

'Jake, how can I? They would think it very peculiar.' What would she wear? No longer could she fit into some of the tighter of her gowns. It would have to be the plum again, she thought, unless she had a new one made. Did she dare? Jake would wonder why, with so many gowns already, she needed another.

'Cleo?'

'She looked up, startled.

'What's the matter? You're frowning.'

'Am I?' She straightened her skirt again nervously. 'I was just wondering what to wear.'

He looked at her. 'Oh? What about the apricot one? I love the way the buttons tease, until I want to undo them, one by one—'

'No, I...it's too tight. The plum one, I thought.'

'Too tight?' Now his eyebrows were up. 'Are you getting fat, my dear?'

'No! That is...' She fanned herself desperately with the letter. 'It's warm today, don't you think? The summer seems to go on and on.'

But his eyes were cold and cruel. 'Be careful,' he said softly, each word like a stone falling into a well. 'Be careful you don't get *too* fat, Cleo. Or I might really leave you.'

She could not answer, only stare at him in frozen terror. And then he had stridden from the room, and slammed the door after him. Cleo sank down on to the nearest chair. Her heart was beating so hard it threatened to burst, and she felt as cold now as she had felt hot a moment before. She could never, never tell him. But how could she not?

Terror brought a fresh wave of nausea. If he should leave her now, she would die. And yet, if she truly loved him, wouldn't it be an act of love, to let him go back to the world where he belonged? Unfortunately, Cleo didn't think she had it in her to be that unselfish.

The atmosphere between them had changed. The easy laughter, and closeness of Molly's final performance, was gone. Cleo felt him watching her, and became nervous, dropping things and babbling in a way she would never have thought herself capable of. It was as if he was waiting for her to make a mistake, so that he could go with a clear conscience. He didn't come to her room. She could only think that, at long last, the physical attraction she had held for him had passed. And that soon, very soon, he would pack up and go.

She lay awake, thinking of what she would do and say, when the moment came. It seemed so sudden. They had been so close, at Molly's farewell, and now it had all gone wrong. Perhaps it had been the farewell supper that made him realise what he had been missing. He had compared the two— Molly and the excitement of her life, with Cleo and Belubula. And Cleo had lost.

After all, Cleo wore the plum-coloured gown to the Scotts'. Jake made no comment on it, only a slight bow of his head to acknowledge her glowing beauty. For she did glow, these days, as though an inner peace arid contentment filled her, which was strange, Cleo thought, because she was filled with no such thing. It was a chill night, the sky clear and filled with stars. Cleo pulled her shawl closer about her shoulders, and knew the chill was in her heart as much as in the night air.

The Scotts' homestead was lit like a beacon, and

the garden was filled with coloured lanterns. They had liveried servants, and Jake met Cleo's eyes as they removed their outer garments. What next? he seemed to say. She smiled in perfect understanding, and after a moment he took her arm in his.

Mrs. Scott was there to greet them, her long horse face smiling gravely. Peggy sparkled in blue, her blonde hair dressed in masses of curls. 'Save me,' whispered Jake, as she made straight for him. But Cleo did not think he looked as if he needed saving, when, later, she saw them together, heads close.

There was dancing. Jake came to claim her, and she treasured the moment. Perhaps she would never have another evening like this with him, ever again. And then he was gone again. Seth Barnet danced with her, but he was watching Jake and Peggy with jealous eyes, and Cleo was watching them too.

'She's very pretty,' Cleo murmured.

Seth met her eyes and smiled a little ruefully. 'She's beautiful,' he said. And laughed. 'Not that she's noticed me, Cleo. She's only got eyes for—' He stopped, embarrassed, but she finished it for him.

'For Jake,' she said. 'They do make a handsome couple, don't they? So many people have commented on it. You'd think he wasn't married already, the way they go on about it...' Her voice cracked and, shocked, she fell silent.

Seth squeezed her fingers. 'Not as handsome a couple as Jake and you make,' he said gallantly.

Cleo smiled, but it was an effort.

After the dance, Seth went to get her a drink, and Cleo sat and fanned herself, chatting to his mother. After a moment, Jake found her. He spoke politely to Mrs. Barnet, but something in his face made Cleo nervous, and she was unwilling when he made some excuse and, taking her arm, led her a short distance away.

'What was Seth saying to you, to make you so white?' he said abruptly.

Surprised, she looked into his closed, angry face.

'Well?' he added, and his fingers on her arm were cruel. She smelt wine on his breath, and wondered if he was a little drunk already. Why did he find it necessary to drink so much? Was he so unhappy?

'He was speaking of Peggy Scott,' she said at last, in a voice lacking all emotion. 'He said she was beautiful.'

His fingers tightened again on her arm, and then fell away. He stared at her blankly, and then he sighed. 'Poor Cleo,' he said, and his voice was as dead as hers. 'But they say love is a fickle mistress—although I cannot vouch for the truth of it, never having been in love.'

He looked over her head, around the room. 'There is Mrs. McDowell bearing down on us,' he said, still in that empty voice. 'I will have to leave you to your fate.' And he walked away.

Cleo stood staring after him, trying to understand what he had said, and hearing only 'never having been in love', like a tolling bell in her mind. And then Mrs. McDowell was there, and she had to try and pull herself together.

Mrs. McDowell's talk was full of the lovely dinner, and the grand connections of Mr. and Mrs. Scott. Cleo nodded and smiled, and pretended to be impressed. 'Of course, your husband has connections of his own,' she went on. 'He was telling me earlier. I wonder he does not make it known more widely, Mrs. Raines. It is very helpful, to have friends in influential places.'

Cleo smiled at her glass. 'Jake thinks a man should be judged by his own merits,' she said, 'not by the company he keeps.'

'A novel idea,' Mrs. McDowell said kindly, 'but hardly realistic, my dear.'

Behind them, Mrs. Scott was talking importantly to one of those 'important friends'. 'Of course Peggy would make a great splash in Melbourne,' she was saying. 'We have her first season there all planned.'

'You must be hoping for great things,' the friend said archly. 'If she can be shown in the right quarters.'

Like a horse, Cleo thought acidly, keeping the smile fixed on her face as Mrs. McDowell yapped on and on.

'It is such a pity,' Mrs. Scott was saying. 'That he is already married, I mean.'

'But could you stomach his reputation, my dear?'

Mrs. Scott tittered. 'Oh, yes! He has made great strides to reform himself, and so wealthy, you know, and his family... well, there is nothing to object to there! His breeding is of the best.'

'It would have been a great accomplishment.'

'The richest woman in Victoria,' sighed Mrs.

Scott.

Cleo felt frozen in place, still smiling at Mrs. McDowell. After a moment she dared to turn, and saw Mrs. Scott and her friend, watching Jake and Peggy dance, with long, sorrowful looks on their long, horsy faces.

Eventually, she escaped outside.

The garden was beautiful, and she stood under the soft gleam of the lantern light, breathing deeply. How dared they? How dared they speak so of her husband? They were no more respectable than Annabel Lees! At least she sold herself to make a living, to put bread in her mouth. They were selling Peggy only for the prestige it would bring them!

The anger died. If he divorced her, Cleo, perhaps he would marry Peggy. Would the Scotts overlook a divorce? Jake was very rich...perhaps that would weigh the balance in his favour. She shivered at the thought, hugging her arms about herself. There were paths running through the garden, and she set out along one of them, slowly, trying to gather her thoughts.

She remembered Jake's face, when he had spoken to her earlier, asking her what was wrong. Why had he sounded so...so low? As if something in him had died. Was it because Seth admired Peggy, and Seth was a bachelor, while he was not? But how foolish, when anyone could see Peggy had eyes only for Jake! Perhaps he hoped to make her his mistress rather than his wife. But that would be against the wishes of her family, surely? Cleo put a hand to her brow, no longer sure what to believe.

The path ahead curved into a lovers' bower, covered in fragrant climbing roses. Cleo heard a rustle of cloth, and went to turn back, not wishing to disturb the couple obviously enjoying their privacy within. But it was too late.

'Jake...' The girl's soft laughter. Peggy's laughter. As Cleo stood frozen, the girl stepped back a little, into view. The blonde head was tilted back, the lovely face laughing up at the dark, handsome head bent over her. And then he had swooped down, claiming her mouth in a long, passionate kiss.

Cleo was running. Her skirts caught on shrubs, her hair tangled, and hot tears burned her cheeks. She ran on and on, and yet knew she could never escape what she had seen. Jake and Peggy. Everyone said they were a handsome couple, ideally suited. Pity he already had a wife...

The figure loomed in front of her, and Cleo cried out as he grabbed her arms. 'Cleo!' he said, then, seeing her state, 'Cleo, what is it?'

She jerked away from him, hands shaking as she put them to her face, her hair. 'Nothing, I... nothing is wrong.'

Seth's face was creased with concern, and then his gaze went past her and his eyes widened. Cleo did not need to turn. She stood straight and stiff as a poker, waiting.

'Seth.' Jake's voice, cool and polite as if nothing terrible had just happened. 'Perhaps you would take Miss Scott back to the dancing?'

Peggy brushed past Cleo, and her hand clutched

at Seth's arm in an almost eager manner. The girl's face was pale, but Cleo hardly noticed. She watched them walk away, Seth glancing back once, and then bending solicitously over Peggy.

'Cleo?'

Still she did not turn. He touched her shoulder, and she pulled away, shuddering. Her control snapped, and she spun around to face him.

He was very pale, and grim. The bearer of bad news, she thought.

'We have nothing to say to each other!' she cried.

'Cleo—'

'Nothing, do you hear me?'

'For God's sake, keep your voice down,' he hissed, and put out his hands as if to catch her to him. But she moved back in revulsion, and he dropped his arms.

'I don't suppose you want to know why I did it?' he said matter-of-factly.

'Why?' she repeated savagely. 'Do you need a reason to kiss a pretty girl, Jake?'

'I did it,' he went on, as if she hadn't spoken, 'because I was sick to death of her following me around. I thought I would frighten her so badly she would run a mile. And so I did. She was living in a fantasy world—I gave her a bit of realism.'

Cleo gasped at his audacity. 'Come now, Jake,' she said, with stinging sarcasm. 'Can't you think of a better lie than that? At least admit to me you think she's lovely. She flattered you, and you took advantage. You only promised to be faithful to me for as long as you could, didn't you? Not forever.'

He stared at her and his eyes were black and gleaming with his growing anger. 'I've told you what happened,' he said. 'But you *can't—won't* believe it. I'm tired of beating my head against a brick wall, Cleo.'

'No.' Her voice rose high with hysteria. Her control was going. She began to cry. Jake grabbed her arm and dragged her along.

'We're going home,' he said. 'Get your coat. And for God's sake keep your voice down! Do you want to be ruined all over again?'

'By you,' she sobbed. 'By you, all over again! I wish I had never met you.'

'Well, we both know where that would leave you,' he said, and he sounded weary now. As if he wanted it over, finished, behind him. A new life beckoned, a life without Cleo.

'Perhaps I would be better dead,' she sobbed.

His fingers dug savagely into her arm. 'Perhaps you would,' he said as savagely. 'You've ruined lives other than your own, Cleo.'

His, he meant, and Peggy's. Bitterness made her say, 'Seth wants her, you know... Peggy. I could see it in his face tonight. The way he bent over her.'

Jake turned and stared at her, and he was so white and furious that for a moment Cleo thought he meant to strike her. But whatever it was he controlled it, and turned away, pulling her onward towards the house.

Cleo followed, dragging her feet. If the thought of Peggy and Seth could cause him so much pain, it was the end for her. She could not fight that.

In the end, Jake went in and collected their coats

and made the excuses. Cleo was unwell, yet again.

He did not speak to her on the way home, and she stared into the darkness, the tears drying salty on her cheeks. Her mind had become very clear suddenly. It was a matter of pride, she thought. Jake wanted her gone, and if she stayed until he left her...that would be unbearable. She must be the one to leave. It was the only way.

Once she decided, she could be calm again. She would just look at it as another stage in her life, another turn in the road. She must look forward to the challenges.

The carriage stopped. Cleo did not wait to be handed down, but jumped down and ran up the steps and into the house, and to the safety of her room.

He did not follow. He never would again. And she would just have to grow to accept it, she told herself, as she flung herself sobbing on to the bed.

CHAPTER TWELVE

'MRS. RAINES.' CLEO looked up. Bridget stood by the door, looking nervous. Cleo put down her pen and rubbed her tired eyes. 'What is it, Biddy?'

'Sorry to interrupt...'

'I'm glad you did. Do we really spend so much money every month at Belubula?' Bridget smiled, then closed the door. Cleo frowned. 'Whatever is the matter? Is it Jake?' Fear made her face pale, but Bridget shook her head.

'No, he's still at the mine, far as I know.'

'Well, what is it? Out with it, Biddy!'

'Mrs. Raines, I've been biding my time, and biting my tongue for weeks and weeks now, but I really must speak.' Bridget rushed on before Cleo could interrupt, 'For Lord's sake, woman, why haven't you told him?'

Cleo let out her breath slowly. 'You've guessed?' Bridget made an impatient movement. 'I've seen enough in my life to know when a woman is carrying a child. You should tell him, Mrs. Raines. Why don't you?'

Cleo shook her head and looked so sad the other

woman came over and put her arm about her.

'There, there,' she whispered, stroking Cleo's hair.

'Tell Bridget what's wrong, my dear.'

Cleo felt suddenly like a child again, being comforted in her mother's arms. She had had to grow up too quickly when her mother died, perhaps that was her trouble. She had not been allowed to stay a child long enough.

'He would not be happy,' Cleo breathed, 'if he knew.'

'But, my dear, you are wrong!' Bridget cried. 'He is a kind man, a good man. Of course he would be happy!'

'Oh, he's kind enough, in his own way. But Bridget,' and her voice broke, 'it is over between us.'

Bridget, surprised, wrapped her arms around the suddenly sobbing Cleo. To see someone she had thought so cool and self-assured, so confident of herself, suddenly broken by her hurt and misery!

Bridget murmured, 'There, there,' trying to comfort her. 'But why should you think such a thing?' she asked at last. 'It is plain that Mr. Raines loves you more than anyone else in the world. You just have to watch him when you come into a room. He lights up.'

Cleo shook her head, trying to pull herself together. 'You're wrong, Biddy. So wrong. He's not steadfast, it's not in his nature. I can't blame him for that. He needed me once, but that time is past. He needs someone else now, and I am just in the way of their happiness.'

Bridget took a sharp breath. 'It's you who are wrong! I could tell the first time he brought you to Belubula, that he was keener on you than a mouse on cheese—'

'Oh, Biddy!' Cleo didn't know whether to laugh or cry.

'And I doubt very much if anything has changed since. If I know Mr. Raines, he's keener than ever. And when he knows you're having a baby, he'll be walkin' on air.'

She shook her head slowly, sadly. 'You don't understand.'

'No, I don't. If you mean to leave him, then you will break his heart. And, besides, where would you go?'

Cleo sighed, and pulling away from Bridget stood up. 'Melissa would have me. She and Douglas will be returning to Melbourne—I could go with them.'

'That woman,' Bridget sneered. 'And do you think Mr. Raines will not go and bring you back?'

Cleo's eyes were dark and bleak as she looked out of the window. 'I think he will be... relieved,' she whispered.

The knock on the door startled them.

'Now, who in the name?' Bridget began, rushing to open it. 'Mr. Barnet!'

'Seth?' Cleo started forward, for Seth's eyes were wide with excitement.

'Cleo,' he said. 'My mother was in Nugget Gully; she's just returned. There's trouble at the mine. Jake's mine. I thought you'd want to know. The miners are refusing to work. And most of the troopers are out after some bushrangers who held up the gold coach to Ballarat. Killed two of the troopers escorting it.'

'Oh, no...'

'They're sending to Bendigo for more troopers, but that'll take a while.'

Jake, in danger! Did it matter, that he did not love her? If he was in danger, then she must be with him.

'I must go out there,' Cleo said. 'Will you take me?'

'Of course. But it might be dangerous.'

Bridget caught her arm, her eyes searching. 'Take care,' she whispered. 'And remember, it's not just you now.'

Cleo smiled. 'I'll take care.'

Seth helped her into the dray he had ridden over in. It was rougher than the gig or the carriage, but Cleo clung on to the side of her seat with one hand, and on to her hat with the other. A hot breeze was whipping over the land today, rising a willy-willy of dust, spiraling and catching up the leaves and twigs in its path. Dead leaves crackled, and the magpies sat on the branches, beaks open, waiting for the cool of evening. The perspiration was already running down Cleo's back, and her hair stuck to her face.

'Why are they striking?' Cleo said harshly. 'Jake is the best mine owner in Nugget Gully.'

'I know that. But some of the other bosses aren't so generous, and discontent spreads. Don't worry.' His hand closed over hers. 'We'll get there in time.'

In time for what? Cleo wondered. But she smiled bravely. 'You're a good friend, Seth.'

His mouth curled a little ruefully. 'Oh, yes, a friend in a million.'

He loved her. Cleo saw it in his eyes, and was sorry. So sorry, for his love was as hopeless as her own. 'Seth,' she said softly. 'Peggy is beautiful, isn't she? Why don't you visit her more. . . or there must be other girls about. You must meet more of them.'

The dray rattled over a culvert in the road. 'Yes. I think I must. I've even been thinking of taking up land further north. They're opening it up for selection, and they say it's good farming country.'

'Oh, Seth,' Cleo murmured, 'don't let me drive you away.'

He smiled at her gently. 'You're not, Cleo. I just feel it's about time I got out on my own.'

Cleo opened her mouth to tell him she would be leaving anyway, but did not. How could she tell him about Jake? And if she did, he might think there was hope for him, and she knew there was not. There had only ever been Jake, and that was how it would remain until the end of her days.

The town was oddly quiet, and Cleo felt her body tensing. The hot north wind gusted down the main street, tossing up dust, caking them with a fine red grit. Cleo licked dry lips. The mine poppet heads could be seen in the distance, running in a crooked line, following the quartz reef.

The Lucky Strike was silent, rising into the

hazy, dusty sky. Cleo drew her scarf about her face, covering her mouth and nose as the powdery dust from the mullock heaps swirled about them. All the mines were quiet, in their strange, nightmare landscape. It seemed very odd after the thunderous pounding of the gold batteries she had heard last time she was here.

'There it is.'

Cleo shaded her eyes. The Queen of Egypt, Jake's joke. Above the rattle and jolt of the dray on the rough track, she could hear shouting. As they cleared the crest, Cleo could see the mine before her. Like the others, the workings were quiet, the battery silent. A great crowd had gathered about the wooden huts on the rise.

The miners clustered together, and they were shouting. Behind them, there were as many spectators from Nugget Gully, their skirts and coats flapping in the hot, gusty wind. And at the hut, almost surrounded, was Jake.

The miners were waving their arms and calling out, and as they drew closer Cleo could hear, among the myriad sounds, 'More money, more money, more money,' over and over again. Seth drew the dray to a halt. Cleo scrambled down, and began to push her way through the silent spectators. They stood, watching, while Jake was up there, alone. Why didn't they help him?

The gun shot was so loud that Cleo almost jumped out of her skin. Some women screamed. There was a deafening silence, and then she heard Jake's mocking voice. 'That's better.'

Over the heads, on the rise upon which the

huts were built, Cleo saw him standing. He had a pistol in his hand, and his face was as calm and controlled as if he were addressing an audience at the music hall rather than an angry mob.

'You, Tom Tredinnick,' he said, pointing at one of the miners. 'And you, Jones. What are you doing here? Don't your families have new shoes and plenty of food on the table every night?'

There were some murmurs, and then an angry growl. 'Aye, but not everyone can say the same.' The voice went on. 'There's those of us working our guts out for a few shillings. We want fair pay for a fair day's work, for everyone!'

They all cheered, but another voice broke through the noise. 'What about Nathan Heard? He died because the shaft was so badly shored up. It was rotten, and everyone knew it but the boss wouldn't replace it.'

More shouts of agreement, and the noise threatened to swamp them again. But Tom Tredinnick waved his arms for silence. 'Mr. Raines,' he said, and his voice had a note of desperation in it. 'We're not sayin' as you're one o' those who do such things. You've been fair to us. But there are others who don't care like you, and something has to be done about them. And if that means we've got to break a few heads, then that's what we'll do!'

Now the voices rose again into a jumble of sound. Cleo felt Seth's hand on her arm, pulling her back when she tried to break through the crush. She could hear Jake shouting, but not what he said. Her terror threatened to engulf her; what if he was hurt, or, worse, killed?

'I must reach him,' she whispered. 'I must!'

And then, suddenly, behind her she heard the thunder of hoofs. Dust blew like a cloud over them. People began to run, screaming. Guns were fired, and the acrid smell of gunpowder stung her nostrils. She saw the uniforms of the troopers through the dust and confusion. Someone pushed her, and Cleo fell to the ground. A horse's hoofs pawed the dust close to her head. Cleo screamed, and flung her hands up over her face. Then something exploded like fireworks in her mind, and she knew only darkness.

***

For a time, Cleo drifted. It was very warm for Plymouth, she thought. She stirred on the bed, frowning. And the mattress seemed very hard and lumpy. There was an ache in her back, but a worse one in her head. Cleo gingerly lifted a hand to it, and felt a lump above her ear, and her hair was matted and stiff, as if she had been bleeding...

Her eyes opened wide.

She could see daylight through the slates of the roof, and if she turned her head... The headache became knives, stabbing. Cleo groaned and clutched her head.

'Cleo?' A cool hand on her brow, and Melissa's green eyes frowned down at her. 'Are you all right? The doctor is coming. Just lie still.'

'Jake,' she said, and was surprised by the croak which was her voice.

'He's outside. Don't worry, he's all right. There was a bit of a scuffle, that's all. Douglas believes in action, not talk.' Melissa raised an ironic eyebrow. 'But your husband refused to lay any charges, and now he's thrashing out some deal or other with the miners.'

Cleo struggled to rise. 'I must see him.'

Melissa pushed her flat again. 'You'll be sorry when you do. He was furious when Seth carried you up here, while Douglas's war was going on. You'd better play up that knock on the head as long as you can.'

Cleo held her head, trying to make sense of everything. She had fallen, and hit her head, and... the baby! Pray God she had not injured the baby. Her hand slid down to the swell of her belly, but it was still there. She let out her breath and tried to pull herself together.

'What are you doing here?' she whispered, turning again to Melissa.

Melissa flushed. 'I... well, I was just—oh, hell!' and she laughed at Cleo's startled look beneath the dirt and sweat and streaks of dried blood. 'You look terrible. Here, let me get some water and try and clean you up a bit.'

The water was cool and refreshing on her face. 'You haven't answered my question,' Cleo said again, after a moment.

Melissa grinned. 'I was afraid for him. I made him bring me. There, that's the truth.'

Cleo felt her spirits sink even lower. 'Jake?'

Melissa laughed again. 'No, for Douglas! Don't faint again, please. I know it is a shock to hear it, but I have a new obsession, and it is Douglas. And I didn't even realise it, until we heard that those two troopers had been murdered by the bushrangers who held up the Ballarat Gold Coach.'

Cleo managed to smile. 'I'm sure I would be pleased for you, if I could feel pleased for anyone at the moment.'

Melissa shook her head, and stood up. 'There,' she said. 'You look more like the Cleo we know and love.'

Cleo tried to sit up, and was able to do so without too much difficulty. Her headache had faded to a dull, distant ache, and the sickness had gone from her throat. 'I really am glad for you,' she said, pushing back her tangled hair. A tear trickled down her cheek. Melissa, worried, bent over her.

'Cleo? Are you in such pain? Where is that wretched doctor!'

Cleo sniffed, and wiped her face. 'No. At least, not the sort of pain a doctor could mend. It's just you suddenly finding your happiness, while I... I have lost mine, if I ever had it.'

Melissa frowned. 'I think you are delirious,' she retorted. 'You love Jake Raines. Aren't you happy with him?'

Cleo looked down at her hands. 'He doesn't love me, though, Melissa. Oh, he was kind. I am tired of hearing how kind he is! But I could not live on pity and now... well, circumstances demand that I must make a decision. I think, for both our sakes, I should leave him. And for that I need your help.'

Melissa looked astonished, opened her mouth as if to berate her, and then stopped. 'Cleo,' she said at last, 'you know I would do anything in my power to help you.'

Another tear trickled down Cleo's cheek. 'Then take me to Melbourne with you, when you go,' she said huskily.

'What's this about Melbourne?'

Melissa had been blocking Cleo's view of the door. She had not seen Jake enter until he asked his question. Melissa spun about nervously, and Cleo hastily wiped her eyes. Jake looked hot, and dust caked him almost as badly as it had Cleo. But his eyes were black and angry, and Cleo knew he had heard too much.

'Jake!' Melissa peered out of the door beyond him. 'Is everything all right? Where are your miners?'

Jake frowned impatiently. '*My* miners have gone home. I've agreed to state their case to the other mine owners. And to take it further, to Parliament, if necessary. They were desperate; they had nowhere else to turn. How could I blame them?'

'How indeed?' Melissa mocked. 'I'm sure Douglas would rather have rounded them all up and put them in gaol. But then that's what he's paid to do! I must go and find him. Cleo?'

Cleo met her eyes. 'I'm all right. You go and find Douglas.'

Melissa went out, closing the door. Cleo looked at the floor—it was of hard-packed earth.

'I asked you about Melbourne,' that harsh voice repeated. It was unlike Jake's voice and, when she lifted her eyes to his, his face too was grim and unfamiliar.

'I am going to Melbourne,' she said, 'with Melissa and Douglas.'

For a moment she thought he was going to explode, but instead he turned away, his back straight and stiff, and began to rearrange some papers on the table. 'And may I ask why?' he said, and his voice was as stiff.

'I...I cannot say.'

Slowly he turned, and his eyes were bleak. 'You cannot say?' he whispered. Then, harsh and rasping, he went on, 'The only reason I can think of is that the child you are carrying is not mine.'

Shock made Cleo's eyes wide and dark. 'You knew!' she gasped.

His scorn was a tangible thing. 'Of course I knew. I'm not a fool. I was waiting for you to tell me, I thought you'd have to eventually. But instead you meant to sneak off to Melbourne. For once in your life tell the truth, Cleo! Is it mine, or is it Seth Barnet's?'

Shocked, Cleo swallowed before the white look of his face. 'Yes,' she whispered. 'It's yours. You know it is, Jake! There's only ever been you.'

He looked uncertain, and it came to her suddenly that he might not believe her. And that it hurt agonisingly to think he should think her a liar. Was that how he had felt, when she hadn't trusted him, time after time?

'I thought it might be Seth's child,' he said hollowly, and laughed shakily, running his fingers through his hair. 'You seemed very friendly, the two of you. And I was away often enough. How could I blame you? And then, that night at the Scotts', when you were so upset about him and Peggy. You said you thought he wanted her. As though something had ended for you. I thought then, that you and he... And I knew I had lost.'

Cleo blinked at him in disbelief. 'Jake,' she whispered. 'Seth was my friend, that is all. I was upset because of Peggy, yes. But *you* and Peggy.'

'Me and Peggy?' he repeated, frowning at her.

'Yes! You...you never wanted to marry me,' she burst out. 'Why should you want a child? How *could* I tell you? When it would send you away from me?'

Jake shook his head. The anger seemed suddenly to empty out of him. 'You don't understand,' he said, quiet now. 'I always meant to have you, and if that meant marriage...' His smile was a grimace. 'You played into my hands, with the partnership. I thought, in time, I would win you over. But you've never trusted me, or forgiven me for ruining your life, have you? I saw that, at the Scotts' the other night, and I knew I had finally lost. I had thought, even if the child was Seth's, I could forgive... I could try. My life has hardly been blameless! But you wouldn't even let me do that. You just cried, because Seth was flirting with Peggy. If you love him so much, Cleo, do something about it! Don't sneak off the Melbourne; go to him. I can't hold on to you, if you love him so much.'

Cleo pressed her hands to her mouth. 'How can

you be so cruel?' she gasped, and suddenly the tears were trickling down her cheeks and she didn't seem able to stop them.

'Cleo?' He sounded puzzled.

'I told you, it's your child!' she sobbed. 'And I don't love Seth.'

'Cleo...' Slowly his arms came around her, and he held her hard against his big body. He began to stroke her hair, gently. 'I held you like this before, remember?' he said softly. 'In the storm? You rarely lower your guard, Cleo. I can't get near you, except in bed. Then you're real, and alive. Other times, you're cold as ice, and I can't reach you. I wanted you to show me the warmth you show to those you love. I couldn't believe that in time you wouldn't grow to love me. Women usually do,' he added, and mocked her, or himself.

Cleo pulled, back, and stared up into his face. 'I was afraid,' she said, frowning. What was he saying to her? She hardly dared to listen, in case yet again her hopes would be shattered. 'I told you I was afraid of being hurt. It was the truth. You can hurt me, Jake, more than anyone else in the world.'

'Can I?' He put his finger to her lips. 'Cleo, it's ironic, isn't it? Don't laugh,' and he mocked himself, 'but I've known so many women— the truth now, Cleo. I have known a great many. And yet I've loved none of them. I had begun to believe love did not exist. Until you.'

that wounded my pride, Cleo. And I wanted to show you that you were wrong, that you were lying to yourself. But you wouldn't admit it. And so I stayed away from you, pretending I didn't care, when I wanted to be loving Cleo caught her breath.

'At first,' he went on, 'I thought you were so obviously not my type that I was attracted by that. That I wanted you because you were unattainable—a madness bound to pass. But it didn't. You were always there in my thoughts. And I realised that this was love, and if I wanted you I had to change my ways. And it wasn't difficult after all, because all women had become boring except for you. The night of our wedding, I wanted to hurt you. You had said things you every moment. It was so much worse, Cleo, once I'd had you. But pride kept me away. How could I beg for favours, when you hated me?'

Cleo shook her head in wonder. 'I dreamt about you, every night,' she whispered. 'I thought I must be as bad as Annabel Lees! I longed to tell you, but I was afraid. That was why I said those things.'

'Oh, Cleo, why didn't you say? The night Freddy came to your room... I asked you then to release me from that promise. I dared you to say you cared. If you had given me the slightest hope, I would have told you I loved you then.'

'You said you would try to be faithful,' she said, and her voice shook. 'You said things I thought were...harsh.'

'I was angry. But I told you the truth. Love might go as quickly as it had come. I know now I was wrong.'

'Oh, Jake.' Cleo took a deep, shaking breath, and smiled at him as though her heart were overflowing. 'That night at the Scotts', I thought it was the end for me. You and Peggy, and the way you spoke... I thought you must want her very much, and that I must let you go. And all the time, you thought Seth and I...'

He met her eyes, suddenly intent. 'Cleo,' he said softly, 'is it Seth? Do you love him?'

'No, I told you! Listen, Jake, please. How can I love Seth? I love you. I always have. I thought if you knew you would hurt me. I thought, if I clung to you, you would despise me or grow to hate me. I thought you would leave me, Jake, when you were bored with me.'

He was looking at her like a man who had been shot. 'You love me?' he repeated, and shook his head. 'You could have anyone you want, Cleo, but you love me?'

She laughed with sudden joy, and put her hands either side of his face. 'I love *you,* Jake Raines,' she said, looking into his dark, dear eyes. 'I love you, respectable or not, now and forever.'

And suddenly his mouth quirked into that smile he seemed to reserve for her alone, and his eyes gleamed. 'My delight,' he said, and bent to kiss her passionately. 'Promise me,' he murmured, after a long moment, 'no more holding back, Cleo. If you love me, you must trust me.'

'I promise,' she whispered, and knew it was one promise she would not find hard to keep. 'Jake, will you be bored, with me and Belubula? You fit so well into life with Molly and...and...I thought, that night at the music hall, you were so—'

'Cleo.' He gave her a little shake. 'I am tired to

death of Molly and all the nonsense that goes with her. The cheap laughter and lies, the living in the public eye, the uncertainty of it all. When will you believe me when I say that I long for the peace of your arms? I want to be an ordinary man. I want a woman to love and who loves me.'

Slowly, slowly, the words sank into her mind, and Cleo believed him. It really was her dream come true! Her smile warmed him, like a glowing flame, and promised much happiness to come.

About the Author

KAYE DOBBIE HAS been writing professionally ever since she won the Big River short story contest at the age of 18. Her career has undergone many changes, including Australian historical fiction under the name Lilly Sommers, to romance written as Sara Bennett and published in the US and Australia. Her books have been translated into many languages. She is currently writing under her 'proper' name, Kaye Dobbie, and is published by Harlequin (Mira) Australia and Weltbild in Germany.

Kaye lives on the central Victorian goldfields with her husband and four very important cats.

Visit her website and sign up to her
Newsletter for the latest:
www.kayedobbie.com
www.facebook.com/KayedobbieAuthor

Lightning Source UK Ltd.
Milton Keynes UK
UKHW020737170521
383859UK00014B/908